Kate Fortune's Journal Entry

*My crash was **no** accident. And in order to find out who sabotaged my plane, I'm pretending to be dead.*

In the meantime, I'm looking out for my family. I'm so pleased they're enjoying the gifts I left them in my will. Take my grandson Kyle. As a boy, he used to come visit me at my Wyoming ranch. One summer he fell in love with that darling Samantha Rawlings. I'll never understand why he impulsively up and left to marry a society girl.

Kyle needs to get away from the city and settle down. He's a restless playboy because he's forgotten what's important. That's why I left him the ranch. And to guarantee he doesn't sell it, he needs to live there six months to offically inherit it.

That should be just enough time for him to reunite with Samantha and discover the secret she's been keeping for ten years....

A LETTER FROM THE AUTHOR

Dear Reader,

Some things are just meant to happen. That's what I thought
when I was asked to contribute to FORTUNE'S CHILDREN.
I was thrilled and honored to be a part of the group of authors
creating stories about this very special family, and I was
thankful that I was asked to do a story surrounding a ranch, a
rich playboy and a secret baby.

I'm a fifth-generation Oregonian and grew up surrounded by
cousins and grandparents, as well as great-aunts and uncles.
My grandparents and great-grandparents lived on farms
complete with cattle, chickens, sheep and hogs. My cousins
and sister, Natalie Bishop (another Silhouette author), and I
played on the banks of a small creek that wound through a
thick stand of old growth timber, chased each other on deer
and sheep trails, or swam in the Molalla River. It was a
magical, special childhood. We weren't nearly as wealthy as
the Fortunes, of course, but we had that same sense of
togetherness and love that wound through our generations, the
common and tightly woven bond of family.

I felt it was fitting that this, *The Millionaire and the Cowgirl*,
should be my fortieth book for Silhouette—a novel
celebrating love and trust and the meaning of family. I'm
thrilled to be able to contribute and hope you enjoy reading
about Samantha, Kyle and Caitlyn.

I feel this is a special book, a milestone in the fifteen years
I've written for Silhouette. Many of you have written me,
asking for more stories with a Western setting, where the
characters live on ranches, and this is for you. I hope you love
this series as much as I do.

Enjoy!

Lisa Jackson

Lisa Jackson

FORTUNE'S
Children

LISA JACKSON
The Millionaire
and the Cowgirl

Silhouette Books

Published by Silhouette Books
America's Publisher of Contemporary Romance

To my dad, from whom I learned
dignity and laughter

 SILHOUETTE BOOKS

THE MILLIONAIRE AND THE COWGIRL

Copyright © 1996 by Harlequin Books S.A.

ISBN 0-373-38903-5

Special thanks and acknowledgment are given to Lisa Jackson
for her contribution to the Fortune's Children series.

This edition published by arrangement with Harlequin Books S.A.

® and TM are trademarks of Harlequin Books S.A., used under license.
Trademarks indicated with ® are registered in the United States Patent
and Trademark Office, the Canadian Trade Marks Office and in other
countries.

Visit Silhouette Books at www.eHarlequin.com

Printed in U.S.A.

LISA JACKSON

lives with her family in the Pacific Northwest. She has been writing for over twenty years. Her books have appeared on the *New York Times, Publishers Weekly* and *USA TODAY* bestseller lists. Her free time is spent with friends and family.

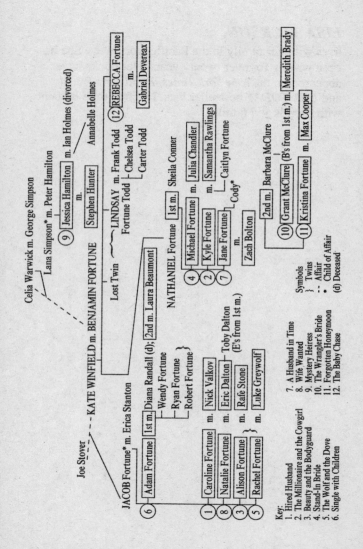

Key:
1. Hired Husband
2. The Millionaire and the Cowgirl
3. Beauty and the Bodyguard
4. Stand-In Bride
5. The Wolf and the Dove
6. Single with Children
7. A Husband in Time
8. Wife Wanted
9. Mystery Heiress
10. The Wrangler's Bride
11. Forgotten Honeymoon
12. The Baby Chase

Symbols
} Twins
-- Affair
• Child of Affair
(d) Deceased

FORTUNE'S *Children*

Meet the Fortunes—three generations of a family with a legacy of wealth, influence and power. As they unite to face an unknown enemy, shocking family secrets are revealed…and passionate new romances are ignited.

KATE FORTUNE: When the powerful matriarch of the Fortune clan is believed to be dead, she and a mysterious stranger play matchmakers in the lives of her children and grandchildren.

KYLE FORTUNE: Playboy millionaire. Can this city slicker turned cowboy rectify mistakes of the past…and make a future with the one woman he's never been able to forget *and* the daughter he never knew he had?

SAMANTHA RAWLINGS: Feisty cowgirl. Could she ever forgive Kyle for breaking her heart and marrying another woman? Would he be able to forgive her for keeping a ten-year-old secret?

ALLIE FORTUNE: Gorgeous Fortune Cosmetics spokesmodel. Men want her only for her money and her body. Is her beauty a blessing…or a curse?

LIZ JONES—
CELEBRITY GOSSIP

The rumors are true! Megamillionaire Kate Fortune, CEO of Fortune Cosmetics, has died in a tragic plane crash. Sources tell me Kate's daughter Rebecca suspects foul play and is looking into hiring a private investigator.

Close friends say the family was devastated at the reading of her will. In addition to her major assets, Kate apparently left special mementos. To her grandson Kyle, the most eligible bachelor in town, she left her Wyoming ranch. So saddle up, all you bachelorettes! To hook this guy you're going to have to play cowgirl, because Kyle has to stay on the ranch for six—yes, six!—months to inherit it. I wonder about this wild condition. But as everyone knows, Kate always had a trick—and a master plan—up her sleeve....

What impact will Kate's death have on the massive Fortune empire? And if someone *is* out to get the Fortunes, who's next on their target list?

Prologue

Bbbbrrring!

The school bell rang sharply, announcing the end of the day for the students of Whitecomb Elementary in Clear Springs, Wyoming. Within minutes laughing, chattering children swinging lunch pails and book bags began streaming from the long, redbrick building. Two flags, one for the United States, the other for the State of Wyoming, snapped from a pole near the front entrance of the school. Yellow buses waited near the side entrance by the parking lot and spewed blue smoke from their tailpipes.

From a van parked in front of a small cottage on the opposite side of the street, a stranger, a man who didn't belong anywhere near this elementary school, peered anxiously through the window. He stared past the caravans of trucks, cars and minivans that idled in the asphalt lot as parents waited to pick up their precious cargos.

"Come on, come on," he muttered.

Surely he would catch a glimpse of the girl in question, the one on whose slim, nine-year-old shoulders his partner's hopes rested.

What if she no longer went to school here? What if

she and her mother had moved? His fingers curled over the steering wheel in a death grip. Damn, it was hot, even though he was parked in the shade of a solitary oak tree, whose branches stretched over the fence guarding the small house.

He cracked open the window just a bit and a breath of hot, dusty wind whispered through the van. A dog somewhere up the street barked, grating on his nerves, but still he waited. He'd promised that he would see this child for himself so that he could report back to his partner that she was alive and well.

Suddenly a blond girl with wild hair and big smile dashed from the building. Long legged, her teeth a little too big for her face, she was one of those children who would blossom with age, a cute girl who promised rare beauty in adulthood. Caitlyn Bethany Rawlings, only child of never-married Samantha Rawlings.

He felt a moment's relief as he watched Caitlyn and the rest of the students in Mrs. Evelyn Johnson's fourth-grade class join the other kids already climbing onto the buses or threading through the line of parked cars.

Caitlyn, chattering to a dark-haired, shorter girl, was dressed in jeans and a T-shirt. Tangled curls, so like her mother's, framed a small, tanned face. Freckles dusted her nose, and her eyes, round and blue, squinted until she spied her mother's sorry-looking pickup. With a frantic wave to a couple of friends, she dashed between two parked station wagons and climbed into the passenger side of the vehicle.

Caitlyn was jabbering excitedly to her mother. It was, after all, the last day of school. There was much to say, plans to be made for the summer, he supposed, though little did either female know that their carefully laid plans were about to change in light of his partner's agenda.

He stared through the grimy back window of the Rawl-ingses' truck.

Samantha, listening to her daughter as she flipped on her turn signal, drove out of the parking lot and followed the parade of cars and trucks that headed through the small Wyoming town for the last time this school year.

They passed the stranger's van and he turned away, hoping not to be seen or recognized. Coming to the school in broad daylight was taking a big risk. There was always the chance that someone would catch a glimpse of a person who didn't belong in this small, tightly knit community located at the base of the Teton Mountains. But some chances had to be taken. They were risky, but necessary, if this first part of the plan was going to work.

And come hell or high water, the plan was going to work. Lives depended upon it. Important lives. The lives of the Fortune family.

One

She hasn't changed a bit.

The thought struck Kyle Fortune deep in his gut, bringing back memories best left forgotten as he eased his foot onto the brake of the old Chevy pickup. Bugs spattered the grimy windshield, and the interior was breathless—baked by the unforgiving Wyoming sun.

Samantha Rawlings. The girl he'd left behind. A woman now. Hell, who would've thought she would be the first person he'd run into here in Nowhere, Wyoming? So his luck hadn't changed any. "Damn you, Kate," he growled under his breath, as if his feisty grandmother—the woman who had arranged this little trek back to the family ranch at the base of the Tetons—could hear him even though she was dead. That thought almost brought him to his knees.

Bald tires rolled to a stop. "God help me." In the flash of an instant, a memory long distant seared through his mind, and he saw Samantha as he had a long time ago, lying in a field of bent grass and wildflowers, her red-gold hair fanned around her face. Her body was tanned except for the most private parts, sweet breasts rising skyward, with pink nipples that pointed proudly up at him as he kissed her everywhere—loving her with the wild abandon of youth, never giving a thought to the future, only wanting to plunge himself into her warmth and make love to her forever.

He hadn't seen her in over ten years, and yet his insides tightened and air already hot enough to blister the paint from the hood of his old truck and bleach the color from the grass seemed to sizzle a bit more as he crossed the gravel lot. A cloud of dust settled around his new, too-tight boots.

She didn't even flick a glance in his direction. Too intent on the stubborn-looking colt on the other end of the short tether she held firmly in her hands, she didn't seem to know he'd driven up. They stood eyeball-to-eyeball, a spirited mite of a flame-haired woman and a determined Appaloosa, all rippling muscles and gleaming, sweat-soaked coat.

Sam wasn't giving an inch. Mule-headed as ever, Kyle decided. Her chin was a little more pointed than it had been at seventeen, her lips, now set in a determined line, fuller and her breasts, hidden beneath the faded gingham of her Western-cut shirt, seemed larger than he remembered. But that hair—blond with fiery red streaks—was still the same, still scraped back into a ponytail, with a few wayward locks framing her sweaty face. "You listen to me, you miserable, overpriced piece of horseflesh," she growled, barely moving her lips. "You're going to—" She stopped short as her concentration was broken by Kyle's shadow, stretching past the rail fence and over the hard, dry ground to crawl across the toes of her boots. Her eyes sliced a glance in his direction and she audibly gasped, her fingers losing their tenacious grip. "Kyle?"

Sensing his advantage, the horse twisted his great black-and-white head and stripped the reins from her hands. With a triumphant whistle, he reared and pivoted, a magnificent stallion who had won again. "Hey, wait, you blasted, miserable..." But the stallion was already gone, kicking up dust as he raced to the far end of the corral and the shade of a solitary pine tree.

"Great! Just great! Now look what you've made me do!" Stalking to the fence, she stripped the rubber band from her hair and stuffed it into the pocket of her tight, faded jeans. "Thanks for messing me up!"

"It's not my fault you lost control of the horse." So her tongue was just as sharp as ever. It figured.

"Sure it is." Squinting against the sun, she eyed him up and down. "So the prodigal grandson has returned. What happened? Lose your Ferrari in a poker game? Take a wrong turn on your way to Monte Carlo?"

"Something like that."

Leaning over the top rail of the fence, she blew her bangs out of her eyes. "You know, Kyle, you're the last person I ever expected to see again. Ever." Hot color caressed high, sculpted cheekbones and sweat dripped from the tip of her nose.

"I guess you haven't heard."

"Heard what?"

He felt a grain of satisfaction to be the one to break the news. "Believe it or not, I'm the new owner of this place."

"You?" She stared straight into his eyes, as if checking for lies, as if she expected him to disregard the truth or stretch it to his own advantage. "*You* own the Fortune Ranch? Just you? No one else?" Was there a note of disapproval in her steady tone?

"The whole spread."

"But—"

"You didn't know?"

She actually paled, the dusting of freckles on the bridge of her nose becoming more visible. "I—I knew that one of Kate's children or grandchildren would probably end up with the..." Her eyes moved from his face to the vast acres of rolling pastureland, dry and brown in midsummer. Clumps of sagebrush were scattered along the fence line and a tumbleweed rolled lazily past the weathered barn. Sam swallowed hard as her gaze settled on him again. "I mean, someone was bound to inherit it, but I never once thought... Oh, for the love of Mike, why you?"

"Beats me."

"You're a city boy now, aren't you?" Her chin rose a little bit, as if she were suddenly defiant. "You haven't set foot here in years."

"About ten," he agreed, and saw her gaze shift away, as if she, too, didn't want to think about that last summer they'd shared. It seemed a lifetime ago, though his blood still raced a little at the sight of her. That would have to change.

"So you're here...why? To live?" she asked, wrinkling her brow as if she couldn't believe it.

"For the time being. There's a catch to my inheritance."

"A catch?"

"Kate left the ranch and everything on it—well, almost everything—with the condition that I can't sell the place or even one item of equipment until I've lived here for six months."

Six months! Kyle was going to be her neighbor for the next half year? Sam's knees hitched a little. "But you don't intend to really stay here," she said, panic chasing through her innards.

"Haven't got much of a choice."

There had been a time when she'd hoped to see him again, had planned the day, been ready to tell him off, nail him and call him the bastard he was. But she didn't want it to happen like this, not so unexpectedly, blind-siding her when she wasn't ready. "You'll be here through Christmas?" she asked, feeling as if the wind had been knocked out of her.

"That's the plan."

He looked so cocky, so damned citified in his starched jeans, new hat, polo shirt and polished boots. He had no place being here. Oh, God, now what? Trying to regain her equilibrium and think clearly, she blurted, "But, but what about Grant?" He was the only one of Kate Fortune's grandchildren faintly interested in ranching. Sam reminded herself that Grant McClure wasn't a blood relative, but a stepbrother to Kyle and stepgrandson to Kate. Not that it had mattered during Kate's lifetime. She'd treated Grant as if he were blood kin, though he'd spent little time with the Fortune family.

"Grant inherited a horse." Kyle's gaze traveled to the muscular stallion who was eyeing the intruder with interest. The beast had the audacity to snort at him. "Fortune's Flame."

"Joker."

"What?"

She nodded toward the stallion. "That's him. They've called him Joker from the time he was a foal. Always in trouble, and with his odd markings—" she motioned to the splashes of white on the animal's coal black face "—it just seemed to fit."

"And what do you call him?"

"Today?" she said with a twisted smile. "Demon, for starters. I have other names, but they're not fit for mixed company." Again she blew a stubborn strand of hair off her face as Kyle laughed, the sound rich and deep, like the first crack of thunder in a spring storm.

Why hadn't Kyle aged poorly? Why was he trim and

fit, his face more chiseled now that all trace of boyishness had disappeared? Where was the hint of a belly? The graying of his hair? The softness of a rich man who didn't have to raise a finger? Instead he was all hard angles and tight skin, slim in the waist and hips, wide across the shoulders. If anything, time had been inordinately kind to Kyle Fortune.

"I haven't met a horse yet that you couldn't handle."

"Joker, here, just might be the one," she said, though her mind wasn't on the conversation, not when there were so many raw emotions racing through her, scraping against her heart. "He'll be the death of me, I swear."

"I doubt it, Sam. The way I remember it, you liked nothing better than a challenge."

"Funny. That's not what I remember."

All the laughter disappeared from his eyes. "No? Then what?"

Oh, Lord. Her heart squeezed painfully. "You don't want to know."

"Try me."

"Already have. It didn't work out."

His lips flattened over his teeth and his jaw turned to granite. "You know, Sam, we don't have to start out this way."

"Sure we do." *Oh, Kyle, if you only knew.* Naked, gut-wrenching emotions tore at her and she could barely breathe. Life just wasn't fair. Why was Kyle Fortune, the one man on this earth she'd sworn to despise, so damned sexy, even in his pressed Levi's and the Ralph Lauren shirt that stretched a bit over his shoulders? He probably worked out in some gym, lifted weights until the sweat ran down his body as he eyed the women in their leotards, thongs and bodysuits. Kyle had always attracted females—like horse dung attracted flies. *Including you,* she reminded herself grimly.

Dusting off her hands, she climbed to the top rail of the fence. ''Since you're here and all, I guess I can go home. I was just watching the place, playing overseer until Kate could hire a new foreman. Then she…'' Sam couldn't say the word, couldn't believe that Kate Fortune—feisty, fun-loving, full-of-life Kate—could actually be dead. Though the woman had to be in her seventies, she'd been nowhere near the grave when a hellish plane crash over the rain forests of Brazil changed everything and snatched away Kate Fortune's life.

''How's your dad?'' Kyle asked, and Sam's heart felt as if it were suddenly filled with lead.

''Gone. He died about five years ago.''

''Oh. Sorry. I…'' He lifted his hands. ''I didn't know.''

She shook her head. ''Doesn't surprise me. You don't know much about anything here in Clear Springs, do you?'' His eyes, blue as the summer sky, clouded a bit, and though she knew she was being cruel, she couldn't help but ask, ''Why in the world would Kate leave you this ranch when you've made a point of avoiding it for so long?''

A muscle came to life in his jaw. His fingers clenched, then straightened, and his gaze drilled into hers as if he was offended that she would be so direct. Finally he shrugged and looked away. ''Beats me,'' he admitted, and she believed him. He squinted as he took off his new hat, showing off thick brown hair that was streaked by the sun. It ruffled in a breeze that swirled through the paddock and bent a few long weeds clustered near the fence posts.

''You know, I really liked your grandmother,'' Sam

said, thinking of the strong-willed woman who ran a cosmetics company in Minneapolis with an iron-fisted grip and yet was known around these parts for her rhubarb pie. An independent woman of many talents, Kate loved her family fiercely and had been determined throughout her life to make her mark, not only in business, but with her children and grandchildren as well. She'd loved her ranch nearly as much as she loved Fortune Cosmetics. "I can't believe that I'll never see her again."

His head jerked up, as if she'd hit a painful nerve.

"Look, what I'm trying to say," she added, tongue-tied for one of the first times in her life, "is that I'm sorry she…she's gone."

"Me, too," he said with a heartfelt sigh, then scowled, as if talking about Kate's death was too painful a topic. Clearing his throat, he hitched his chin in the stallion's direction. "So what were you doing with the horse?"

"Trying and failing, thank you very much, to teach him to walk on a lead. He's the most valuable stallion on the spread, and several ranchers in the area have been asking about hiring him as a stud. The problem is he's got a mind of his own and, like a lot of men I know, doesn't much like being told what to do. He hates the lead, refuses to be loaded into a trailer and is a general pain in the backside," she added, but smiled. Truth to tell, she admired Joker and his fierce independence. Though his bloodlines were pure, it was his attitude that often teased a grin from Samantha's lips.

As if on cue, the stallion lifted his head, flared his nostrils and let out a neigh as a mare, her spindly-legged foal prancing behind, grazed closer to the paddock where Joker was penned.

"He does like the ladies," she observed.

"A mistake."

Shooting Kyle a sharp glance, Sam felt her smile disappear. "Experience talking?"

His jaw tightened a bit. "Look, Sam, I know I—"

"Forget it," she said, cutting him off swiftly. "Ancient history. Let's not discuss it, okay?" *But you'll have to, won't you? You can't just ignore the past—not now, not when he's back in Wyoming, not when he deserves to know the truth.* Her conscience was sometimes a royal pain in the neck. Sure, she had no choice other than to confide in him, but not yet. Not now. "Let's just take care of the horse." With that she stalked across the paddock, and Kyle followed. She talked in soft tones to Joker, and he responded as he always did, by bolting to the far end of the corral. Sam's nerves were stretched tight as she approached the beast again, but this time the fire was out of him, and as quickly as a dime flips when tossed into the air, Joker gave up and allowed Sam to lead him back to the stables, where she unsnapped the tether and fed and watered him.

To her consternation, Kyle didn't leave her side. As if he were fascinated by her handling of the horse, he followed her into the stables and eyed the old building that was now his—concrete floor, rough cedar walls, hayloft stretching over the row of stalls and tack room where saddles, bridles and halters gave off the warm scent of oiled leather.

"You live in your folks' place?" he asked, peering around curiously. Sunlight filtered in through windows thick with grime. Dust motes played in a few feeble rays of sunlight that pierced the interior.

"Yeah."

"Alone?"

"With my daughter," she said, closing the stall door. The latch clicked into place and seemed to echo in the stillness, broken only by a frustrated fly buzzing near the window and her own wildly beating heart.

"I didn't know you were married."

"I'm not."

"Oh." He probably thought she was divorced, and for now, until her equilibrium was restored, she'd let him think what he wanted. He could bloody well leap to whatever conclusions his fertile mind conjured up.

She was used to speculation. Raising a child alone in a small town was always grist for the ever-grinding gossip mill. Over the years people had made a lot of wrong assumptions about her—assumptions Sam never bothered correcting. "Mom moved into town when Dad died, but Caitlyn and I—"

"Caitlyn's your daughter?"

She nodded tightly, afraid of giving away too much. "We wanted to stay out here. I was raised in the country and I thought she should be, too."

"What about her father?"

A roar like a wind through the mountains in the middle of a winter storm surged through her brain, creating a headache that pounded behind her eyes. "Caitlyn's father," she repeated. "He's—he's out of the picture." Silently calling herself a coward, she grabbed a brush to stroke Joker's sleek coat.

"Must be tough."

If you only knew. "We manage," she said, throwing her back into her work as nervous sweat began to slide down her spine. *Tell him, Sam, tell him now! You'll never have such a golden opportunity again. For God's sake, he deserves to know that he's got a child, that he's Caitlyn's father!*

"I didn't mean to suggest—"

"Don't worry about it," she interrupted, moving to the

other side of Joker and sending a cloud of dust from the animal's rump. She worked feverishly, her mind racing, her mouth as dry as Sagebrush Gulch in the dead of July.

"If you don't watch out, you'll rub the spots right off of him."

She realized then how intent she'd been on her work. Even Joker, usually never distracted from feed, had crooked his long neck to look at her. "Sorry," she muttered and tossed the brush into a bucket. Kyle was making her nervous, and the subject of Caitlyn's lack of a father was always touchy. Today, in the hot, dark stables, with the very man who was responsible for impregnating her and leaving her alone, Samantha felt trapped. She let herself through the stall door and tried to ignore the way he sat upon the top rail, as he had ten years before, jeans stretched tight over his knees and butt, heels resting on a lower rail, eyes piercing and filled with a sultry dark promise as he watched her. But that was crazy. Those old emotions were gone, dried-up like Stiller Creek in the middle of a ten-year drought.

"Sam..." He reached forward and touched her arm, his fingers grazing her wrist.

She reacted as if she'd been burned, drawing away and throwing open the door. A shaft of bright summer sunlight pierced the dim interior and a breath of hot, dry air followed along. Hurrying outside, she heard his footsteps behind her, new boots crunching on the gravel of the parking area, but she didn't turn around, didn't want to chance looking into his eyes and allowing him to see any hint of what she was feeling, of the bare emotions that surged through her just at the sight of him. Damn it, what was wrong with her? "I—I've been coming over here, doing my dad's old job, acting as foreman ever since the last guy, Red Spencer—he'd been here for seven years or so, I guess, before Dad retired—anyway, Red took over for Dad when Dad couldn't handle the job, but he left a couple of months ago. Moved to Gold Spur, I think it was, to be close to his son and daughter-in-law. Kate asked me to keep an eye on things and I agreed, but now that you're back you won't be needing me—''

"Sam!" This time his fingers found her wrist, clamped tightly and spun her around so fast she could barely catch her breath. "You're rambling, and near as I remember, that's not like you."

"But you don't know me anymore, do you?" she said, her anger, ten years old and instantly white-hot, taking control of her tongue. "You don't know a damned thing about me, and that's because it's the way you wanted it!"

"For the love of—"

She yanked back her hand. "All the records are in the den." Making a sweeping gesture toward the house, she kept walking to her truck. "It looks like your tractor might need a new clutch, there's a buyer from San Antonio interested in most of your cattle, I've got a list of people who want Diablo—er, Joker—as a stud. The hay's in early this year and—"

"And you're running scared."

"What?" She whirled and faced him, fury pumping through her bloodstream, hands planted on her hips.

"I said you're—"

"I heard what you said, I just couldn't believe it. You," she said, eyes narrowing in silent, seething anger as she pointed a furious finger at him, "of all people have no right, *no right* to accuse anyone of running!" Throwing her hands into the air, she looked up at the blue sky with its smattering of veil-thin clouds. "You're unbelievable, Kyle. Un-be-liev-a-ble!" Turning on a well-worn heel, she stormed to her truck, threw the rig into gear and ripped out of the parking lot, leaving Kyle in his fancy new boots, tight jeans and designer shirt to eat her dust.

''Is somethin' wrong?'' Caitlyn, sitting on the far side of the old pickup, pinned her mother with blue eyes so like her father's as the truck sped into town.

Tar oozed on the shoulders of the old country road. Hot air blew threw the open windows, catching Caitlyn's already tangled wheat blond hair.

''Wrong?'' Samantha's heart tightened as she shifted down for a corner. The sun was sitting low on the horizon and waves of heat shimmered from the asphalt, distorting the false fronts of the Western-looking buildings. Clear Springs paid homage to the latter part of the nineteenth century with its architecture.

''Yeah, you've been acting funny ever since you picked me up.'' Caitlyn wasn't having any of her mother's double-talk.

''I suppose I have,'' Sam admitted, remembering how Kyle had rattled her cage. She'd been still fuming as she'd retrieved her daughter from a friend's house.

''Why?''

''I just saw an old…friend today. It took me a little by surprise.''

''So?''

Yeah, right. *So?* ''And I have a headache.'' That wasn't a lie. From the second she'd laid eyes on Kyle Fortune, her head had been pounding.

''Your friend gave you a headache?'' Caitlyn shook her head, still not buying her story. ''You look mad.''

''Mad?''

''Uh-huh. The same way you looked last year when

you found out that Billy McGrath had his birthday party and invited everyone but me and Tommy Wilkins.''

Sam's blood boiled at the memory of that incident. ''Well, that was wrong and Billy's mother knew it was wrong and… Oh, well, it's all water under the bridge now.'' Samantha reached toward the dashboard and grabbed her sunglasses. At the time she'd wanted to throttle bratty Billy and his snob of a mother, who had decided that two kids out of a class of twenty-one weren't good enough to attend the birthday swimming party. The two kids who were whispered to be illegitimate.

''So why'd your friend make you mad?''

''He didn't…he just showed up unexpectedly and it surprised me,'' she hedged, then tapped Caitlyn's smudged nose. ''I've got to stop at the bank and the post office, but then we can get an ice cream at The Freeze.''

Caitlyn's eyebrows smoothed. ''How about a sundae?''

''Why not?'' Sam exclaimed as she passed the sign welcoming visitors to Clear Springs, Wyoming. Maybe it was time to celebrate. It wasn't every day that her daughter's father landed back in town. Oh, God, how would she ever tell him that he was Caitlyn's dad? What would he do? Laugh in her face? Call her a liar? Be so stunned that his lying, silvery tongue would be finally stilled? Or would he see the naked truth with his own eyes and decide that it was time to become a father? If he wanted even partial custody, there was no way she could fight him. Against the Fortune family money and bevy of lawyers, she wouldn't stand a chance.

Sam's throat was suddenly dry as sand. She pulled into a parking space and told herself not to overreact, that Kyle was only here for six months, that even when he found out that Caitlyn was his daughter, it wouldn't matter. He would be reasonable, wouldn't he? He had to be. But what about Caitlyn? How would she feel about the man who was her father?

Samantha couldn't lose her child. Not to anyone. Not even to the man who had sired her.

Two

"What a mess." With a snort of disgust, Kyle eyed the handwritten ledgers. The musty journal was spread open on the old oak desk that had been in this den for all the years he could remember. The oaken behemoth had belonged to Ben Fortune, Kyle's grandfather and Kate's husband, though Kyle couldn't remember a single time he'd seen Ben sit in the timeworn leather chair. No, this ranch had been Kate's haven from the fast pace of the city, but these damned journals were a mystery. Why no computer system? No link to the Internet? No modem? No accounting program? This wasn't like his grandmother, a woman who had lived her life ahead of her time, who'd used a cell phone and fax machine as easily as she splashed on perfume. Kate Fortune had been connected by computer to all of her late husband's companies, including factories as far away as Singapore and Madrid. Though she'd spoken the language of the wildcatters working for Ben's oil company, she flew her own private jet. If any ranch out in the wilds of Wyoming should have a damned PC and modem, it was Kate's spread. The lack of telecommunications just didn't make sense. Unless Kate came here to get away from the rat race and preferred the leisurely pace that had worked for ranchers for decades.

The phone rang, and Kyle snatched up the receiver,

half expecting to hear Samantha's husky voice on the other end of the line. He tensed. "Kyle Fortune."

"Well, whaddya know!" Grant's voice boomed across the wires as Kyle settled back in his chair. "I heard a nasty rumor you were back in town."

"Bad news travels fast."

"Especially in this family."

Amen, Kyle thought. The Fortunes had always been a close-knit lot, but ever since Kate's death, Kyle had felt a newfound kinship with his cousins and siblings—a camaraderie born of shared grief for a loved one lost.

"Mike called and said you'd taken a company jet to Jackson, so I figured you'd show up sooner or later."

"Just in time to get a look at that beast you inherited."

Grant chuckled. "Fortune's Flame."

"Fortune's Folly, if you ask me."

"I'll take him off your hands as soon as he'll ride in a trailer. I know Samantha's been working with him."

"Seems as such."

Sam. Why couldn't he quit thinking about her?

"I suppose you know that Rocky's thinking about moving out here?"

"Rocky? As in Rachel?"

"Your cousin and mine."

Kyle hadn't seen Rachel since the reading of the will in Kate's lawyer's office. Usually adventurous, with a quick smile, Rocky had been as sober as the rest of the family that day. Dark circles had shadowed her brown eyes and she'd nervously fingered the charm her grandmother had bequeathed her. She'd seemed lost at the time, but then they all had.

"So my horse is okay?"

"I ran into Sam as she was working with him. The stud looked full of the devil."

"He is." Grant chuckled.

Glancing out the window as twilight caressed the land, Kyle said, "Sam's got a kid."

"Yep."

"Said the father was out of the picture. I didn't know she'd been married."

"Wasn't."

"So where is the guy?"

"Beats me. I never asked. Wasn't any of my business," Grant said. Unspoken but implied was the message *and it's none of yours, either.*

Kyle heard the quiet reprimand in Grant's tone but ignored it. "No one knows?"

"Well, I suppose Sam knows, and Bess, her mother. Some of the gossips in town try to point the finger at Tadd Richter. You remember him?"

"Yeah. Never met him, but heard he was a local hood."

"He ran with a fast crowd, rode a big motorcycle, drank and was always in trouble with the law. His folks split up and he ended up in jail, or a juvenile home somewhere near Casper, I think. Anyway, Sam had hung out with him right before he left town and then...well, she turned up pregnant. Not that it's any of your concern. She's kept quiet about it all these years and I figure she's got her reasons.... Anyway, I just called to welcome you to Wyoming."

"Thanks."

"It's not a bad place, you know."

"Never said it was."

"But you weren't too happy to have to move here."

Kyle stared through the panes to the stand of aspen guarding the banks of Stiller Creek. "I don't like being told what to do. Not even by Kate."

"It won't be so bad. You might find you like it out here, discover what it is you're running from or looking for. You never know."

"Nope, you never do." Kyle felt his temper flare a little. Never one to mince words, Grant had let it be known that he hadn't approved of Kyle's rootless lifestyle in Minneapolis.

"Maybe you need to slow down a mite."

"Maybe," Kyle drawled, though his jaw tightened. He didn't need a lecture. He knew that he'd thrown away a few years of his life, dabbling at this business and that, making a little money, sometimes losing a lot. Marrying the wrong woman. Working for the family and getting fired was the latest disaster. He didn't want to be reminded of that failure, nor could he explain the restlessness that had chased after him since boyhood, the feeling that he couldn't stay in one place too long. And, he suspected, six months in Clear Springs with Samantha living next door was going to be far too long.

"I'll be by in a couple of days and see that you're not mistreating Joker."

"Yeah, more likely that stallion will be the end of me."

"Or Sam will."

Amen.

"She's a bossy one. Likes to run things her way."

"I figured that much out already."

"Just remember, she might bug the hell out of you, but she knows a lot more about ranchin' than you do."

"I'll keep that in mind."

"You do that. See ya tomorrow."

Kyle hung up, scowled at the ledgers on the desk and slammed the book closed. *Sam.* He hadn't thought about her in years, wouldn't let himself, but ever since he'd set foot in Wyoming, he couldn't get away from her.

"Damn it all to hell." Rotating his neck, he winced as a vertebra near the top of his spine popped. *Tadd Richter—what had Sam seen in that lowlife?* And why did Kyle care? It was old news.

His coffee, bad instant stuff when it was hot, was now cold and looked as if it might gel. Kyle ignored the cup. The old chair groaned as he stood and walked to a cupboard where, once upon a time, Ben had kept his liquor. Empty. "Strike two." No computer and no liquor, not in this den with its yellowed, knotty pine walls, faded prints of rodeo riders and braided rug tossed over an ancient plank floor. It was as if life out here in godforsaken Wyoming hadn't changed in the past fifty years. "Thanks a lot, Kate," he grumbled, though the ranch in summer had always held a special spot in his heart—a spot he'd rather not remember.

Jet lag hadn't settled in and probably wouldn't. The plane ride from Minneapolis to Jackson hadn't been all that bad, nor had the trip out to the ranch in his hastily purchased, used pickup. No, it wasn't the travel that bothered him so much as the feeling that he was being manipulated. Again. By his grandmother. From her damned grave.

Snapping off the desk lamp, he walked in his stocking feet through the long hall that ran the length of this rambling, two-story house, the place where he'd spent many of his summer vacations. Sometimes the family had taken trips to faraway and exotic places—Mexico, Jamaica, Hawaii or India. But the summers he remembered best, the ones he cherished, weren't when he was ensconced in some opulent hotel boasting five-star restaurants, mineral springs and connecting pools. No, the best summers of his life he'd spent here, learning how to rope calves, saddle horses, brand the stock, skinny-dip in Stiller Creek and sleep under the blanket of stars in the vast Wyoming sky.

Kyle walked up the steep, uncarpeted stairs to the second floor, where a warren of attic rooms was housed. At the end of the hall was the bunk room in which he and his cousins had slept. He felt the worn wood of the door and touched the gouge where Michael had broken the lock when Kyle and Adam had locked him out. Kyle had been about twelve at the time. Michael, a year older and full of piss and vinegar, wasn't about to let a little latch keep him from breaking open the door and seeking some kind of vengeance for his brother catching him off guard and nailing him with a stream of ice-cold water from the garden hose.

Smiling, Kyle remembered Michael, dripping from head to toe as he'd crashed through the door and sprawled into the room, clunking his head on the end of one of the bunks and nearly knocking himself out.

It seemed like a lifetime ago. Before he'd started shaving, before he'd really noticed girls. Before Sam.

Snapping on the light, he walked into the room and eyed the bunks, three sets now without sheets, mattress ticking faded, tucked under the eaves and in the dormers. Nowhere in sight was the carton of cigarettes they'd swiped from their grandfather, the *Playboy* magazines that one of the ranch hands had "loaned" the boys or the bottles of booze they'd hidden deep in their dresser drawers when a local cowboy had, for a stiff fee, bought them whatever kind of rotgut whiskey they could afford.

Running his hand over one of the bed frames, he stopped at the window they'd used for escape. The ledge was located close to an ancient apple tree with wide branches, and the boys had rigged an elaborate system of ropes and pulleys to lower themselves to the ground or climb back up. They'd thought they were so smart, but, Kyle suspected, their grandmother probably knew everything that was going on. She was just too clever to have missed all of their shenanigans.

"Son of a bitch," he growled, his fist curling in grief. To think that she was gone—really gone—caused a raw emptiness deep in his soul. What had she been doing, flying alone in the damned plane, looking for some rare plant in the Amazon rain forest? She'd never made it. Her plane had exploded over Brazil somewhere, falling to earth in a horrifying ball of flames. Her charred body had been shipped back to the States, where her stunned children and grandchildren had fought their disbelief and dealt with the fact that the most influential force in their lives was suddenly gone.

Opening the window, Kyle let in a late-evening breeze and stared across the rolling acres—his acres now, he reminded himself. Well, they would be in six months, if he could hack it here that long. It wasn't as if he was unhappy to leave Minneapolis; his life there had stagnated and he'd never really found himself, never settled down, never held a job long enough to count. No, he'd been restless by nature, and maybe that's why of all her grandchildren, Kyle had been picked by Kate to inherit this ranch. It was probably the old lady's way of forcing him to put down roots.

Hell, he remembered the funeral and the closed casket covered with floral sprays, the church packed with mourners, the family members draped in black and fighting tears. Then later, stunned, barely able to speak, they'd sat around a huge table in Kate's attorney's office and listened while Sterling Foster, seated at the head of the table, his hands folded on Kate's last will and testament, had eyed them all. "Kate Fortune was a remarkable woman, mother of five children—though only four were raised by her," he began, his gaze moving slowly around the table. "Grandmother of what—twelve? And a great-grandmother as well." He smiled sadly. "Though widowed for ten years, she was still the driving force behind Fortune Cosmetics. She survived the death of a husband, Ben, as well as the loss of her child...well, you know all this. First, she instructed me to give everyone the charms she'd collected at the times of your birth. I've taken them from the sculpture in the boardroom that displayed them all." He passed a silver tray with white envelopes around the table, and when the platter reached him, Kyle found his name typed neatly on one of the packets. *Oh, Kate,* he thought sadly as he tore open the envelope and withdrew a silver trinket.

Sterling cleared his throat and lifted the neatly typed papers before him. "I, Katherine Winfield Fortune, being of sound mind and body..."

Everyone's attention was on the lawyer, and Kyle felt his muscles tense. This was all so wrong. It was as if the world had suddenly stopped and shifted beneath his feet.

His sister Jane sat next to him, her fingers tightening over the sleeve of his coat, the antique lace of her cuff smudged with mascara where she'd wiped her eyes. She'd tried to be brave, but her lower lip continued to tremble and she'd clung to him for support. A single mother, she was supposed to be able to stand on her own, to face the challenges life threw at her. But none of them—sons, daughters, grandchildren—could believe that they'd lost someone so dear and integral, the foundation of their lives.

"Oh, God," she moaned, a strand of cinnamon-colored hair falling out of its barrette.

He placed his hand over Jane's and met Michael's somber gaze. Michael's eyes reflected his own misery. Michael. Always responsible. Where Michael had always done the right thing, Kyle had been the screwup. Michael shouldered responsibility; Kyle ran from it.

Jane seemed to gain some starch in her spine. Blinking and straightening her shoulders, she reached for the water pitcher on the table and poured herself a glass. At a signal from Allison, she poured a second glass. Allie the beauty, a model and spokesperson for Fortune Cosmetics, the rich girl with the thousand-watt smile. Now her pretty face was drawn and pale as she sat wedged between her brother and twin sister, Rocky. Even Rocky's normally animated expression was lifeless in her grief.

Rocky seemed to gain a little strength from her only brother, Adam, who, as Sterling droned on, absently patted her shoulder. Adam was the oldest child and only son of Jake and Erica Fortune. Surrounded by sisters, Adam was someone Kyle used to look up to, a kindred spirit— a rebellious son. Adam had turned his back on the family fortune, knocking about the country for a few years before he joined the military, only to give it up when his wife died. Now Adam was a single father with three children and trying to cope.

Kyle didn't envy him. Hell, he didn't envy anyone here today. Tugging at his collar, he tried to concentrate.

Sterling, catching his eye for a brief instant, flipped the page and kept reading in his soft-spoken drawl. Kyle liked the guy. He seemed to shoot from the hip and rarely minced words. Reading glasses were propped on the tip of his nose, and his white hair, impeccably combed, gleamed silver in the gentle light thrown by brass fixtures.

"And to my grandson Grant McClure, I bequeath Fortune's Flame, a registered Appaloosa stallion...."

Kyle watched for a reaction from his stepbrother, but Grant continued to stare out the window, never once flinching at the sound of his name. Grant seemed as out of place here in his jeans, Western-cut jacket and Stetson as a dusty pickup in a parking lot filled with BMWs, Cadillacs and Porsches. Kyle silently wagered with himself that his cowboy stepbrother couldn't wait to climb on a plane, shed the lights of the city and fly back to the harsh life he loved in the middle of nowhere—Clear Springs, Wyoming.

Next to Grant, Kristina, the only child of Nate and Barbara, Kyle's father and stepmother, fidgeted in her chair and bit her lower lip nervously while trying to appear interested. Spoiled beyond belief, she tossed a strand of blond hair over her shoulder and looked like she wanted nothing more than to flee from the stuffy attorney's office. She caught Kyle's eye, sent him a silent message, then glanced away.

He didn't blame her. They'd suffered through the funeral, graveside service and a catered buffet afterward for the closest friends and family of Kate. Hundreds of sympathy cards, a veritable garden of flowers and sprays and tens of thousands of dollars in checks to Kate's favorite charities had been arriving in a steady stream. Then there was the press and the speculation about her death, how she'd flown the company jet alone over the jungles of South America, somehow lost control and perished a horrible, mind-numbing death....

Kyle ground his teeth together.

"...And to my grandson Kyle, I leave the ranch in

Clear Springs, Wyoming, with all livestock and equipment, aside from the stallion, Fortune's Flame...." Kyle had barely been listening until the stipulation was read: "...Kyle must reside on the ranch for no less than six months before the deed and all other necessary paperwork is transferred into his name...."

It was just like his grandmother to bequeath him the ranch—the one oasis of his childhood—with strings attached. He heard his brother Michael's swift intake of breath, probably because of the value of the ranch and the fact that Kyle had never made anything of himself—not really.

Later, Michael had spoken to him alone, given him some speech about responsibility, taking control of his life, making the most of the opportunity Kate had given him.

Kyle hadn't listened much. He didn't need lectures. He knew he'd fouled up and he didn't figure it was any of Mike's damned business what he did with his future. It was his to gild or ruin.

But his brother was right about one thing. Now Kyle had a chance to prove himself by living here on the ranch, making the necessary repairs and eventually selling it all for a tidy profit, though that probably wasn't what the old lady wanted.

"What did you expect?" he said to the empty room, as if his grandmother could hear him. "Did you really think you could control me from the grave? Did you? Well, you're wrong. I'm gonna sell this place like that...." He snapped his fingers and reached for the latch of the window, but as he closed the pane, he glanced out at the starry night, past the old orchard to the neighboring ranch, where a lamp glowed brightly in one of the windows.

Sam.

An unexpected jolt of emotion caused his heart to kick. For a fleeting instant he wondered if his grandmother had planned to place him in such close proximity with the one woman who could make him want to strangle her one instant and make love to her the next. But that was impossible. No one, but no one, had known about his affair with Sam—well, only Sam and himself—and that was the way it would always stay.

He stared at the warm patch of lamplight, a welcoming beacon, it seemed, and gritted his teeth as he realized he'd like nothing better than to walk across those moonlit fields, pound on her door and take her into his arms. He'd kiss her as he used to, with the same passion that had steamed through his blood and brought his manhood springing to attention years ago.

But crossing the fence line to the Rawlings place was the last thing on earth he planned to do.

Turning on his heel, he nearly slammed his head on a low-hanging crossbeam before he stalked out of the room. He felt cornered and manipulated and frustrated as he thought about Sam. As if his grandmother was listening from her spot on the other side of the pearly gates, he grumbled, "Okay, Kate. You've won. So I'm here. Just tell me one thing. What the hell am I supposed to do about Sam?"

Three

"Great, just great." Sam kicked off her boots on the back porch, where a moth was beating itself senseless against the exterior light. She stole a glance past the barbed-wire fence to the few visible acres of the Fortune spread and wondered again what Kyle was up to.

All afternoon and evening she'd been fighting a blinding headache that had developed when she'd first set eyes on Kyle Fortune after ten long years. Throughout her chores she'd thought about him, wishing she'd never have to deal with him again, while knowing deep in her foolish heart that she had no choice.

Why had Kate—a woman Sam had admired for her courage and clear vision—seen fit to leave the place to him, when she had more than a dozen descendants to choose from? Kyle was the least fit to run the ranch, the most unlikely candidate for adopting Wyoming as his home. Why not Grant, who had never left Clear Springs? Or how about Rachel, who many people in town thought was so like her grandmother? Rocky, Kyle's cousin, was adventurous, a pilot, for crying out loud, and she'd always loved Clear Springs. But no, Kate had chosen Kyle and then strapped him to the place for six long months—right next door to Sam.

Padding to the kitchen sink, she muttered under her breath, cranked on the faucets, then splashed cold water on her face, letting it drip onto her blouse. "Criminy," she said under her breath before taking a long swallow from the faucet. If she had any brains or courage, she'd call Kyle, tell him she needed to talk to him, and then, once she was face-to-gorgeous-face with him again, admit that they had a daughter, a beautiful tomboy of a girl.

"Oh, right. And then what?" she wondered aloud as she wiped her sleeve over her mouth. Kyle would either turn tail and run—if history served to repeat itself—or he'd demand proof of paternity and then, once the results of the blood tests were announced, probably expect no less than partial custody. "Damn it all to—" She stopped short when she caught a glimpse of Caitlyn's reflection in the window over the sink. "What're you doing up?"

"What're you doing cursing?"

Sam sighed and straightened the sleeves she'd pushed up over her elbows. With the special smile she reserved for her daughter, she lifted a shoulder. "Okay, you caught me," she admitted. "I'm upset, I guess."

"Because of your friend?" Caitlyn was eyeing her oddly. Her nine-year-old face was puckered in concentration, her Fortune blue eyes silently accusing.

"Yeah, because of him."

"You tell me not to let other people bother me."

"Good advice. I guess I'll take it. Now, why don't you explain why you're up so late? I thought you went to bed an hour ago."

"Couldn't sleep," Caitlyn said with a shrug, but the lines of concern didn't smooth from her forehead.

"Why not?"

"It's hot."

"And...?" Sam prodded, walking up to her daughter and, with gentle hands, turning her toward the stairs leading to her bedroom.

"And..." Caitlyn worried her lip.

"What is it?"

"It's Jenny Peterkin," Caitlyn finally admitted with a scowl.

"What about Jenny?" Samantha didn't like the topic of the conversation. Jenny was a spoiled ten-year-old who had been the bane of Caitlyn's existence since second grade.

"I think she called me."

"You *think?*"

"Yeah. While you were in the barn, the phone rang and someone asked for me and said they were Tommy Wilkins, but it didn't sound like him and I heard laughing." She swallowed and looked at the floor.

"What did Tommy or Jenny or whoever it was say to you?"

"That I'm—I'm a bastard."

Oh, Lord, give me strength. "You know better than that, Caitie girl. As for the people on the other end of the phone line, they're just a pack of cruel ninnies," Sam said, aching inside for her daughter. "They don't know a thing about you." She bent down and wrapped her arms around Caitlyn's shoulders. This wasn't the first time her daughter's lack of a father had been brought to her attention and it probably wasn't going to be the last, but each time it hurt a little more.

"Is it true?"

"What?"

"I looked up the word in the dictionary and—and I am one. I don't got no daddy."

"It's true I wasn't married to your father, but you've got one, honey. Everyone has a daddy."

"Where's mine? Who is he?" Caitlyn's lower lip trembled slightly and fat tears filled the corners of her eyes.

"He's a man who lives far away. I told you that."
Why now? With Kyle so darned close, why did those little snots have to bring up Caitlyn's lack of a father now?

"You said I could meet him someday."

"And you will."

"When?"

With a sad smile, Sam said, "Sooner than I want you to, I'm afraid."

"Will I like him?"

Sam nodded. "I think so. Most people do."

"But not you."

"It's more complicated than liking him or not. You'll see. Now, would you like a snack before you go back to bed?"

Caitlyn's eyes narrowed, as if she knew that she was being manipulated. At nine she wasn't as easily distracted as she had once been. "But, Mom—"

"The next time Jenny or Tommy or whoever it is calls, you tell them they're to leave you alone. No, better yet, don't say anything, just give me the phone. I'll handle them. Now, are you okay?"

"Yeah, I guess." She sniffed back her tears and the trauma, at least for the moment, seemed to have passed. Sighing loudly, Caitlyn walked to the window and looked in the direction of the barn. She ran her finger along the sill. "I was thinking." She slid her mother a sly look.

"About?"

"You promised me a horse for my birthday, remember?"

"That I did, but your birthday isn't until next spring."

"I know, but Christmas is before that."

"Still half a year away." *Six months—the same amount of time that Kyle had to spend in Wyoming.*

Together mother and daughter walked up the narrow

flight of wooden stairs to Caitlyn's tiny bedroom, the very room where Sam had spent her childhood years. She shoved open the window. A slight breeze lifted the faded curtains, carrying with it the scents of dry hay and roses from the garden. Crickets chirped, their soft chorus interrupted by an occasional moan of a lost calf or the mournful howl of a coyote high in the mountains.

Caitlyn tumbled into her bed—the canopied twin that Sam had slept in—and tried to stifle a yawn. "Love ya," she murmured into her pillow, in that moment looking so much like Kyle that Sam's throat ached.

"Me, too." Sam kissed her daughter on one rosy cheek, but before she could snag a pair of dusty jeans and a T-shirt from the floor and depart, Caitlyn stirred.

"Leave the light on."

Sam grabbed the dirty clothes, but didn't move from the room. "Why?"

With a lift of her shoulder, Caitlyn sighed. "Don't know."

"Sure you do. You've slept in the dark since you were two." The hairs at the nape of Sam's neck lifted. "Is something wrong?" she asked, "Something more than Jenny Peterkin's phone calls?"

Caitlyn bit her lip, a sure sign something else was troubling her.

Still holding on to the wrinkled laundry, Sam lowered herself to the foot of Caitlyn's bed. "Okay, honey, stop pussyfootin' around. What is it?"

"I—I don't know," Caitlyn admitted, her face drawing into a worried pout. "Just a feeling."

Sam's throat went dry. "A feeling? Of what?"

"Like—like someone's watching me."

"Someone? Who?"

"I don't know!" Caitlyn said, pulling the hand-pieced

quilt to her neck, though it was over ninety degrees in the little room.

"You saw someone?" Oh, dear God, was someone stalking her child? It happened to famous people in the city, but sometimes perverted creeps followed children.... Please, please, God, no!

"I didn't *see* anyone but...it's just like, you know, when you *feel* that someone's staring at you. Sometimes Zach Bellows looks at me funny, and even though his desk is behind mine and I can't see him, I *know* he's watching me. It's creepy."

"Of course it is," Sam said, her heart pumping wildly. "But if you didn't see anyone... When did this happen?"

"A couple of times at school, and then once when I was at the store."

"Was anyone with you when this happened? A friend or a teacher or someone who might have noticed who was watching you?" Sam asked, trying like hell not to panic, when her stomach was twisting into painful knots.

Caitlyn shook her head.

"So why are you...worried tonight?"

Caitlyn chewed on her lip. "I—I just feel weird."

"Well, that does it!" Sam pasted a smile on her lips, though her insides were churning. "You're sleeping with me. And don't worry about anyone watching you. We've got the greatest watchdog in the world and—"

"Fang?" Caitlyn laughed, the concern disappearing from her eyes.

"Yeah, and I lock all the doors and windows at night. This is all probably just your imagination, anyway. Come on."

Dragging the quilt with her, Caitlyn scurried into the bedroom across the hall and jumped onto Sam's double bed. She burrowed deep in the covers. "Can we watch TV?" she asked, a glint in her eye.

"I thought you were tired."

"Please?"

Wondering if she'd been conned by the youngest flim-flam artist ever to walk the planet, Sam agreed. She double-checked the locks on the doors, made sure that Fang was in his favorite position near the base of the stairs, then stole a glance through the kitchen window to the Fortune ranch. The night, illuminated by a quarter moon, was serene, not sinister; the only immediate problem looming in their future was Kyle Fortune. Sam climbed the stairs, listening to the third step creak as it always did, but knowing that her life and Caitlyn's would never be the same.

Kyle swatted at a pesky horsefly with his clipboard as he walked through the stables and eyed the barrels of grain, tack, veterinary supplies, tools and bales of hay. Though it was early morning, not yet nine, he'd already been to the barn, three sheds, the machine shop and pump house. He intended to compare the notes and figures he'd scribbled down to the ledgers in the den, then input the data into the computer he'd ordered over the phone. Laptop, modem, software and printer were supposedly on their separate ways. The Fortune Ranch was finally going to join the twentieth and twenty-first centuries.

The stables seemed musty and close, the thick air already gathering heat. Sharp odors of horse dung, sweat, urine and oiled leather mingled with the familiar scent he'd always associated with this place. Aluminum buckets, pitchforks, shovels and rakes hung from hooks on the walls. Along with the fire extinguisher was a kerosene lantern, ready to be lit should the electricity fail.

He heard Joker, the only stallion fenced near the build-ings, let out a piercing whistle. The stud was bad news, Kyle had determined, but he would miss the spotted beast when Grant decided to haul him to his place. Kyle would always associate the Appaloosa with seeing Sam again.

With that nagging thought clogging his brain, he slid his sunglasses from his pocket and onto the bridge of his nose as he stepped outside. Harsh sunlight glinted off the metal roof of the machine shed.

The stallion neighed again.

"It's okay, boy," a kid's voice intoned.

Kyle stopped dead in his tracks. Balanced on the top rail of the fence was a girl—somewhere between eight and twelve, near as he could guess—talking to the damned horse. Fiery blond hair sprang from the restraint of a once-upon-a-time ponytail, and her arms and legs, sprouting from cutoff jeans and a yellow T-shirt, were tanned and long. Boots covered her feet, and dust and grime spattered her clothes. He couldn't see her face, as she was turned the other way, concentrating on the horse.

"What're you doin' here?" Kyle asked, and she visi-bly started, nearly toppling from her perch as she glanced over her shoulder.

"Who're you?" Blue eyes over a spray of freckles were indignant.

"I think that's my line." He walked forward, studying her, and realized in an instant that she was Samantha's kid. She had the same proud tilt of her chin, the same full lips and straight, slightly upturned nose.

"I'm Caitlyn," she said with an edge of defiance, as if he dared challenge her. Like mother, like daughter. "Caitlyn Rawlings."

"Glad to meet you. I'm Kyle Fortune." She stared at him without so much as flinching, holding his gaze fast, unlike most kids he knew. "I know your mom. Is she here?" he asked, his eyes scanning the parking lot for Sam's truck.

"Nah." The kid squirmed a little, as if she either didn't trust him or knew she was somewhere she shouldn't be.

"No?" He leaned against the fence, staring at the imp who was so like her mother. "But she does know you're here?"

Caitlyn gnawed on her lower lip, as if contemplating a lie. Instead she hedged. "Kinda."

"Well, either she does or she doesn't."

The girl's eyes, a shade of summer blue, slid away. "She thinks I walked over to Tommy's house. He lives over there...." She pointed a finger to the west. "But I took a shortcut through the fields and..."

"Ended up talkin' to Joker."

"Yeah. I'd better hurry," she said, as if she suddenly realized she might be in trouble. She hopped to the ground and dusted off her hands, then hesitated. "Fortune? Like Mrs. Kate?"

"She was my grandmother."

The kid grinned. "You were lucky."

He couldn't argue the point. "She left me this ranch."

"So you live here now?" Her mouth rounded in awe and those blue eyes sparkled like sunlight on a mountain lake. "Wow, you *are* lucky."

"You think so?" He glanced around, noticed the weather vane mounted over the roof of the stables—a running horse—as it turned with the wind. "I guess so. Anyway, I'll be here for a while. Until Christmas." Why did he feel compelled to tell her his life story? Probably the clarity of her eyes. And deep down, he'd always liked kids.

"What then?"

"I'll probably sell the place."

"Why?"

"It'll be time."

"If I owned it, I'd *never* sell it. My mom says it's the best ranch in the valley."

"Does she?" Kyle couldn't help but be amused. An interesting kid, this Caitlyn Rawlings. Precocious, smart and, he suspected, a little cunning.

She was already walking backward toward the lane. "I gotta git. Mom'll be callin' over to Tommy's if I don't phone her first and tell her that I got there." Whirling on her heel, she made tracks down the lane, and Kyle watched her go. Instinctively he knew she was a tomboy who caught grasshoppers, splashed in creeks, probably shot a .22 and built forts out of hay bales. He doubted if she ever played with dolls, dressed up in her mother's old clothes or hosted a tea party. Yep, he thought, watching her slide between two strands of barbed wire and start running across the western acres, she was definitely Sam's daughter.

"Well, look at you," Grant said as he stepped through the screen door and eyed his stepbrother half an hour after Kyle had met Caitlyn. "If I didn't know better I'd think you were an honest-to-goodness cowboy."

"Right," Kyle drawled, sarcasm dripping from the single word.

"Got any coffee?"

"Instant."

Grant's grin inched a little wider. "What? No espresso or cappuccino or whatever the hell it is you city slickers drink?"

Kyle snorted. He couldn't argue. His day in Minneapolis had usually started with a double *latte*, though he wasn't about to admit it here. But he had to concede that his damned cowboy boots pinched a little and his jeans, newly purchased at the local dry-goods store, were still stiff with sizing. "Look, insult me all you want. I'm just bidin' my time until I can sell the ranch and move on. This is day one of the next one hundred and eighty."

"Noble of you," Grant observed.

"Who ever said I was noble?"

"No one. Believe me."

"That's what I thought." He'd never been one to pursue noble causes, didn't know why anyone cared. Oh, sure, he held a grudging respect for people who fought for something they believed in, but he wasn't surprised when the fight backfired and the erstwhile heroes got their teeth knocked in. Kyle figured as long as he didn't break any laws or step too hard on anyone's toes, nothing else much mattered. His only regret, and one that he'd buried deeper than he cared to admit, was Sam. Seeing her again reminded him just how close he'd been to her. But that was a long time ago. They'd been kids. They'd been as wrong for each other then as they were now.

Grant hung his hat on a peg near the back door, then slid into a chair at the old maple table, the same ladderback one he'd claimed as a kid, as Kyle poured them each a cup of the stuff he called coffee. "So you saw Sam again," Grant said as Kyle handed him a mug that was hot to the touch.

"Yesterday. She was workin' with that devil you inherited."

"Only one who can handle him."

"That so?"

"Sam's become quite a horsewoman."

Was there a note of awe in his stepbrother's voice?

For some unnamed reason Kyle experienced a jab of jealousy. Not that he had any reason to care. "I suppose she has."

Grant took a long swallow of coffee and wrinkled his nose. "No one bothered to teach you how to cook."

"Tell me about Sam." Sitting on one worn, maple seat, he propped the heel of one boot on the chair next to him.

"She's been a godsend. When Jim got sick, she took over. Stepped right into her dad's shoes. He taught her everything she knows about ranchin', which is one helluva lot, and when he died, she ran things here as well as at her own place." He swirled the contents of his cup and frowned. "Kate depended on Sam to keep things going when she wasn't around, even though she hired one guy—Red Spencer—as foreman. He wasn't as sharp as Jim, and Sam helped out when she could. Then Red retired and everything fell on Sam's shoulders. Kate paid her and tried to find someone else, but no one was as honest and straightforward as Samantha Rawlings. No one else really cared about the ranch and then…well, Kate died and Sam stepped in."

"Sounds like she walks on water." This time Kyle was certain he'd heard a hint of reverence in his stepbrother's voice.

"Don't tell her that."

He twisted his cup in his hands. "Or else you're half in love with her."

Grant grinned and ran a hand through his short, sandy brown hair. "Me? No way, and I pity the poor fool who is. She's one mule-headed lady. I like my women a little bit less short-tempered."

"Oh, yeah, right." Kyle wasn't convinced and didn't bother hiding his feelings. Grant had been a bachelor for years, but he wasn't immune to women—especially the smart, good-looking kind. Like Sam. "I met her kid today."

"Caitlyn?"

"Mmm. She was here less than half an hour ago. Looks a lot like her ma."

"Yeah. Same temperament, too. Kinda has a way of weaseling her way into your heart."

"Like Sam does?"

Grant grinned and his eyes glinted. "Why would you care?"

"I don't."

"Well, speak of the devil," Grant said at the sound of a truck roaring down the lane. A plume of dust followed the old Dodge as it rumbled to a stop near the house. "I think I'd better see how she's gettin' along with Joker."

"The devil horse? Not too well, if yesterday's exhibition was any indication."

"You want to try a hand with him?"

"Hell no. The farther I am from that mean bastard, the better I'll like it. If Kate hadn't seen fit to let you have him, I would have probably sold him to the glue factory," Kyle said, but a smile tugged at the corners of his mouth.

"Sure." Grant finished his coffee, but his eyes never left the window and Sam's truck.

"Look, I have to live here for the next six months, but I don't think there was anything in my legacy about risking life and limb trying to train some self-important stud how to follow on a lead rope."

"I assume you're talking about the horse and not about me." Grant was still staring out the window, and Kyle let his own gaze follow as Samantha hopped to the ground and blew her bangs from her eyes.

"Take it any way you want," Kyle said. "You know, she looks mad enough to spit nails. I think I'll go check on my horse."

"Chicken."

Grant reached for his hat. "You bet. I made a promise to myself years ago that I would never sit around and be chewed out by a woman before ten in the morning. It starts the day off on the wrong foot." His eyes narrowed as he rammed the hat on his head. "You know the saying about someone getting a bee in her bonnet? This may just be a guess, but from the looks of her, I'd say Samantha has a hornet's nest in hers."

Samantha slammed the door of her pickup. Her jeans were tight and black, her shirt faded denim with the sleeves rolled to her elbows, as if she were ready for a fight. Her lips were compressed into a firm, determined line. Before Grant could walk out the back door, she stormed in, the screen door slapping shut behind her.

Kyle felt a smile stretch across his face, though he wished he could hide his amusement, because if looks could kill, he'd have dropped dead the second she swung her furious green gaze in his direction.

"Mornin', Sam," Grant drawled.

"Mornin'," she offered.

"I was just leavin'."

"Wait. I was gonna call you," she said, laying a hand on Grant's arm—so friendly and intimate it made Kyle's teeth grate. "What do you want to do about Joker now that Kyle's back?"

"I'll move him in the next week or so. No hurry. By that time I assume he'll walk docilely up the ramp into the trailer."

Sam couldn't help but grin, and Kyle felt an unwanted

kick in his gut. How many times had she, a tomboy of seventeen, trained that smile on him?

"I guess that's up to Kyle. He's in charge now." Her smile faded and was replaced by her original expression, the one plastered on her face as she'd marched grimly to the porch. Tiny white lines pinched the corners of her mouth, a deep furrow was wedged between her eyebrows and the skin over her cheekbones was stretched as taut as a hide ready for tanning as her gaze landed full force on Kyle again. Some of the starch seemed to leave her for a second before she said, "I just came by to pick up some of my things. Now that Kyle's here, it doesn't make much sense for me to hang around."

She breezed past Grant.

"Samantha? Wait a minute. You're not giving up on Joker, are you?"

"Maybe Kyle can handle him."

"In his dreams," Grant replied.

"No way." Kyle lifted his hands. "I want nothing to do with that beast."

She muttered something under her breath that had to do with spoiled brats and silver spoons.

"We had a deal," Grant reminded her.

"Cancelled when Kate left the place to your brother."

"Hey—this isn't my fight," Kyle proclaimed, and Sam pinned him with a look that all but called him a citified, useless, low-life coward.

"For the love of..." She clawed stiff fingers through hair that was pulled tightly away from her face. A few strands fell into her eyes. "Okay, okay," she said to Grant. "I'll handle Joker. It'll take a couple of days, but then I'm outta here."

"What's wrong?" Grant glanced from Kyle to Sam. "Lovers' spat?"

The color drained from her face. "I just have enough to do over at my place."

"Fair enough." Grant didn't look like he completely bought her story, but he didn't seem anxious to press the issue. "As long as I can pick up Joker before Clem James's mare goes into heat."

"No promises. I'll do the best I can."

"All I can ask." Grant squared his hat on his head. "I've got to run into town for a part for my damned tractor. I'll see ya around." He slapped the side of the doorframe with a tanned hand as he sauntered out, then hesitated on the porch, the screen door propped open by one shoulder. "Oh, I meant to tell you, Kyle, Mom called this morning. Rebecca's gone off on some toot about hiring a private investigator to look into the cause of Kate's plane crash."

"I thought it was all just an accident, faulty equipment or something."

"Yeah, that was what everyone assumed, but you know our aunt. She doesn't believe in letting sleeping dogs lie."

Kyle felt a sensation akin to dread. Rebecca was the youngest daughter of Ben and Kate, and though she was technically his aunt, she was only a few years older than he. A mystery writer, Rebecca had earned her reputation of having a vivid, sometimes wild imagination. "So what does she think?"

"Who knows? If you ask me, she should quit working herself up over everything and settle down."

"Oh, like you?"

Grant shot him an unreadable look. "Just don't be surprised if she gives you a call. See ya around, Kyle. Sam."

Samantha watched him leave and felt a moment's hesitation. She was alone with Kyle. Again. Which was what she wanted. Or was it? As Grant drove away, she was suddenly aware that the air in the house seemed thicker, dense with silent emotions, and she had trouble drawing a breath. Being this close to a man who had once had the ability to break her heart was just plain stupid.

"For the life of me I can't figure out why Kate left this place to you," she said, untying the knots that suddenly took hold of her tongue. "Grant or Rocky—"

"I know, I know. You've already pointed out that nearly anyone in the family would have been a better choice."

She angled her chin upward and met his eyes. "I think so, yes."

"Even Allison?"

Her lips twitched at the mention of Kyle's beautiful and sophisticated cousin, Rocky's twin, a woman who was meant for the glitter and fast pace of the city.

"Even Kristina."

"Not Kris!" he teased.

"Absolutely! Your sister might be spoiled, but at least she knows what she wants in life!" Sam had never been one to keep her opinions to herself, especially not with Kyle. "I think your grandmother was out of her mind when she left this place to you."

"I couldn't have guessed."

Damn his sexy drawl and drop-dead grin. "You know what else?" she asked.

"I have a feeling you're going to tell me whether I want to know or not, so let's hear it." His crooked smile stretched across his jaw and she had the urge to slap him. He was goading her, whether he knew it or not. Well, he'd asked for it. She would gladly give it to him with both barrels.

"You're not gonna make it six months, Kyle. You're

gonna turn tail and run before your stint here is through. You've never suffered through a winter here, have you? Sometimes the electricity gives out, and if you can't get the generator going you have to rely on firewood for warmth. You have to break a trail through hip-deep snow to the stables, melt water for the stock and live on oatmeal, canned beans, potatoes and apples that you've hopefully had the brains to keep in a fruit cellar. There's no TV, no radio except for a transistor if your batteries aren't low and no four-wheel drive big enough to get through to you. It's just you and your wits, tryin' to survive against Mother Nature, and in your case I'll bet she'd win hands down!''

"How much?"

"What?"

"How much are you willing to bet?'' he asked, his eyes suddenly dangerous. He crossed the short distance between them and glared at her with an expression as stormy as a winter thundercloud. Hot breath fanned her face.

"I don't need to put up a wager, because you're already gonna lose. You're not going to inherit this place because you, Kyle Fortune, never could stick with anything long enough to see it through. That's why Kate attached strings to her bequest, and it's a good thing she's dead because you would disappoint that old lady the day the going got rough and you decided to take off." She glared up at him, challenging him, and he saw it then— a shadow crossing her eyes, a tremble in the pinched corners of her mouth, an emotion she was trying desperately to hide.

"Is that what you came over here to tell me?"

"I just came for my things." She started for the den,

but he grabbed her arm, his fingers tightening over the crook of her elbow.

"I don't think so."

"Let go of me, Kyle."

"There's something more, Sam. Something that's bothering you. Big-time." No one had ever been able to get to him like Samantha Rawlings. One sultry look from her and he melted; a quick lash of her tongue and his temper rocketed into the stratosphere; pain showing in her green eyes and he wanted to kill the bastard who'd hurt her.

One side of her full mouth lifted in a sarcastic smile. "Gee, Kyle, how perceptive of you. Could it be—let me see—the fact that you took off from here ten years ago, left me without so much as a goodbye, didn't call or write, just sent a formal invitation to my family to your wedding?"

His breath whistled through his teeth. "God, Sam."

"You asked." She yanked her arm from his fingers and stormed through the kitchen to the hallway. He caught up to her just as she was leaving, a jacket under one arm, an address book and coffee mug in her hand.

"I think we should talk."

"Too late." But again that shadow flickered in her gaze and her steps faltered for a second.

"It's never too late."

She let out a soft grunt of defeat. "Oh, Kyle, if you only knew."

"Knew what?"

Whirling to face him, she dropped her mug. It crashed to the floor and splintered into a thousand pieces. "Oh, for the love of—"

"Forget it." His fingers once again tightened on her arm.

"What?"

"I'll sweep up the mess later." He felt a second's premonition, as if he were on the edge of a bottomless emotional abyss and the gravel he was standing upon was slowly crumbling beneath his boots. "You were about to confide in me."

She swallowed. "This—this isn't the time. There's a lot to say. Most of it won't mean a thing, but...well, some things are important."

"What things?"

Oh, God, could she bring herself to say it? To tell him that he was a father? Come on, Sam, now's the time. Quit being such a coward!

He was staring at her, waiting, icy blue eyes narrowed on her face. Her heart thundered in her ears. How many times had she envisioned just this moment, dreamed of telling him the truth, even gone so far as picking up the telephone or starting a letter, only to drop the receiver in disgust or wad the unfinished page in her trembling fingers?

"I know I left abruptly," he said, prodding her.

She let out a sarcastic sound.

"You probably thought we had a future, and we should have, but—"

"Don't!" She shied away from the truth again and ducked past him to the door.

"Sam—"

"Another time, okay? We can rehash the past some other time, but right now I don't have a minute to spare. I've got to pick up Caitlyn and—and I'll come back later to work with the horse."

"I met Caitlyn this morning."

"You what?" Whirling, she felt her face drain of all color. *He'd met Caitlyn? Oh, dear God.*

"She stopped by on her way to—to…"

"Tommy Wilkins's house?"

"That's right. Seems like a nice enough kid. You did a good job with her."

"Oh, uh, thanks." She could hardly speak. Licking her lips, she silently called herself a coward, but couldn't find the nerve to tell him the truth. "Look, I've got to run." She headed for the door again.

"You know, Samantha, I never meant to hurt you." His words stalked her, trod across her soul. Her own footsteps faltered and her heart felt scraped bare. A huge lump formed in her throat. "Don't worry about it," she said over her shoulder. "You didn't."

She heard his boots ringing on the floor behind her. She dashed out the back door, ran across the porch and hurtled down the two dusty steps before he caught up with her. A huge hand clamped over her shoulder. "Samantha."

Heaven preserve me.

"Help me out here."

"I can't." She was dying inside, wanting to tell him, to wound him, to hurt him, and yet she couldn't, not this way, not until she knew that both she and Caitlyn were ready. Oh, God, what a mess!

"You keep running from me."

"I guess I learned well. Had a good teacher."

He stepped in front of her, his shadow falling over her face. "What's going on?"

"I just think it's a sin that a woman as smart as Kate would leave this ranch to a citified playboy who doesn't know the front end of a horse from the back end."

"You're a lousy liar."

"And you're a lousy lover!"

His mouth fell open and she bit her tongue. That

wasn't what she'd meant to say, but she wasn't going to retract the words. Their brief affair had been hot, wild and breathless. She'd been a virgin, and he'd been eighteen, randy as a nearly-grown colt. She swallowed hard against the memories and the tingles to her skin. "Just leave me alone, Kyle."

"No way."

"I mean it. I'm not a naive, seventeen-year-old girl who worships the ground you walk on anymore."

His jaw tightened.

"You want the truth? You got it!" Ten years of fury grabbed hold of her tongue. "I thought I loved you, Kyle, and you didn't care a lick about me. Oh, sure, I was a lot of fun, a good time whenever you were in the mood for a quick one in the hayloft or down by the creek, but certainly not someone to marry or care about."

"God," he whispered.

"I wouldn't have cared, Kyle, wouldn't have given one good damn, but within three or four months, you got married just like that." She snapped her fingers in his face, ignoring the old pain throbbing in her heart. "And you didn't even have the guts to call. Because I meant so little."

A muscle ticked in the corner of his eye.

"Just some stupid little country girl who was good enough to make it with, but not good enough to—to..."

"To what? Marry?" He angled his face toward hers. "Is that what you wanted?"

I just wanted you to love me. "I guess I did at the time. I believed in commitment. Lucky for me you were so fickle. Otherwise I might have made the biggest mistake of my life!"

"If you were so interested in commitment, what about Caitlyn's father?"

"Don't even ask," she warned, backing up.

"You brought it up."

"I think it would be best if we kept my daughter out of this conversation." She didn't wait for a response, just walked around him and climbed into the cab of her truck. A yellow jacket buzzed wildly over the dash, bouncing against the windshield, nearly tangling in her hair in its flight out the open window.

Sam's cheeks felt hot and her pulse was dancing crazily as she glanced in the rearview mirror. Kyle hadn't moved. He stood tall and rigid, his legs planted wider than his shoulders, his straight hair ruffling in the breeze as he stared after her.

Her heart gave a painful kick. Tears threatened, but she willed them away. Her fingers tightened over the wheel as she silently cursed the day she'd met Kyle Fortune and his too-damned-sexy smile.

Four

"Women," Kyle grumbled, dusting his hands together, as if in so doing he could get rid of Sam and the way she'd already gotten under his skin. It was useless. Somehow, someway, in less than twenty-four hours, she'd managed to invade his mind and slip back into his blood. He had a bad feeling he wasn't going to purge himself of her easily. He looked at the stallion, which was standing nearly motionless, staring at Kyle as if he were some sideshow attraction. "Women are the single most interesting creation God ever came up with, as well as the most infuriating. Especially that one." Kyle glanced over his shoulder, but spied only the dust settling onto the gravel driveway. Samantha was long gone. He should have been elated, but wasn't. Her barbs had stung.

He had been a jerk. An eighteen-year-old, self-important, rich son of a bitch. Full of piss and vinegar, and horny as all get-out. He'd dated his share of girls back in Minneapolis—rich debutantes who went to private schools, who drove Porsches and BMWs, who spent their summers touring Europe and their winter vacations in the Bahamas. Girls with smiles fixed by orthodontists, noses bobbed by plastic surgeons, figures kept svelte by binging and purging. Most of them were smart, some were funny, a few even rebelled and wore clothes from secondhand stores or army surplus. But none was like

Sam. She was the proverbial breath of fresh air in a stale ocean of upper-crust dissatisfaction.

Short and sassy, with her untamed, strawberry blond hair unrestrained except for a single rubber band holding it away from the perfect oval of her face, she was different from every other girl he'd met. Samantha's level gaze hadn't so much as flickered with interest at the rich boy visiting his grandmother's ranch, where Sam sometimes helped her father with the chores. But Kyle had really noticed her for the first time that summer, and the fact that she'd practically ignored him only sparked his interest, adding fuel to an already simmering fire. He'd shown off for her, smiled his killer grin, and while leaning against a fence and chewing on a match, had watched her walk from the stables to the toolshed, noticing how her hips swayed and her tight buttocks moved beneath worn Levi's that left little to his overactive imagination and testosterone-filled brain.

She'd grabbed whatever tool she was looking for—a wire cutter or some damned thing—and as she sauntered back, said loudly enough for him to hear, "Why don't you take a picture? It lasts longer."

Though his ego had been deflated, he'd done just that. Swiping Jane's camera, he'd snapped roll after roll of Samantha Rawlings, the girl seemingly unimpressed with his Corvette, his tennis trophies, his acceptance into Cornell University or any damn thing about him. Her eyes, green as a forest in morning, remained cool, her lips never curved into a smile at one of his jokes and when he dared touch her, she raised already arched eyebrows to disdainful new heights. She refused rides in his car, pretended not to notice the fact that he often stared at her, didn't seem to give two cents that he took out other girls from town. The more she ignored him, the more intrigued he was, but it was only when he confronted her in the stables, where she was checking the feed and water for the brood mares, that he started to understand.

"You don't like me much, do you?" he asked, vaulting onto the top rail of one of the stalls.

"Don't think much about it." Her back was to him as she measured oats into the manger, pouring the grain from an old coffee can, but he caught a whiff of wildflowers over the oat dust.

"Sure you do."

"Geez, you don't have an inflated opinion of yourself, do you?" She tossed him a look that silently said *grow up*. The barn was shadowy, with only a few shafts of light piercing the dusty windows. It was quiet inside, except for the rustle of straw as the horses moved and the grinding of equine teeth mashing grain.

"I'd just like to get to know you better." Were his hands actually sweating on the top rail of the stall?

"Sure."

"Why don't you believe me?"

She turned and gave him the once-over, then shook her head. "Because you want to get to know me and every other girl in Clear Springs." Patting the painted mare, whose nose was already sunk deep in grain, she left the stall, scooped another measure of oats into the can and entered the next box, where an anxious sorrel let out a soft nicker of anticipation.

"I play the field."

"I'm not even in the game." She threw the latch behind her and began talking in soft, dulcet tones to the horse. With knowing fingers, she patted the mare's rich coat as she poured out the grain. It galled Kyle that Samantha Rawlings paid more attention to the animals than she did to him.

For a while, nothing changed that one unalterable fact. But Kyle was nothing if not persistent.

During the first few weeks he was at the ranch, Samantha didn't give him the time of day. His grandmother, who spent part of her summers in Wyoming, offered him little advice except once, when she'd caught him sweating, gulping down a bottle of Coke and watching Samantha through narrowed eyes. Sam was helping shoe one of the more rambunctious of the colts on the spread, and Kyle, sitting on the porch railing, his back propped against a support post shoring up the roof, didn't hear the screen door open or his grandmother's light tread on the worn floorboards. "Sam's not like most of the other girls you know, or haven't you noticed that yet?"

He nearly jumped out of his skin, so intent was he on watching Samantha. Soda splashed down the front of his shirt. "Meaning?" He couldn't stop the heat that stole up the back of his neck.

"It'll take more than a flashy car and a thousand-watt smile to get her attention. She's been seeing Tadd Richter, you know, a boy who has nothing, so don't expect her to be impressed with what you have. It's what's inside you that counts."

Kyle didn't believe it. What would his grandmother know? She was *old,* for crying out loud. A widow.

However, his usual tricks—paying attention to other girls, cruising through town in his hot car, joking with her whenever he could—hadn't broken through the thick armor surrounding Sam's heart.

"You could try being yourself," Kate suggested, her blue eyes twinkling as if she were privy to a very deep secret—one that involved him. She slapped him affectionately on the shoulder as she'd done for as long as he could remember.

"Myself? I am."

"Are you?" Arched brows lifted in disbelief. "Think about it, Kyle," she advised and added, "And don't leave the Coke bottle out here to attract the bees. Put it in the garage where it belongs."

He'd gritted his teeth and held back the urge to tell her to butt out of his life. Even at eighteen he knew that she only wanted the best for him. Besides, she was just getting over Grandpa Ben's death from a massive heart attack that even lucky, tough-as-nails Ben Fortune hadn't been able to survive. This trip to Wyoming was her first since her sons, Uncle Jake and Kyle's father, Nathaniel, had stepped into the old man's shoes. Kate was on the board of the company, of course, and had overseen the transition, but was finally taking a few weeks off, just long enough, it seemed, to stick her nose into his life.

Ignoring his grandmother's suggestion, he spent the next two weeks trying to catch Sam's attention. But Samantha, it seemed, was impervious, and the more she ignored him, the more obsessed he became with her.

At night he'd spend hours lying awake, hands under his head as he stared through the open window at the stars, conjuring up images of her—images that always made him so stiff it hurt. He wondered what she looked like beneath her frayed cutoffs and T-shirts. Her breasts weren't all that big, probably about the size of his palm, and yet he'd give every dime he owned just to catch a glimpse of her topless. Would her nipples be dark and large or small and pink, quick to pucker? In his mind's eye he envisioned her body, wet from swimming in Stiller Creek or slick with sweat and hot with desire, but always warm and comforting deep inside. He thought about grabbing her and kissing the pout from her lips, scaling her ribs to touch those hidden breasts, yanking down the zipper of her jeans and delving inside her panties to touch her moist warmth, but knew he could never go through with it.

Had any other boy kissed her, touched her breasts, undone her pants? His fingers curled into a fist of frustration. What about Tadd Richter, rumored to be a low-life hoodlum who lived outside of town in a trailer? Did she kiss him?

He groaned to himself and considered driving into town and meeting Shawna Davies. He'd dated her a few times, known that all he had to do was kiss her and say a few kind words and she would let him do whatever he wanted. Trouble was, he wasn't interested. It wasn't just that she'd already made it with half the boys around Clear Springs, it was that ever since he'd first laid eyes on Samantha Rawlings, no other girl turned him on. "Idiot," he uttered, loudly enough for his brother to hear.

"You said it, not me," Mike said from the lower bunk, where his mattress squeaked as he turned over.

"Go to sleep."

"I'm tryin'."

Hell, what a mess. Kyle knew he had two choices: he could either forget Sam or try to break down her defenses. Most girls melted at the sight of him. Those who weren't charmed by his looks usually came around when they realized he had money and plenty of it. Girls like Shawna Davies. But he didn't want Shawna. For the first time in his life he didn't want anyone else. Just one girl interested him. The one he couldn't have.

"Quit drooling," Michael joked the next afternoon. They were riding over Murdock Ridge, eyeing the herd of white-faced cattle grazing near the banks of the creek. Red tails switched at the ever-present flies, and calves cavorted near their mothers, but it wasn't the cattle that drew Kyle's attention, not when in the next field Samantha was helping her father hitch a trailer to an old John Deere. The idling tractor was puffing exhaust into a blue, cloudless sky, and Samantha, not realizing she was being watched, was bent over, gazing up at the underside of the engine, her jeans stretched tight over her rump as she stood in the dry stubble of the already mown field.

"I'm not drooling," Kyle muttered under his breath, but his gaze never left her.

"Right." Mike, a year older and light-years more advanced when it came to the opposite sex, pulled on the reins and eyed his brother. "Boy, have you got it bad."

"I don't have anything bad—"

"Like hell. You're as hungry as they come, and she won't even give you the time of day, will she?" Mike's grin stretched into a wide leer. "I never thought I'd see the day when some girl—especially someone so...well, homespun and sharp-tongued—could get the best of you, but I like it." He nodded to himself as Kyle's temper snapped. "I like it a lot."

"She's not homespun."

"Compared to Connie Benton, Beverly Marsh and Donna Smythe?" Mike chuckled as he mentioned three of the girls Kyle had dated in the past year. "Sam's homespun, all right. Not your type."

"My type?"

"Rich, beautiful snobs."

"You don't know anything."

"No?" He glanced at Sam and his smile faded. "Look, leave her alone, will ya? She doesn't need your kind of trouble."

"You know, Mike, you're a real pain in the ass."

"So you're just figuring that out? You're a lost cause,

Kyle.'' Laughing, he yanked on the reins, gave a whoop that caused Sam to glance over her shoulder, then kicked his horse, which took off, sending clods of dirt flying.

His ears still ringing with his brother's warning, Kyle rode to the fence, swung out of the saddle and climbed through the rusting strands of barbed wire. He couldn't help but notice that the corners of Sam's mouth tightened as he approached. She looked angry enough to eat glass, but Kyle wasn't one to let a little female ire bother him. He motioned to the tractor. ''Need some help?''

''No, thanks. We're fine.'' She gave him a stiff, cool smile.

''Sam, where're your manners? We could use some help, let me tell you.'' Jim, Samantha's father, walked around the side of the faded green rig and rested one hand on the cracked plastic seat, while with the other, he took out a dusty handkerchief and wiped the sweat from his face. ''Damned alternator. This here tractor's been a good 'un. Given your granddad a lot of years and no trouble, but she's gettin' tired, I guess.'' Sighing, he jabbed the rag into the back pocket of his overalls. A short man with a perpetual day's growth of silver beard, Jim Rawlings had lived in Wyoming all of his life, as had generations of Rawlingses before him. ''We're just finishing up hauling hay from this field. Jack and Matt took the last load back to the barn, but then the tractor started givin' us some trouble.''

Kyle swung out of the saddle. ''Let me take a look at it.''

''No! We—we can handle it.'' Samantha was adamant.

''You know somethin' 'bout tractors?'' her father asked, and for the first time, Kyle heard the slur in his words and caught a faint whiff of whiskey.

''A little.''

Sam tried to step between her father and Kyle. "Listen, don't bother. We're fine, really." She enunciated each word emphatically, as if hoping her father would get the message. When he didn't respond, she turned back to Kyle, her fixed smile out of place on her anxious face. "Jack and Matt will be back in a little while." Squinting hard, she stared at the horizon, as if by sheer will she could force the two hired hands to appear. "Don't bother."

"No bother." Kyle's gaze met hers, and he noticed a flutter of her pulse in the damp hollow of her throat.

"But this is our job. We can handle it."

"I work on cars—"

"It's not quite the same."

"Sure it is." Kyle wasn't about to be bullied, even though he saw the panic rising in her eyes. She was worried he'd turn her old man in to Kate for drinking on the job.

"Listen to this," Jim said. He tried to climb into the tractor's seat, but his feet slipped and he dropped back to the ground. "Hell," he growled, before he grabbed hold of the rim of the seat and hauled his slight frame onto the cracked cushion. His face was flushed beneath his tan and he mumbled to himself as he lit a cigarette, then twisted the key.

The engine barely turned over, then shuddered into silence. Shooting smoke from his nostrils, Jim tried again, but the battery was dead, and all he accomplished was to create a loud series of clicks that seemed to mock him.

"Son of a—"

"Dad!"

"Deader'n a doornail. Damned—"

Sam's jaw tightened. "Please, Dad."

"It's all right. Kyle don't care if I swear a little. This damned rig—"

"Dad, don't." Sam's cheeks flamed. Her pulse pounded nervously. Drops of sweat slid down her neck to the collar of her shirt. "Just leave us alone," she said to Kyle. "We'll get the tractor back to the shed. Matt knows we broke down and he'll be back soon—"

Jim hopped to the ground and nearly fell, twisting his ankle and sucking in his breath as he steadied himself. Ashes from his cigarette dropped onto his chest.

"He's in no condition to work with any kind of machinery."

"Oh, God," she whispered. "No, no, he's just had a few—"

"A few? For crying out loud, Sam, he's three sheets to the wind! He could hurt himself or injure someone else or—"

"I won't let that happen." She was determined, her shoulders square, her gaze challenging.

"Wha's that you say?" Jim mumbled.

"Nothing, Dad," Samantha answered, silently imploring Kyle with wide, frightened eyes. For the first time he saw a vulnerable side to her and understood why she'd been so quick to keep him at arm's length.

The growl of an engine split the air. Relief flooded Sam's features as one of the ranch's pickups lumbered into view. "Matt's back, Dad," she said, though she continued to stare at Kyle. "You can go now. Matt will fix everything."

"You didn't tell your grandmother." Sam's voice jolted Kyle, and he glanced over his shoulder to find her standing not ten feet away from him. He'd been alone at the creek, propped against the trunk of an aspen tree, smoking a cigarette he didn't really want, considering the long summer ahead of him. Dusk was quickly turning to nightfall, and fish were beginning to rise, forming ripples.

"Didn't see any reason to." His pulse jumped at the sight of her. Her hair was down, framing her face in loose curls, and she'd exchanged her usual faded jeans for white shorts and some kind of gauzy blouse that she'd tied beneath her breasts. "Kate wouldn't be too happy if I told her the foreman was a drunk."

"He's not—" she began, then stopped. "He, uh, starts and quits. Most of the time he's clear as a bell, and then something sets him off and he starts drinking. It'll stop."

"You're sure?"

She hesitated a second too long. "Yep."

"What if he doesn't?"

"He will."

For the first time in his life Kyle felt sorry for her, always covering up for her dad, pretending life was normal and not the roller coaster he guessed it really was. He ground out his cigarette on a flat rock. "How can you be certain he'll give it up?"

Sam sighed loudly as a breeze rustled through the trees, turning the silvery leaves and catching in her already tangled hair. "Mom will threaten to divorce him if he doesn't."

"And that works?"

"It has so far." She sat on the dry vegetation beside him. The scents of wildflowers and soap mingled in the air and teased his nostrils. Plucking a blade of grass, Samantha began shredding it into tiny pieces, which she tossed into the breeze and watched settle on the dark waters of the creek.

"You can't keep covering up for him."

"I know."

Mesmerized by her cute little pout, he had trouble keeping his mind on the conversation. "Kate'll find out."

"I said I know."

"Then what?"

"We'll take care of everything. Look, let's not argue about it, okay? Dad has a problem. He knows it, and Mom and I know it, but we're taking steps to keep things under control. He had a little slipup the other day, and he's worried that he blew it by letting you see him...well, kind of out of control. It won't happen again."

"You've got a lot of faith in the old boy."

"I know him. He loves his job. Loved working for your grandfather and worships the ground Kate walks on, so don't worry about it, okay? I just came by to say thanks for not ratting on him."

She started to leave, but Kyle's fingers encircled her wrist. As he did so, he felt her pulse fluttering beneath her smooth skin. "That's not the only reason you came looking for me."

"It isn't?" She turned startled eyes his way before she seemed to read his thoughts. "Oh, for Pete's sake, Fortune, don't flatter yourself."

"Shouldn't I?"

She stared at him long and hard, and the skin beneath his fingertips began to warm. Her lips puckered, and he couldn't help but imagine kissing her so hard that neither one of them could think. "You've been coming on to me since day one, but I hoped you got the picture that I'm not interested."

"I think you're scared."

She laughed. "Scared? Of you? Why? Because you're the boss's grandson? Because you're from the big city? Believe me, you don't scare me, but your ego does. You really think you're something.'' Hitching her chin up a fraction, she asked, ''Just what is it you want from me?''

''Maybe a chance to get to know you better.''

''As I said, I'm not interested.''

''Why not?'' He eyed her thoroughly. ''Is it because of Tadd?''

''Tadd?''

''Heard you were seein' him.''

''He's...'' She shook her head and sighed. ''Tadd's just a friend. Everybody thinks he's a creep, but he's not really. He's okay. Just mixed-up.''

''He's in trouble a lot.''

''So are you. Maybe a different kind, but trouble nonetheless.''

His grip tightened. ''If it's not Tadd or some other guy—''

''There is no other guy.''

''Then why do you keep avoiding me?''

She hesitated, then slowly drew her arm back. In the nearby trees an owl hooted soulfully. ''You want reasons? Okay, I've got plenty.'' She wagged a finger in front of his nose. ''One, I don't date men I work for.''

''You don't—''

''Two—'' she held up two fingers ''—you don't even live around here.'' Another finger sprang to attention. ''Three, you're spoiled rotten, and four, you run with a fast crowd. Too fast for me.'' She let her hand fall to her side and lifted a shoulder. ''I didn't come down to argue with you. Look, thanks for keeping your mouth shut about Dad. I—we appreciate it, and you have my word and his that he won't drink on the job again.'' She got up and stepped away from him. ''I'd better get back.''

''No, wait! Sam!'' he called as she walked up the bank. Scrabbling, he ran after her, catching up as she whistled softly to a dun-colored mare grazing on tufts of grass that grew near an outcrop of rocks. "Don't run away."

"I'm not running."

"Sure you are."

"Oh, right, because I'm scared."

He stared at her mouth as she swallowed nervously, as if her throat was suddenly dry as dust. "Yeah. Just like me," he murmured.

"Oh, no—" she whispered, as he lost his head completely and kissed her hard enough to cause his head to spin. She stiffened in his arms for a heartbeat, then seemed to melt as surely as butter. Suddenly warm and pliant, smelling of lavender, she leaned against him. His heart pounded furiously, echoing in his brain so that he couldn't hear the water lapping at the shore or the soft nicker of her horse.

When he lifted his head, she looked up at him with heavy-lidded eyes for an instant before she shook her head as if to clear it and pushed him aside, stepping out of his embrace. "Oh, no!" Her gaze was clear as springwater and realization dawned in her eyes. "No!" Angry with herself, she ran the back of her hand over her mouth, not as if she was erasing his kiss, but more like she wanted to be sure her lips were still in place. "This was a mistake."

"Why?"

"Because—because..." Her fingers fluttered in the air nervously before she forced her hands into the pockets of her shorts. "Because you're a spoiled rich kid."

Unable to argue, he lifted a shoulder.

"Used to getting what you want."

"Most of the time," he admitted, feeling a slow, confident smile stretch across his jaw.

"Not this time, Fortune," she said, as if his name tasted sour. "You'll never get me!" Her voice quavered as she gathered up the reins again and climbed onto her horse. With a twist of the strap and a shout, she was off, disappearing into the twilight and leaving a plume of dust in her wake.

"Oh, Sam, yes I will. You know it and I know it." He was certain then that it was only a matter of time before he made love to Samantha Rawlings. "Patience," he muttered under his breath as the moon rose in the darkening sky and a bat swooped over the creek. "We've got all summer."

But telling himself to bide his time was an exercise in futility. The summer was slipping away and soon he'd be back in Minneapolis with the rest of his family. Even his grandmother, Kate, was getting restless. She'd come to Wyoming to sort out her life and "take a big breath before I tackle running the company," she'd said, but everyone knew she was using the time to work through her grief. Though her marriage to Kyle's grandfather hadn't been made in heaven, they'd managed to hold it together. Kyle didn't know all the details—his father and grandmother were both tight-lipped about personal things—but Kyle had gleaned a little over the years from his mother, Sheila, who had been Nathaniel's first wife and who had used every opportunity since their divorce to spread a little venom about the Fortune family whenever she had the chance.

Kyle had once felt that his mom had gotten the shaft when she and Nate had split, but over the years, he'd changed his mind, as had Michael and Jane. They compared notes and found that more times than not, their mother changed her story, stretched the truth or just plain lied to put the Fortunes, especially her ex-husband and his mother, Kate, into a bad light. Sheila Fortune was a bitter woman who continually complained that she'd been mistreated, hadn't gotten a fair shake and had been "screwed" by the Fortune attorneys when it came to the divorce settlement.

But Sheila had never worked a day in her life, lived in an expensive condominium in a building she owned, thanks to the Fortune money, and had personal cooks, maids and groundskeepers to wait on her hand and foot. As time wore on, Kyle's opinion of his mother shifted, and when he compared her to Sam and her family, a bad taste filled his mouth.

Sam avoided him for nearly a week, but he wasn't going to let her get away with only one little kiss—heart stopping though it had been. He pursued her with the determination of a hungry wolf following a lone doe. He caught her in the stables feeding the stock, at her house helping her mother make jam, in town at a little dive of a drive-in, where she ordered a raspberry malted milk shake, whatever the hell that was. The Burger Haven looked as if it was on its last legs. The orange Naugahyde seats of the booths were cracked and taped, a single air-conditioning unit, rammed into a window and held in place by plywood, wheezed painfully and the floor matched the counter in cigarette burns.

"Don't you get tired of following me around?" she asked as she paid for her milk shake and turned toward the door. Her father's grimy, once green pickup was parked in the dusty lot near Kyle's sports car.

"I'm not following you."

"Sure." She tossed him a look that called him a liar as she swept through the screen door. He left his unfinished Coke on the counter and caught up with her outside, where the sounds of engines rumbling through town and the smell of exhaust hung heavy in the air.

"Okay, so maybe I like running into you."

"Maybe you're bored."

"Not with you."

Her lips wrapped around the straw of her drink and she studied him with such intensity he wanted to squirm. "Give it up, Fortune. You're not my type."

"Bull."

"You think just because your last name is—"

He stepped closer, grabbed her wrist and inadvertently sloshed red milk shake over her blouse, spattering her breasts. "I think I just want to get to know you better."

"No way! Now look at my blouse—" She halted abruptly as Kyle eyed the stain that spread across the yellow fabric. In a split second he imagined himself licking away the icy red concoction from breasts that were firm and high, proud nipples waiting to be touched by his tongue. "Forget it!" she said a trifle breathlessly.

"Can't." He kissed her then, wrapped his arms around her and pressed anxious lips to hers. He heard her drink fall, felt it splash against the back of his legs, but he didn't let go, and for the first time she kissed him back, her lips warm and seeking, her mouth opening to the plunder of his tongue.

A shudder ripped down his spine and his blood was instantly lava hot. His groin ached.

He deepened the kiss, mindless of the fact that they were standing on the sidewalk on the main street of town, with traffic rolling by, pedestrians stepping around them, patrons in the nearby buildings watching them.

As if a bucket of cold water had been poured over her, Sam finally pushed him away. "Not here," she said under her breath as she slid a glance to the tinted windows of the Burger Haven.

"You name the place."

"No. Look, I can't get involved. Not with you or anyone else."

"Samantha, please, give me a chance—"

She glanced down at her shirtfront, shook her head and forced her eyes to meet his again. "No way."

"But, Sam—"

She backed away. "Leave me alone."

"I can't."

"Then do me a favor, will ya?" she asked, her jaw set. "Go to hell, Kyle Fortune, but please, don't take me with you."

But he did. One hot summer afternoon when the bees were swarming in the cottonwoods and he'd been setting fence posts all day, he found her. Alone. Swimming in a bend of the river where the water turned dark and deep as it pooled in a lazy swirl.

Her clothes were strewn in disarray on the riverbank and her body was visible through the clear ripples, tanned arms and legs, white abdomen and breasts, dark nipples that pointed skyward as she floated on her back before curling under the water again.

He should leave. Pretend he hadn't crossed the fence line in the hopes of meeting with her. Act as if he'd never seen her triangle of red-blond curls at the apex of her legs glittering with dewy drops as she surfaced and dived.

His guts clenched and desire, so hot he could barely breathe, twisted anxious fingers through his insides.

Sunlight spangled the water where the shadows didn't reach and her body, slim and small, limber and lithe, was shaped perfectly, from the tiny nip of her waist to the swell of athletic hips and trim ankles. What he would give for one taste of her…to press his hot lips to her wet skin and touch her as she'd never been touched. No doubt she was a virgin, and Kyle would love to make a woman of her, to show her the delights of lovemaking, to hear her moan in pleasure before he entered her.

His heart was thundering as she splashed like a water nymph, completely unaware that he was watching. Throat dry as cotton, he slid around a huge boulder. Resting his hips against the dusty rock, he cleared his throat loudly enough to startle the blue jays in the branches overhead.

Samantha surfaced and tossed the hair from her eyes. "What—oh, for God's sake, what're you doing here?"

"Watching you."

"You don't give up, do you?"

"Not when I want something, no."

"Oh, Lord. This—this is private property."

"Oh. Then I stand corrected. I'm trespassing and watching you." Swallowing a smile, he noticed the flush that climbed up her cheeks and the way she had trouble treading water while trying to cover her breasts with one hand and the top of her legs with the other.

"Leave."

"Not yet."

"I'll sue you."

"Sure."

"Then my dad will come looking for you with his shotgun."

Kyle laughed. "I don't think so."

She was getting truly angry now. He could see the flicker of fire in her eyes. "You're embarrassing me."

"With a body like that you shouldn't be embarrassed."

"With a line like that, you should be."

He laughed again and reached for her clothes. She let out a strangled cry. "Don't you dare—"

"What?" Scooping up cutoffs, blouse, bra and underpants, he straightened.

"If you leave me stranded without anything to wear, I swear, Kyle Fortune, I'll come up when you're sleeping and cut out your sick, black heart or some other piece of your anatomy that you're fond of."

"Would you?" He hadn't thought of stealing her clothes, but the idea did hold some appeal. She was swimming to the shore now.

"In a heartbeat."

"That would be something to see."

"You're a spoiled, self-important, rich son of—"

"Who has your clothes. You know, Sam," he drawled, crossing his arms over his chest and letting her garments hang from his fingers, "considering the situation, I wouldn't be hurling insults if I were you."

She wasn't listening. Apparently deciding she had nothing to lose, she waded out of the water, her gorgeous body dripping on the dry ground. Shaking with indignation, her jaw set in determination, she approached him. "You're a creep."

"You don't really think so." His eyes held hers as he held out her clothes. "I wasn't going to take them."

"Bull." She snatched her cutoffs and stepped into them, leaning over and letting her breasts, so white and beckoning, dangle a little. They shook as she wiggled into the frayed garment, and the erection he'd been fighting sprang to attention.

With the hiss of a zipper, his view of her hips and the dewy curls at the joining of her legs disappeared. Within seconds she'd yanked her T-shirt over her head and pulled her hair through the neckline. Then she snagged her bra and underwear, shoved them in her back pocket and glared at him. "Why do you insist on humiliating me?"

"Because you won't give me the time of day."

"So this is all because of your bruised ego?" She reached for her boots. "Lots of girls are dying to be with you. Go play Peeping Tom with them."

"I don't want lots of girls."

She froze. "Sure you do."

For the first time, the truth hit him hard in the gut. "I just want you."

She visibly started, her eyes seeking his as she nearly dropped a boot. "No way."

"Yep." Without another thought, he reached for her. "And believe me, I'd change things if I could."

"No, Kyle, don't—" she said as his lips claimed hers. She trembled beneath his touch, and an answering tremor slid through his body. "Please..."

"Please what?" he asked, but she didn't say another word.

Her response was to open her mouth and give in to the weakening of her knees. Together she and Kyle tumbled to the cracked, dry earth strewn with pebbles and rocks, and there on that hard surface, with water lapping against the bank and wind rustling the leaves of the cottonwoods, he discovered the true meaning of making love. With anxious fingers, hot, hard body and a new awareness of his soul, he stole her virginity and left behind a piece of his heart.

Even now, years later, he remembered her lying beneath him that first glorious time. Her wet hair fanned around her tanned face, her eyes were wide with inexperience and a little fear and her skin quivered beneath his touch as he slowly entered her and found a little bit of heaven he hadn't known existed.

Five

Why now? Sam wondered. *Why ever?* Geez, she didn't need this! She slapped together a tuna sandwich, nearly ripping a hole in one slice of wheat bread as she spread mayonnaise. The window over the sink was open, and she spied her daughter climbing in the lower branches of an apple tree in the backyard. "Caitlyn! Lunch."

"Comin'!" With the agility of a true tomboy, Caitlyn swung from the branch, landed lithely on the ground and in a swirl of dust raced to the back steps. Fang, their mutt of a dog, was on her heels.

"Leave your boots on the porch."

"I know, I know." Caitlyn wedged the heel of one boot off with the toe of the other.

"And wash—"

"My hands and face."

"Right."

The screen door creaked open, then slammed shut as Caitlyn slid across the cracked linoleum in her stockings, then disappeared into the bathroom. Fang, tail wagging, settled into his spot by the ancient wood stove. Rusty pipes groaned and water splashed loudly in the bathroom as the timer on the old stove buzzed.

Armed with pot holders, Sam retrieved a bubbling strawberry-and-rhubarb pie from the oven. She wasn't much of a cook, and the crust was singed around the edges, but the sweet aroma of hot fruit and cinnamon filled the air.

Caitlyn slid back into the room, a grin stretching across her face. All her worries about being watched by some unknown individual seemed to have faded, and she'd received no prank calls since the last one from Jenny Peterkin. Life once again seemed stable for Sam and her daughter. Except for Kyle Fortune. Like it or not, he was a flesh-and-blood problem that Sam would have to face.

"Can I have a piece?"

"Later."

As Sam set the pie on the window ledge to cool, Caitlyn plopped onto the worn straw seat of her chair. "When's Sarah's mom gonna get here?"

"Anytime." Samantha cast a glance at the clock as she poured a half glass of milk and set it on the table. "Eat quickly."

Caitlyn was already digging into the sandwich, biting into the bread with teeth that were still a little too big for her mouth. At nine, she was a bit gawky, her arms and legs growing faster than the rest of her, but in Sam's eyes she was gorgeous.

"Tell Sarah's mom that I'll pick you up after the lesson." Samantha took her seat and reached for half a sandwich. "I shouldn't be late, but if I am, you and Sarah—"

"I know, I know. Don't swim in the river alone, don't take a ride with anyone else and—oh, she's here!" The sound of tires crunching on the driveway drifted in through the open window, and Fang scrambled to his feet and let out a quick couple of barks.

"Already? She's ten minutes early." Which was unusual. Sarah's mother, Mandy Wilson, was forever running behind schedule, juggling four kids and a part-time job. Yet Mandy insisted upon doing her share in the car pool to the canoe lessons the girls had wanted to take this summer.

"Fang, hush!"

The rest of her sandwich forgotten, Caitlyn took a long swallow of milk, scrambled out of her chair, snagged her backpack from a hook near the back door and started outside, only to stop dead in her tracks.

"Oh. It's not Sarah." Disappointment was evident in the droop of her shoulders.

"No? Then who...?" But Samantha didn't have to ask, because she knew the most likely person to land at her back door was Kyle Fortune. Her heart lurched and she nearly dropped the glass of ice tea she'd lifted to her lips.

How could she have such bad luck as to be thrown face-to-face with him again so soon? She wasn't ready for this, but then, she probably never would be. Forcing some steel into her spine, she glanced outside to the shaft of sunlight bouncing off his dusty truck's door. If he only knew how much she had loved him ten years ago and how cruelly he'd broken her heart. Their dizzying affair hadn't been planned; stupidly, they'd fallen head over heels in love, except that in Kyle's case love never lasted more than two weeks. Samantha believed in love for a lifetime. She was, beneath her tough-as-nails veneer, a true romantic. Foolish, foolish girl!

She slid back her chair and walked to the porch, where Caitlyn, always curious, was studying the stranger through eyes so like his own he had to see the resemblance. Unaware that it was his own daughter scrutinizing him, Kyle sauntered up the back steps, and Sam braced herself as she walked outside. The reflective sunglasses guarding his eyes were streaked with dirt, as if he'd really done some work at his ranch. A forest green shirt, sleeves rolled up his forearms, was stretched tight across his shoulders and tucked into a waistband that hung low on his hips.

Samantha's throat turned to sand, and though she tried to say something, anything, no words came. *Oh, God, oh, God, oh, God.* Her thoughts were as much of a prayer as she'd whispered since her father's funeral.

"Hi, Caitlyn," he said, with that same crooked grin Samantha had fallen in love with years before.

"Hi," Caitlyn replied.

"You haven't been over to see Joker and me again."

"Mom wouldn't let me," Caitlyn replied, slicing a triumphant look at her mother.

"I, uh, thought it wouldn't be a good idea." Samantha's voice was wooden, and she felt as if she were having an out-of-body experience. She was saying the right things, acting as if nothing in the world was wrong, when inside her head there was a dull roar, like the sound of a distant but deadly waterfall growing closer and louder and more dangerous by the second.

"She can stop by whenever she feels like it."

"Really?" Caitlyn asked in delight.

"Wait a minute." This conversation was moving much too fast for Samantha.

"Sure. Anytime. It's a deal."

Caitlyn's eyes gleamed.

"Want to shake on it?" he said, bending down and offering Caitlyn a big hand.

Sam leaned against the siding of the porch. Her legs were suddenly untrustworthy as she watched her daughter's tentative little palm being swallowed by Kyle's huge fingers. The moment was monumental, but it wasn't supposed to be this way. No, there should be more of a permanent connection, a deeper understanding, a special love. But then, neither father nor daughter knew the truth, did they? Sam had made sure the two of them had been protected from reality. Only she could comprehend the magnitude of the moment. Tears burned behind her eyes.

Father and daughter.

Dreamer. Damned fool romantic. Haven't you grown up yet? They'll never be part of any kind of true family.

"It's a deal, Mr. Fortune." Caitlyn's grin was wide, showing off her large teeth.

"You can call me Kyle. Mr. Fortune makes me sound like an old man." He bent down to look at Caitlyn's face a little more closely as he released her hand. "If you call me Mr. Fortune, I might get mixed up and think I'm either my father or my brother, and believe me, they *are* old, at least a lot older than I am." He flashed a blinding smile in Caitlyn's direction, and Sam could barely breathe. Then his expression changed—subtly at first, a question pinching the corners of his mouth. The same question, an inkling of something he couldn't quite put his finger on, shaded his eyes.

He knows! He sees his own face reflected in her gaze! Sweat broke out on Sam's skin, and her heart was pounding so wildly beneath her ribs—like a bird battering itself against a cage—that she couldn't move.

Her fingers curled automatically. *He has the right to the truth. So does Caitlyn. You have to tell them!*

Slowly, as if he was looking into a murky pool just as the water began to clear, the doubts marring his face disappeared. Within a heartbeat he knew. Sam was sure of it.

Tell him. Tell him now! Tell them both! Oh, God. Sam's palms began to sweat and she opened her mouth, just as a horn blasted and Mandy Wilson's minivan, jammed with her kids and the family dog, roared down the lane. The silver vehicle slid to a stop near the barn. From the kitchen, Fang let out a reluctant woof.

"Gotta go," Caitlyn said, yanking on her boots. Within seconds she was racing across the dry grass of the yard to the gravel parking lot wedged between the house and the stables.

"Wait!" Kyle stared after her, dumbstruck.

"Be careful," Samantha said, somehow managing to wave to Mandy, who poked her head out the driver's-side window. "I'll pick the girls up when they're finished."

"Good. I'll be home with the rest of the brood."

Caitlyn disappeared into the van. The wide sliding door that Sarah had been holding open slammed shut with a thud that seemed to echo in Sam's heart. *Here it comes,* she thought, lifting her hand as Caitlyn waved from the open window while Mandy drove off.

"She's cute," Kyle said slowly, staring after the mini-van as it cruised down the driveway. His brow was furrowed slightly, his lower lip protruding as if he were deep in thought. "How old is she?"

"Nine." Samantha's throat clogged.

A few long, silent seconds ticked by. Kyle slid his sunglasses off his nose and hung them from the closure of his shirt. Sam's heart pounded painfully over the drone of insects and the chirp of birds. *Oh, God, he knows. He has to know.* Fang wandered to the door and scratched to be let out.

"When's her birthday?"

Sam's heart cracked. "Come in, Kyle." He was already putting two and two together and coming up with three—two parents and a child. Their child. Opening the door, she cocked her head toward the kitchen as Fang ambled onto the porch and disappeared into the shrubs. "I've got ice tea and pie and—"

"I don't want any tea."

"Well, there's something stronger. My dad left a couple of bottles of whiskey in the den and—"

"She's mine, isn't she?" Storm clouds gathered in his eyes, and his smile, once so warm, faded into a grim, bitter line as cold as the Tetons in winter.

"Dear God." Sighing, she turned away from the damning questions in his gaze, the silent accusations etched in the planes of his face. Sam's legs felt as if they might not hold her as she looked into the kitchen where Caitlyn had played as a child, building forts under the table, stacking blocks near the pantry, asking a million and one questions when she wasn't running through the house like a whirlwind. Life as they'd known it was about to change forever.

"She is, isn't she?" He kicked a tired old porch rocker out of the way. It banged against the side of the house. Fang barked.

Sam's fingers tightened over the worn handle of the screen door. "Look, Kyle. We need to talk. If you'll just come inside—" She began to open the door wider, but quick as a mountain lion pouncing, he slammed the screen shut with the flat of his hand, grabbed her roughly, and with strong fingers digging into her shoulders, whirled her around, forcing her to stare into the fury of his face.

"Answer me, damn it! Is she my daughter or not?"

Sam's temper snapped like a brittle twig. "Yes, Kyle, she's yours. Of course she's yours!" She knocked his hand away and glared up at him. "My God, couldn't you see it in her eyes, the bridge of her nose, the curve of her chin?"

"I had no idea—"

"Did you honestly believe that I would be involved with anyone so quickly after you? Did you?"

"People thought Tadd Richter—"

"I *never* slept with Tadd, Kyle. The only man I was ever with was you! How could you think that I'd be with anyone, Tadd or anyone else, so soon after you and I... Oh, God, this is hopeless!"

"I don't know what you did."

"And why was that?" she asked, her temper igniting like gasoline to a match. "You were the one who turned tail and ran as fast as you could. Before I could blink, you married another woman."

"Sam—"

"You're not blind, Kyle. Caitlyn's the spitting image of you! She's got Fortune stamped all over her! She's yours, Kyle, like it or not. Now can we can go inside and talk this over civilly or do you want to have your tantrum right here on the porch?"

His jaw worked. "Does she know?"

"What do you think?" Sam yanked open the door and stepped inside the kitchen, which was warm from the blistering heat of the day and the still-cooling oven.

Running a hand around his neck, Kyle swore loudly as he followed her inside. "I can't believe it."

"Then don't."

"I mean...oh, hell, I don't know what I mean," he admitted, shaking his head while visibly trying to rein in his anger. He'd always been a hothead, known for getting into his share of arguments, fistfights and wrestling matches. But this was different. They both knew it. "Why didn't you tell me? Didn't you think I had the right to know?"

"No." She gripped the back of one of the chairs.

"No?" he repeated. "*No?* Are you out of your mind? What planet have you been living on? These days fathers have rights, too. Or haven't you kept up with custody cases lately?"

A chill settled deep in Sam's heart. *Custody.* Surely he wasn't thinking about suing her for parental rights. Not Kyle, the eternal playboy. What would he want with a nine-year-old girl who would only foul up his life? But no matter how hard Sam argued with herself, she couldn't help but feel fear—the deep, gut-gnawing kind of trepidation that steals sleep and causes a person to sweat in the middle of winter. "You gave up all your rights to my daughter a long time ago."

"I didn't know about her." A vein was beginning to throb at his temple. "How could I have given up anything?"

"You gave her up when you gave up on me."

"I didn't—"

"You got married, Kyle," she said again, feeling that old ache in her heart, the one she'd tried so hard to bury.

The air grew still. Only the steady ticking of the clock in the living room and the hum of the refrigerator broke the silence. His grim countenance grew darker, and Sam's fingers ached from holding on to the chair in a death grip. "That's right," she said softly. "By the time I'd screwed up my courage and gone to the doctor, after skipping two periods and finally taking one of those home pregnancy tests, your wedding invitations had already been mailed."

"But you could have told me—"

"When? At your bachelor party? Or maybe at the rehearsal dinner...no, better yet at the wedding itself—you know, the part of the ceremony where the preacher asks the rhetorical question about any man knowing a reason why the bride and groom shouldn't get married? Maybe I should have stood up then and announced that I was carrying the husband-to-be's baby?'' She couldn't stop the sting in her words, couldn't stop feeling the same pain and bitterness she'd felt when she'd spied the engraved wedding invitation lying open on this very table. Her father had brought in the mail, and her mother had opened the cream-colored, embossed envelope. Samantha, having just visited the doctor to confirm her suspicions, had spotted the invitation and felt as if she would faint. She remembered the words branded into her brain: *Mr. and Mrs. Donald P. Smythe request the honor of your presence at the marriage of their daughter, Donna Joanne, to Mr. Kyle James Fortune....*

The room had spun. Samantha had dropped the damning invitation onto the table, her knees suddenly weak, her stomach churning. Then, by sheer force of will, she'd run to the bathroom, where she'd promptly lost her lunch and been forced to confide in her mother that she was going to have Kyle Fortune's baby. It had been their secret, one they'd never shared with her father, or anyone else.

And now Kyle knew the truth. ''Why don't you sit down? I'll pour you some tea or whatever. There's pie and—''

''I don't want any damned pie!'' His voice thundered through the house, and he kicked a chair across the room. It crashed against the wall. ''Damn it, Samantha, you just told me that I'm a father. I've got a daughter who's half-grown and doesn't know that I exist. My whole life is turning upside down and inside out and you want me to eat pie?''

''I'm just trying to stay calm.''

''Why? This isn't a calm kind of conversation, Sam.''

Fine. If that's the way he wanted it, then he might as well hear it all. The battle lines had already been drawn.

"Were you ever going to tell me?" he asked, raking fingers angrily through his hair, as if he were trying and failing to hold on to the shreds of his composure.

"Yes."

"When?"

"Right before I told her."

"Which was going to be—?"

"When she turned eighteen."

He stared at her as if thunderstruck, rooted to the yellowed floor, then shook his head slowly from side to side. "Eighteen?"

"Yes."

"When she was grown?"

"Mature enough to understand."

"Son of a bitch!" He walked to the sink and stared out the open window. "Didn't you think she might want to know that she had—has—a father, that she had the right to be told the truth, that it's a crime to keep this kind of information in the dark?"

"But it wasn't a crime to chase someone all summer long, break down her defenses, convince her that you were the most special man to ever walk the earth, make her love you so much it hurt inside and then leave her to marry another woman?"

"It wasn't like that."

"Save it for someone who believes it, Kyle." Sam's throat ached; her entire body was drained.

"I cared for you and—"

"Don't start, okay? Just don't start. I was stupid, a naive romantic, but I'm not seventeen any longer and I'm immune to you now." She walked to a cupboard on the far side of the sink, opened the door and, standing on tiptoe, yanked down a dusty bottle. "I don't know about you, but I need a drink." She eyed him over her shoulder.

"No one ever *needs* a drink."

"Sure they do. The last one I had was the day Dad died, and before that I can't remember. But today, I definitely need a swallow of something with a kick. Besides, I don't need any lectures on morality from you." She found two glasses, splashed some kind of aged Kentucky blend into both, then handed him one. "Cheers," she mocked, clinking the lip of her jelly-jar glass to his. "It's not every day we can celebrate being parents."

Jaw tight, eyes narrowed with a seething, condemning fury, he said, "Maybe I should propose a toast."

"Why not?"

"To Caitlyn." His voice was husky as he clinked the lip of his glass to hers. Sam felt a catch in her throat. Gaze locked with his, she took a sip and nearly choked as the fiery liquid splashed against the back of her throat. "I hope I get to know her a lot better."

"You have six months."

"Nope." He finished the whiskey in one quick swallow. "I've got the rest of my life."

"What's that supposed to mean?" The world was tilting again.

He set his glass in the sink and sighed loudly. "Just that there's a lot of lost time to make up for."

"Now wait a minute. You can't just waltz back to Wyoming and bulldoze your way into a little girl's life."

"Wrong, Sam," he said, with that same damn arrogance he'd always worn like some kind of medal. "I can do anything I sure as hell please."

"Because you're a Fortune?"

"Nah." He walked to the door and kicked it open.

"Because, unless you're the fastest liar this side of the Mississippi, I'm Caitlyn's dad."

"For crying out loud, Kyle—"

"Where is she?" He was striding to his pickup, reaching into his pocket for his keys as he crossed the yard and gravel parking lot.

"At the river—with a guide."

"The river?"

"She's taking canoe lessons with Sarah, her friend."

"Humph."

He reached his truck.

"Wait a minute! What do you think you're doing?" Sam demanded, panic squeezing her heart in a death grip.

"I'm going to meet my kid."

"Now?"

"I think I've waited long enough." He wrenched the door open. "You comin'?"

"You bet I am."

He slid his aviator sunglasses onto his nose. "Hop in."

"But—but I'm not ready. I don't have my purse or—"

"Don't need it. Either get in the truck or get out of my way."

"For the love of God, Kyle, listen to you. Think!"

He climbed into the cab, his jaw clenched, the corners of his mouth tight, his eyes hidden by reflective lenses. Sam didn't like the feeling of being manipulated. She'd always prided herself on making her own decisions, but right now she didn't have much of a choice. With a flick of his wrist, he started the engine. "Okay, okay," she yelled, dashing around the front of the pickup. "But we're going to do this my way."

He snorted in disgust as she slid onto the truck's seat. "I think you've had it your way long enough."

"I was only thinking of Caitlyn."

"Like hell." Ramming the truck into first gear, he tromped on the accelerator, sending a spray of gravel from beneath the tires as he cranked hard on the steering wheel and headed down the long drive. Sam's heart was beating like a drum. Sweat trickled down her spine, and dread, forever her shadow, chased through her insides, making it impossible to breathe.

"Where do they put in?"

"Bittner Point Park. The dock is near where Stiller Creek runs into—"

"I remember." He slowed at the mailbox, checked to see that the country road was clear, then stepped on it. Obviously he wasn't going to waste one more second.

Sam snapped her mouth shut and stared through the window. Aspen trees dotted the foothills, their leaves shimmering in the tiny breath of wind. Cattle and horses grazed on the bleached grass, and miles of barbed wire separated the road from the fields flanking the highway. The sky was clear and blue, only a few wispy clouds crowding around the tallest peaks of the mountains. Nothing had changed, except that her life and her daughter's would never be the same.

"Tell me about it."

She glanced at him, guessing at his thoughts. "About what—raising Caitlyn?"

"Finding out you were pregnant."

"Oh." She pretended interest in the countryside, which was flashing by in a blur of fence posts.

"Well, it wasn't good news, at first. I was scared. Kept thinking that I was miscalculating or just late with my periods, hoping I was wrong. I, um, wasn't one of those women whose cycle was like clockwork, but by the second month, I was pretty sure. I took one of those home tests, and when that proved positive, I saw a doctor, then told my mother." She rubbed her palms on her jeans. "She, uh, wasn't too happy."

"I'll bet not."

"She wanted to know the father's name, and I told her, after having her swear that she'd never reveal it, not even to Dad and especially not to Kate—or to you."

"You should have—"

"You were getting married, Kyle, or don't you remember?"

"The marriage was annulled within a year."

"But I didn't know that then, did I? And the day I found out I was having your baby, my family was invited to your damned wedding. All I knew was that you were marrying a girl you'd known all your life, one with the correct breeding and social position, one that was right for you—some debutante who came with her own damned pedigree." She'd never met Donna Smythe, only seen the wedding photograph in the local paper. But Kyle's bride had been beautiful—tall, reed slim, with short dark hair and an exquisite white lace gown with a train that seemed to go on for miles. In the picture, Donna had been smiling up at her bridegroom, who, dressed in a long-tailed tuxedo, seemed a far cry from the boy with whom Sam had skinny-dipped and made love under a star-sprinkled Wyoming sky.

She swallowed the old pain as he guided the truck into the shady park. Cars, trucks, RVs and empty boat trailers were parked at odd angles on the dusty asphalt. One family was picnicking near the river, and kids waded and splashed on the shoreline where a few trees cast shadows over the ripples. Sam reached for the handle of the door, but Kyle's hand clamped over her arm, restraining her.

"Wait."

"For what? I thought you were hell-bent on seeing this through."

"I am," he admitted in a low voice, deep brackets framing the corners of his mouth. "I guess it's only fair, since you're finally being honest with me, that I tell you what really happened."

"That would be a good start," she said, dread mingling with curiosity.

His lips compressed, as if he was already regretting confiding in her. The fingers of his left hand drummed on the steering wheel. "Oh, hell, Sam," he said, staring at her through his dark lenses, "the truth of the matter is that I married Donna to forget you."

Six

Sam didn't move. Kyle's statement hung in the hot, dry air, spanning the years that stretched between then and now. A painful ache started in a dark corner of her heart, but she ignored it, nor would she listen to the stupid little voice of triumph echoing through her brain when she realized that he had cared for her. "It doesn't matter."

"Sure it does."

"I don't need any apologies."

"I'm not apologizing, damn it." He swore under his breath and his grip tightened on her arm. "For once in your life, Sam, just listen. Donna had been chasing me for years, ever since junior high school, but I was into playing the field...well, you know."

"I remember."

"When I got back to Minneapolis from Crystal Springs that year, she knew something had happened, that I'd changed. We were at the country club, a friend's engagement party, and she'd gotten a couple of bottles of champagne. We both drank too much, I ended up in her bedroom and forgot to leave. Her folks discovered us the next morning and—"

"To save some of her honor, you said you were engaged." Sam could read it in his eyes.

He shrugged. "That's about it, yeah, even though her old man still wanted to beat the living tar out of me. I didn't really want to be tied down, but I decided it was for the best."

He lifted his sunglasses from his face and stared at her with those blue, blue eyes. "I even thought I could forget about you."

"Which you did."

He nodded crisply. "Yeah. Eventually."

All her fleeting hopes, which had risen so stupidly, crashed back onto the cold, cruel stones of reality. He didn't love her; he never had. Why had she naively expected more? He was, after all, just a man, a selfish rich man used to doing things his way. His fingers, still surrounding her arm, had tightened, and his gaze delved deep into hers, as if searching the darkest corners of her soul. A breeze ruffled his hair, as it had ten years before, and for a heartbeat they were as they had been—hard, young and impatient, with passion binding them together and the future pulling them apart. As if he suddenly realized how hard he was clutching her, he let go, and Sam fell against the cracked cushions.

"Mommy!" Caitlyn's voice sang through the air. A long canoe holding the two girls and their instructor cut across the shining ripples of the river. Caitlyn, at the stern, was waving wildly, her paddle out of the water and dripping.

Sam was out of the truck in an instant. Shielding her eyes, she waved back at her daughter, and without waiting for Kyle, started toward the landing at a brisk pace. He caught up with her in a few strides, and within seconds they stood at the end of the dock, watching as the girls maneuvered the canoe to the shore.

Caitlyn, hair wet, her little face flushed, climbed onto the pier. "Did you see me?" she asked, excitement gleaming in her eyes.

"I did."

"And me?" Sarah chimed in, her frizzy black curls dripping.

"You bet." Samantha motioned toward Kyle. "Sarah Wilson, this is Mr. Fortune."

"He likes to be called Kyle," Caitlyn interjected.

"Hey, girls, haven't you forgotten something?" Reed Fuller, a strapping forty-five-year-old, was tying the canoe to the dock. Sarah and Caitlyn joined him in securing the thin-skinned boat. As Kyle and Samantha watched, Reed gave the girls a few more instructions. Minutes later they unfastened their life preservers and stowed them in the equipment bags that Reed hauled around in his Jeep.

Once finished, the two girls, chattering like magpies, wedged themselves into the truck between Kyle and Samantha, which was just fine with her. The more distance between her body and Kyle's the better, but seeing Caitlyn's thin, tanned leg pressed hard against her father's jeans-clad thigh was difficult, and Sam wondered as she glanced at their two faces, so alike, how no one in town, not even Kate Fortune, had guessed that Samantha's little girl had Fortune blood flowing in her veins.

Upon the girls' insistence, Kyle drove into town to the old hamburger joint where he and Sam had once met. The place had been owned by several families since then, had served everything from take-out pizza to Tex-Mex cuisine, but was now once again an old-fashioned hamburger-and-milk-shake, mom-and-pop operation.

The kids ordered root-beer floats, which foamed wildly, spangled their upper lips with bubbly mustaches and were devoured within minutes. Kyle drank coffee, while Sam sipped a diet cola and wondered if she'd ever felt so uncomfortable. Caitlyn didn't seem to notice that Kyle was watching her. She barely spared him the time of day until they were in the truck again and driving to Sarah's house, an old cabin that had been added on to four times in the past half century and now had a central hallway and kitchen with three separate wings shooting off from the original structure.

"You related to Mrs. Kate?" Sarah finally asked, studying him with serious eyes.

"Her grandson."

"I knew her," Sarah said, nodding so that her black curls bounced. "My mom sometimes cleaned her house, but that was before she died."

Kyle's lips flattened, his eyes trained on the road.

"I liked her," Caitlyn offered. "She told me someday I could ride Joker."

Samantha shook her head. "That was a long time ago. Joker belongs to someone else now."

"He's still at the ranch."

"I know, but we can't just hop on his back without the owner, Mr. McClure, saying it's okay."

"Grant won't mind," Kyle said, and Caitlyn's eyes shone.

Samantha sensed the conversation slipping into dangerous waters. She was still Caitlyn's mother, the only parent her daughter had ever known. "I'm not sure I want her riding that one. He's stubborn and unpredictable, and—oh, here's the turn to Sarah's house." She pointed to a rutted lane, where wildflowers grew near the fence posts lining the drive and weeds scraped the undercarriage of Kyle's truck.

Several of Sarah's siblings were in the yard. A little boy with dark hair and freckles swung on a worn tire hanging from a branch of an apple tree, while his older brother was hooting at him from the upper limbs. A few cattle, horses and even a couple of llamas were penned in the fields surrounding the old homestead.

Mandy waved from the porch as Sarah wriggled out of the cab.

Then they were alone, the three of them. A should-have-been family. As the truck bounced and jostled down the lane, Samantha's throat tightened. How were they going to break the news to Caitlyn that she had a father, that her mom had lied about him all these years, that at any moment during her lifetime Caitlyn could have been told the truth?

Sam glanced toward Kyle and remembered how much she'd come to love him. At first wary, she'd finally given herself to him heart and soul, believing in the power of love.

She'd asked herself a million times since how she could have been so wrong about him. She'd never thought him capable of so hot-blooded a romance, only to run off and marry another woman before Christmas of that same year. She wondered about his story—that he'd thought it best to marry someone else to get her, a poor country bumpkin, out of his system.

Lord, why did she even care? she wondered, as the truck sped along the highway and her thoughts wrapped around her like a dark, unforgiving cloud. She'd gotten pregnant in late August or early September, suspected the worst in October, confirmed the truth in November, and before she could pick up the phone to tell Kyle the news that he was about to join the ranks of fatherhood, had spied the wedding invitation on the kitchen table. How little had he thought of her?

When she'd heard that the marriage had been annulled less than a year later, she was already a mother and had her hands full dealing with her baby. By then she'd become determined to make it on her own. She had too much pride to claim that Kyle had impregnated her, then been callous enough to run off and marry someone else. The whole Fortune clan, Kyle included, would have thought her just another gold digger looking for a share in the mother lode the family wealth represented. There would have been paternity tests, court battles and hours upon hours with slick-talking lawyers, all out for their own little bit of fame and a lot of money.

At the time, Sam's father was still working for the Fortunes, trying to pay off the mortgage on the Rawlingses' ranch. And Kate was a widow, in charge of all her husband's holdings while at the same time trying to keep her family together. She didn't need the burden of Sam and her baby making a mess of things in a family that was already grieving and fractured. Sam would have been damned before she'd let her precious baby become the subject of more speculation, or cruel innuendos by those in the Fortune family who would have resented Kyle's illegitimate daughter.

Time had slowly slipped away. Kyle never visited the ranch, and Samantha decided it was best if she raised Caitlyn alone. She felt that she was well equipped to mold her daughter into a smart, independent woman, especially since her own parents had been more than willing to help out.

Years later, when Caitlyn asked about her father, Samantha had always squirmed. Never one to lie, she'd explained that the man who had sired her had married another woman and never known that he had a daughter. Sam had never told Caitlyn his name, but had promised her daughter that someday, when she was old enough, she could meet the man who was her father.

When Caitlyn was a toddler or preschooler, keeping

the secret wasn't a problem, but as the years passed and Caitlyn developed into a curious, determined little girl, hiding the truth from her had proved difficult, especially when, at school, Caitlyn had heard words like *unwanted, illegitimate* and that she was probably a mistake. She'd been the object of both scorn and pity.

Samantha's heart had broken for her daughter, so tough on the outside and so soft within. Several times she'd nearly broken down and told Caitlyn about Kyle, but she'd always ended up holding on to her secret for fear that Caitlyn would demand to meet him and start a chain of events involving lawyers, paternity tests, publicity and possible rejection by the one man who should have stood by her side her entire life.

There had been questions, of course, from the time Sam had begun to show. Sam's mother, Bess, had deftly fielded the smirking insinuations, the bald speculation, the notes of disapproval. No one knew that Sam had been involved with Kyle. The few times they'd been seen together were no different from the times he'd been with other girls in town.

When asked, Sam had always explained her pregnancy as the result of a love affair gone sour with a local boy who took off when he found out about the baby. Her father had wanted to know who "the cowardly son of a bitch" was, but Bess had insisted that it wouldn't help things, only hurt them, and that they were all going to love Caitlyn regardless of who her biological father was.

The story wasn't all that far from the truth. Everyone assumed Sam had been involved with Tadd Richter, a local tough whom she had befriended before his family moved away that summer. The few times she'd been seen with Kyle hadn't even raised an eyebrow in a town where many girls at one time or another had caught his attention.

However, Sam believed that, had Kate lived much longer, she would have eventually come to the conclusion that Caitlyn was a Fortune. The family resemblance was just too strong to ignore.

Even Kyle had seen it.

While Kate was alive, she'd shown a special interest in Caitlyn whenever she'd visited the ranch. Oh, God, Sam missed the older lady. She'd been like a grandmother to her, and now, because of her death, it seemed as if Kate had given Kyle the perfect opportunity to meet his daughter. Whether Sam liked it or not.

"You two want to stop by my place?" Kyle asked, bringing her crashing back to the present. Someone had flipped on the radio, and an old Bruce Springsteen tune was fighting a losing battle with static. Caitlyn seemed so much at home in the truck, as if she belonged right here, between the two of them, that Sam had trouble finding her tongue.

"I, uh, think we should go home." Sam rolled the window down a little farther, hoping fresh air would chase away her memories and clear her head. "Caitlyn needs to clean up and—"

"Can I ride Joker?" Caitlyn asked with a shy smile, on the verge of being coy.

Kyle barked out a laugh. "You sure have a one-track mind."

"But would it be okay?"

Samantha tapped her daughter on the shoulder. "I told you that Joker is Mr. McClure's horse now."

Kyle frowned thoughtfully. "I think it would be all right."

"Are you nuts?" Sam asked, astounded. "The horse

won't let anyone lead him into the trailer, let alone let a little girl climb on his back and—''

"I'm *not* little."

"Don't argue with me!" Sam said swiftly, as she saw the turnoff to her lane flash past. "Wait a minute—"

"It's all right. Joker's got a mind of his own sometimes, but we can handle him," Kyle assured her, and she felt her cheeks burn red-hot. How dare he undermine her?

"No, it's not. I said no and what I say goes. As I've told Caitlyn more than once, we're in this boat with only one captain, and I just happen to be it."

He laughed again, the tense lines of his face softening enough to remind her of how much she'd loved him, trusted him, belonged to him. Oh, their affair had been a lifetime ago and she wasn't about to fall into that ridiculous trap again, but there had been a time when he'd charmed her completely, body and soul. He shifted down at the lane to the Fortune Ranch, and as the fence posts and aspen trees sped by, Sam tried to calm herself. Getting upset would only make the situation worse. Kyle parked in the shade of the barn, and as Samantha got out of the truck, Caitlyn scrambled past her, heading for the paddock where Joker was usually penned.

Once her daughter was out of earshot, Samantha whirled on Kyle. "You can't do this, you know," she said through lips that barely moved.

"Do what?"

"Take charge. She's my daughter and I'm the one who raised her this far without any help from you. I don't need it now."

"Don't you?" His smile was downright laconic, and she wanted nothing more than to slap it off his smug, handsome-as-the-devil face.

"No."

One eyebrow lifted challengingly over the rim of his sunglasses. "You might change your tune when I tell her that I'm her natural father."

"You wouldn't."

"I sure would. It's time she knows."

"Just wait, okay?" Samantha insisted, barely able to think. Her mind was whirling, a headache threatened and her chest felt as if it was encircled by ever-tightening barrel staves, determined to shove all air from her lungs. Glancing at Caitlyn, she wanted to cry. Her daughter had climbed onto the fence, her little boots hooked on the lowest rail, one arm wrapped around a post, the other outstretched with a handful of grass as she tried to entice the feisty Appaloosa closer. Joker was having none of it. He tossed his great head and snorted, the odd markings on his face looking more sinister than comical at the moment.

"What're you worried about?"

"Everything," she admitted, swallowing hard. "Her. You. Me. Oh, God, this is such a mess." Her life was suddenly like a vise, with pressure from all sides determined to squeeze her so hard she felt like screaming.

"It's only gonna get worse before it gets better."

"Thanks for the words of encouragement."

"Just tellin' it like it is, ma'am," he drawled. "Now, I think the sooner we tell Caitlyn the truth, the better we'll all feel."

"This will take time."

"I've already lost nine years, Sam."

"And so now you're ready to become a daddy," she mocked. "You, the perennial playboy? You know it takes more than fertilizing an egg to be a real father." Whirling away from him, she stalked toward the stables and her daughter. It was impossible to discuss the subject civilly with him. Of course she'd have to tell Caitlyn the truth, and it would have to be soon, but damn it, she'd tell her on her own terms, in her own manner and when the time was right. Kyle could bloody well learn a little patience. "Come on, Caitlyn. We've got to go."

"But—"

"Now!" Sam insisted. "We can cut across the fields."

"I'll drive you," Kyle offered.

"It's all right."

"I want to ride Joker. You promised." Caitlyn didn't move from her spot on the fence.

"I did no such thing." Sam shot Kyle a look that accused him of getting them into this mess. "Another time, maybe, if Mr. McClure agrees. Now, come on."

"I think you'd better get into the truck, Caitlyn. Please," Kyle said. "Your mama's laid down the law, and you know how bossy she can be when she sets her mind to something."

Caitlyn's lower lip protruded and she tossed Kyle a murderous glance that accused him of being a liar and a traitor along with every other vile thing a nine-year-old could conjure up. "You can't tell me what to do," she said, hoisting her little chin proudly into the air.

"Can't I?" Kyle was never one to let a challenge slide by without a response.

"Just get into the pickup, Caitlyn," Sam ordered, sensing that the conversation was about to turn ugly.

"Do what your mother says."

"He said I could ride Joker, but he lied!" Reluctantly Caitlyn climbed off the fence.

"No, he just did what I asked. Come on now." Sam shepherded her angry daughter into the cab and noticed tears of frustration gathering in Caitlyn's eyes. One little

drop slid down her cheek as Kyle hoisted himself behind
the steering wheel. Caitlyn quickly brushed the tell-tale
tear aside, but the action wasn't lost on Kyle. Grimacing,
he switched on the ignition. *Great,* Samantha thought
morbidly with an eye to her future. The next one hundred
and seventy-odd days promised to be sheer hell.

"Kyle's back," the stranger said into the receiver of
a phone in a tired-looking booth just outside of Jackson.
Graffiti was scratched into the walls—ugly four-letter
words and phone numbers. The air was so hot it was
nearly suffocating, but the booth was better than a cel-
lular phone. Here, it would be difficult for anyone to trace
the call.

"Is he planning to stay?" The voice on the other end
sounded weak, yet determined.

"I'd say so. He doesn't have much choice."

"And Samantha?"

"She's seen him. So has her daughter."

"Well, well, well..."

"Yes," he said, wishing he could find a room with
state-of-the-art air-conditioning. "Everything's set."

"Good. Good."

"Now all we need is a little luck."

"Luck?" his partner reprimanded with a throaty
chuckle. "You should know me well enough to understand that I don't believe in luck. Never have. People
make choices, that's all."

"If you say so," the stranger said. After all, who was
he to argue with someone who had proved that theory
right?

A father!
Kyle stripped off his shirt and caught a glimpse of his

reflection in the mirror over the sink as he reached for his razor. To think he had a kid—a nine-year-old spitfire of a girl who was as beautiful as her mother and, he suspected, just as volatile.

How could he have not known? Never suspected? Why hadn't Sam told him? He felt like a heel.

He hadn't lied to her, though. He'd run like hell the last time he'd left Wyoming. Sam had touched him so intimately—messed with his mind—more than he'd allowed any woman to touch him before, and it had scared him spitless.

He lathered his face, intent on shaving, but memories wouldn't leave him be.

That long-ago summer he'd become obsessed with her and had lost a part of himself—the part associated with male pride—to her. She wasn't his kind of woman, not really. Too stubborn. Too quick with her tongue. Too independent. At seventeen she could shoot a rifle better than he could, rope a steer, vaccinate a herd of cattle, calm a nervous stallion or brand a passel of bawling calves without batting an eye. She hadn't admitted it, but he'd been sure she could castrate a bull without too much trouble as well.

And he'd fallen for her. Hard. Harder than any man should fall for a woman.

At the end of the summer, he'd run back to Minneapolis, where Donna was lying in wait—ready to claim him and chase away his obsession for Sam. All soft and feminine, wrapped in a cloud of expensive perfume and silk, Donna Smythe never argued or disagreed with him. She laughed at his jokes, did what he asked, smiled adoringly and never gave him a tongue-lashing. Unlike Sam.

Donna's entire life seemed to revolve around making Kyle feel good, and about the time he'd decided he couldn't continue the charade, that she was beginning to bore him with all her attention and smiles, they'd been caught in bed together. Like a fool, he'd been cornered into the marriage. To get Sam out of his system, he'd married the ''right'' woman, one of his own station, and he'd been miserable. Everyone in the family had been thrilled for him—everyone but Kate.

She'd pulled him aside, reminded him that he was young, that there were lots of women in the world, that one beautiful socialite might not be the answer. But Kyle's pride as well as Donna's reputation had been on the line. She'd been good to him, and he didn't want her to think she was just another notch in his bedpost. Besides, he'd rationalized, he did care for her, not with the blazing, mind-searing passion he'd felt with Sam, but he did love her in his own way.

The marriage had been doomed from the beginning. Kyle couldn't stand to be tied down, to run with the country-club set, to attend night classes and take a job with the family business as his wife insisted. Donna had been certain that one day he would run his grandfather's financial empire, when he didn't give a damn about it.

Soon after the wedding, when the fights began and it became apparent that Donna's ambitions were miles from his own, Kyle had thought he was trapped forever with a woman he didn't know, a woman who put on a false smile as easily as her lipstick, a woman who looked at him not as a man, but as a prize—*Look what I got! A Fortune heir!* She'd tried to tell him how to dress, what kind of car to drive, where they would move, how to make sure he inherited what was due him—a part of the company. Donna had warned him to keep a wary eye on his brothers and cousins to make sure they weren't kissing up to Kate and thereby insuring themselves larger inheritances.

It had made him sick. She talked about having children and sending them to the best boarding schools in the country. She took him to the ballet and the symphony and stuffy parties at the country club.

Within four months, Kyle was restless. The arguments became full-fledged fights, and the once-pliable Donna became a fire-breathing dragon determined to mold him into what she thought was best. When Kyle balked, she seemed stricken. She reminded him that she'd given up numerous suitors, all from good families, to be married to him. She told him how disappointed she was. He'd come back from Wyoming different from the way he was before he'd left and she didn't know what had come over him. Whatever it was, it wasn't good.

Kyle silently disagreed.

They fought, she cried, he consoled. They made love in the same old passionless manner, until he finally began sleeping in the guest room. It all came to a head one night when he refused to go to a benefit dinner and dance downtown. He'd spent the day with his father at the company, dealing with lawyers, accountants and partners. He couldn't face another minute with the stuffed shirts that were part of Donna's and his crowd.

That night, once again alone in the guest room, he stared out at the lights of Minneapolis, but his thoughts were in Wyoming, where the hills were black and the sky sprinkled with a million stars. He remembered making love to Sam under a pale sliver of moon and wondered why he couldn't conjure up one image of his own wife in the throes of wild, sensual desire.

"You're a louse," he'd told himself, "and you'll probably rot in hell."

The next morning he'd found Donna in the kitchen, her makeup unable to hide the redness in her eyes, a cigarette burning unattended in her fingers. She hadn't bothered to dress, and her pink robe gaped at her cleavage as she sat at the kitchen table near the French doors, where snow had piled on their deck.

"It's over," she said, biting her lip.

"What?"

"Don't act stupid, darling, it doesn't suit. I'm talking about us—you and me—and this damned marriage that you never wanted in the first place."

He couldn't lie, and she'd dissolved in tears, but when he tried to console her, to wrap his arms around her shaking shoulders, she'd shoved him away. She'd already called a lawyer, asked about an annulment rather than a divorce, and the wheels were in motion.

"You'll be free again," she said, finally taking a long drag from her cigarette and spewing smoke toward the ceiling. "That's what you want."

"I think we should talk."

"Why?" She nailed him with her brown eyes. "It wouldn't matter. You don't love me. You've never loved me and this summer...well, I'd hoped you'd changed. You seemed different when you got back from Wyoming, more alive, more interested." Her eyes narrowed thoughtfully for a second, then she shrugged. "Oh, hell, it doesn't matter anyway. I thought I could make you love me, but I can't." Her throat worked, her voice cracked and she blinked hard as she crushed out the cigarette.

"I'm sorry."

"Don't be." Sniffing loudly, she reached into her pocket for a tissue. "I knew you weren't the loving type, not the settling-down kind, so let's just end it. All I want is my pride. I want to be able to say that I was the one who wanted out.''

Kyle agreed, moved out that night, found a furnished apartment and went through the motions of ending a marriage that had never really begun. His sister had tried to talk him out of it. Jane, forever the romantic, thought he was being a spoiled brat, that he hadn't tried hard enough. Older brother Michael had chided him for not being responsible, but told him he'd never thought Kyle and Donna were a good match—Kyle was much too restless. Fortunately, Kristina was too young to be interested in anyone but herself.

Kyle had thought he might catch hell from his father, but Nathaniel Fortune had suffered through one bad marriage himself, to Kyle's mother, and had gratefully kept his opinions to himself.

So Kyle, once the legal strings had been untied, had sworn off marriage for good. Once burned, twice shy, he always figured.

But then he hadn't counted on being a father. He nearly cut himself with the last swipe of his razor.

A father! Without even being a husband. He splashed water over his face and toweled himself off. He'd never figured that he would have a child or that he'd end up seeing Samantha Rawlings again. But now, thanks to this damned inheritance, whether he liked it or not, he was face-to-face with the stubborn woman.

The trouble was her strawberry blond hair, green eyes and pale freckles were just as intriguing to him now as they used to be, maybe even more so. No longer a girl, she was a grown woman with a mind of her own, a ranch of her own and a daughter who belonged to him. As wild as the windswept plains and as sturdy as the mountains rising to the west, Samantha Rawlings was more woman than Kyle wanted to deal with.

But he had no choice.

Seven

"Hello?" Samantha said, answering the phone as Caitlyn, her tanned legs swinging from a kitchen chair, tore into a piece of pie.

No response.

No dial tone.

"Hello?" Sam's heart thumped a little as she waited. Again no answer. "Is anyone there?"

Click.

Whoever it was had hung up. Sam's fingers turned to ice. Surely anyone who had dialed incorrectly would identify himself. So this was a prank. Who was it?

"No one there?" Caitlyn asked, her mouth smeared with red pie filling.

"I guess it was a wrong number." Sam replaced the receiver slowly and told herself not to overreact. Someone had just dialed incorrectly. No big deal.

"It happened before."

"It did? When?" Sam slid into her chair as her stomach lurched.

Caitlyn shrugged. "Dunno. A few days ago."

This was all getting a little spooky. "How about that feeling that you were being watched?" Sam asked, bringing up a subject that scared her half to death as she grabbed the glass of ice tea she'd left on the counter. It was probably just her child's overactive imagination, but Sam couldn't ignore it.

Caitlyn plopped another forkful of pie into her mouth and shook her head. "That hasn't happened for a while."

"Since the last time?"

"Umm."

Silently, Sam let out a sigh of relief. Maybe Caitlyn's feeling that she was being observed was nothing—the product, once again, of a little girl's vivid imagination. Sam had worried herself sick about it. She'd thought about calling the sheriff's office, then chided herself. No deputy was going to come racing out to her ranch just because Caitlyn thought she was being stalked...if that was even the right word. Besides, Sam had more immediate problems to face. Somehow she had to confess that she was a chronic liar where her daughter's paternity was involved. Sam would have to explain to Caitlyn that the new neighbor taking over the Fortune Ranch was her father. But how? She'd been stewing about it for two days, trying to find the right moment, only to realize that there never would be one. But Kyle wouldn't wait forever. He'd made that more than clear.

"Use your napkin," she reminded her daughter as Caitlyn, already dressed in her pajamas, slid from her chair and headed for the living room.

She was back in a flash, gave her mouth and chin a quick swipe with a paper towel, then dashed through the archway again. Fang, from his position near the wood stove, lifted his head and slowly climbed to his feet to trot after her. When Caitlyn had been born, Fang had been little more than a curious puppy who, intrigued with the red-faced, crying infant, had whined and stood on his back legs to peer into the new baby's bassinet. Over the years they'd grown up together, dog and girl, creating a special bond, except that now Caitlyn was young and rambunctious, while the mutt was aging, his snout beginning to gray, his energy level far from what it once had been.

Still uneasy, Sam carried her daughter's plate to the sink. It was now or never. She'd force Caitlyn to turn off the television, cuddle with her on the couch and explain that Kyle Fortune was her father. Simple enough. There would be a million questions, of course—there always were with Caitlyn—but Sam would sort through them and tell her the truth.

She rinsed off the plate, wiped her hands on a dish towel and heard the rumble of an engine. Her heart sank as she recognized Kyle's truck in the drive. ''Great,'' she muttered, bracing herself. If only he could have waited a few more minutes.

Fang let out a couple of barks as Kyle stormed up the steps of the back porch. Sam met him in the doorway.

''Well?'' he asked, not bothering to smile.

''I haven't told her yet.''

''Oh, God!'' He shot a glance inside, then grabbed her arm and tugged, yanking her through the doorway to the dark porch. ''Why not?'' He was so close she could feel the angry waves of heat radiating from him. His fingers tightened over her wrist, and stupidly, her pulse fluttered as an image of him as a younger man, lean and hard and anxious as he pulled her to him, flashed through her mind.

''There—there hasn't been a good time.''

His eyes were mere slits. ''Just like there hasn't been a good time in nine years!''

''Kyle, please understand—''

''What I understand is that Caitlyn's my flesh and blood. Now unless you were lying through your teeth, I have a kid I've never really met—not on a father-to-daughter basis.'' His nostrils flared in the darkness. ''I

have a right to be with my daughter, Sam, a legal right—
to get to know her, to make some plans with her, for her
to know that I exist.''

''Plans?'' she asked, dread inching up her spine.
''What kind of plans?'' The future stretched out before
her in a dark, fathomless void.

''First things first.'' He released her suddenly, threw
open the door and strode into the kitchen.

''Oh, God.'' Sam's head was pounding. He couldn't,
wouldn't... She was after him like a shot, but it was too
late. He'd already entered the living room where Caitlyn,
lying on the floor, was watching television and flipping
through a magazine about horses.

''I think we should talk,'' he announced, and Samantha, in the archway, stopped dead in her tracks.

Caitlyn eyed him. ''About what?''

''Your dad.'' He walked past her and stood near the
fireplace, tall and looming and so unpredictable.

Sam bit her tongue.

All ears, Caitlyn climbed onto the couch and sent a
glance of triumph at her mother. Here at last, she silently
said, was someone who would tell her the truth. ''You
know him?'' she asked Kyle.

''Intimately.''

''Wait, I think I should do this.'' Steeling herself, Sam
walked into the room and sat on the edge of the couch.
Her heart was pounding, her palms suddenly slick with
sweat. ''I, uh, I should have told you a long time ago.''
Somehow her words were coming out steadily, though
inside she was trembling. Damn Kyle for pushing her into
this before she was ready. Caitlyn was staring at her with
big, round eyes, and Sam's heart cracked. ''Your father
is Mr. Fortune.''

"What? Him?" Caitlyn swiveled her head to stare at the man leaning against the mantel. "You?"

"Yes." Even though she was dying inside, Sam felt as if a tremendous weight had been lifted from her shoulders. Her throat worked and tears burned behind her eyes. "Mr. Fortune—Kyle—and I knew each other a long time ago."

"But he lives far away...."

"I spent a summer here on the ranch," he explained. "I met your mother, and we spent a lot of time together. We liked each other a lot and became very close." He lowered himself until he was squatting and staring at her, eyeball-to-eyeball. "I had to leave before your mother could tell me that you were coming along. Things kind of got complicated and your mom and I lost touch."

Caitlyn's eyebrows drew down in a frown. "So you were in love but not married."

Oh, God, help me, Sam prayed without uttering a word.

"Yep." Kyle said it without blinking an eye.

Sam started, nailing him with a glare. "Not exactly. We, um, thought we were in love, honey, but we were too young to know what love was all about." If they were going to be honest, damn it, then the entire truth was coming out. Even if Kyle hadn't loved her, she had, in her own naive way, loved him.

Caitlyn crossed her arms over her chest and sent a damning look in Sam's direction. "You knew his name."

"Yes, but as he said, he didn't know about you."

"Why not?"

"It's not that easy."

"You could have told Mrs. Kate. She would have found him, I bet."

"Yes, but I was young and confused. I thought...I hoped I was doing what was best for you."

"Or for you?" Caitlyn asked, her eyebrows drawing together. In that heart-stopping instant, she appeared older than her nine years.

Kyle cleared his throat. "It's not your mom's fault. I married someone else." He stared at her with honest blue eyes and offered her a smile. "I think I was a little stuck on myself and I made a lot of mistakes. Bad ones. Now it's time to rectify the ones I can."

"What does that mean?" Sam asked, hardly able to breathe.

"That I need to take steps—legal steps—to shoulder some responsibility for Caitlyn."

Things were quickly getting out of hand. "You don't have to do anything of the kind."

"I want to."

"I don't get it," Caitlyn said, licking her lips nervously. "Is something going to change? Am I still gonna live here?"

"Of course you are," Sam assured her, hugging her close. Oh, Lord, she couldn't lose her baby, not even to Kyle. "We're a family."

"And him?" she asked, pointing at her newfound father.

"We're just taking one day at a time. And nothing's going to change, believe me," Sam said over the top of Caitlyn's blond curls as she scowled at Kyle, warning him not to defy her.

He managed one of his slow grins. "The only thing that's really gonna change is that you and I are gonna see each other a lot, get to know each other and make up for lost time."

"What about Mom?"

"Oh, she can come along, I suppose, if she wants to."

"Will we be a family?" Caitlyn asked, and the room grew suddenly still. The clock ticked off the slow, tense seconds. Sam's throat closed tightly, until Kyle finally winked at his daughter.

"Of course we're a family."

"Will we live together?"

"Oh, no, honey." Sam kissed Caitlyn's crown and fought tears when she realized how much Caitlyn had hoped and dreamed to be like the other kids—the ones whose parents were married and still together.

"Why not?"

"Because your father and I aren't married."

"Can't you get married?"

Dear God, stop this torture, please. "No, honey, that's impossible."

"Why?"

"Because Mr. Fortune—er, Kyle and I—aren't in love anymore."

"You told me love lasts forever."

"True love, Caitlyn," Sam said, aware of the weight of Kyle's gaze resting heavily upon her. "True love lasts forever, but it's very hard to find."

Caitlyn shook her head. "Nah, you just have to look harder."

"Maybe she's right," Kyle said. "Maybe we just didn't look hard enough."

Sam swallowed and shoved her hands nervously into her pockets. "It was a long time ago."

"I know, but—"

"It didn't work out. End of story." Her voice was firm, brooking no argument. The tenor of the conversation had to change before she lost her fragile grip on her composure. Running stiff fingers through her hair, she said, "I think this is enough for one day, don't you?"

He glanced at his watch and frowned. "Looks like your mom's right again." He patted Caitlyn's knee. "I've got to run. I'm expecting a call. But I'll be back and we'll start getting to know each other, okay?"

Caitlyn nodded, all the while staring at him with wide eyes. She picked at a piece of lint on the arm of the sofa.

"Is there something you wanted to ask me?" Kyle said.

Caitlyn nodded. "Can I ride Joker?"

"Oh, for the love of Pete!" Sam squeezed her daughter and sighed. "I told you that's not possible—"

Kyle laughed. "As I said before, Caitlyn, you sure have a one-track mind."

"Amen," Sam agreed.

Straightening, Kyle promised, "I'll talk to Grant. And we'll see what your mom says. Good night," he said, and thankfully didn't try anything as foolish as kissing his daughter. Instead he walked out of the room and through the kitchen, closing the door behind him. Sam slowly let out her breath as she heard the sound of his truck disappearing into the night.

Caitlyn twisted in her arms. "You didn't tell me," she said accusingly. "Why not?"

"Because I thought it was best," Sam replied, shaking her head and holding her child fiercely, as if she expected Kyle and the lawyers for the Fortune family to swoop back into the room and, with legal documents and money, wrest her baby from her. "Obviously, I was mistaken."

"I'm telling you, Kyle, something's not right." Rebecca's voice pounded in his ears, and he couldn't deal with her farfetched, half-baked theories about his grandmother's death, not now. Not when he was having his own personal crisis. Drumming his fingers impatiently on the counter, he leaned against the kitchen wall of his ranch house and wiped the sweat from his forehead.

"Mom was a terrific pilot," Rebecca continued.

"But the plane malfunctioned."

"Why? Mom had it checked by her mechanic between each flight. I talked to the guy and he swore it was running like a top the day before she took off."

"It was an airplane, Rebecca. Sometimes they crash."

"Not without a reason."

He could almost hear the wheels spinning in his aunt's mind. She was a little off center, in his opinion, a mystery writer who sometimes seemed to have a problem determining between fact and fiction.

He ran his tongue along his teeth. His throat was parched, his muscles aching from hours of setting fence posts, and he didn't have time for Rebecca's nonsense. "So what are you saying—that the plane didn't go down?"

"I don't know what I'm saying, not yet, except that something's fishy. Mom was too careful to have an accident like this."

"Careful? Kate? Are we talking about the same woman? She took to a dare or a challenge like a fish to water."

"But she wasn't reckless," Rebecca insisted. "Look, I've hired a private investigator to check into the plane crash."

"Yeah, I heard. But, Rebecca, why? It won't bring Kate back."

"This is just something I've got to do, okay? I thought I'd let everyone in the family know."

"I can't believe this."

''Believe it, Kyle, and trust me. Something's rotten in the Brazilian rain forest and I intend to find out just what it is.''

He hung up, picturing his aunt, who looked so much like her mother, with long, curly auburn hair, patrician nose, slim figure... And the same keen intelligence, when she wasn't off on some wild-goose chase, which she apparently was again.

Hell. He didn't have much time for Rebecca's latest mystery, even though it dealt with Kate. Not now, when his own set of problems, the least of which was running this ranch, were more than he could deal with.

Now that he knew Caitlyn was his, what was he going to do about her? Sure, he'd get to know her better, though he sensed instinctively that the little imp would wrap him around her finger in no time. But what about later, when he sold this miserable scrap of land and moved back to Minneapolis or wherever it was he ended up? What then? Or could he stay? Why not? A thousand reasons came to mind but he chased them all away. He'd always loved it in Wyoming and felt as at home here as anywhere on earth.

He walked outside and squinted at the horizon. Fields and sagebrush stretched to the foothills, where pine, spruce and fir trees climbed up the lower elevations of the mountains. He grabbed hold of a rough crossbeam supporting the edge of the roof and swore roundly. Truth to tell, Caitlyn was only part of the problem. The rest was Sam.

''Damn it all,'' he muttered into the wind rising from the east. ''Damn it all to hell.''

''You told me it was wrong to lie!'' Caitlyn exclaimed as she and Sam watered the garden. Stalks of corn and rows of pole beans grew between the house and the barns.

"It was. I know. But I was young and, oh, Caitlyn," she said, squinting up at the sky, where a few clouds floated on a summer breeze. "I made a mistake. What can I say? I'm sorry."

"Are you?"

"Yes! Why won't you believe me?"

"'Cause you're a liar." Caitlyn, in a foul mood from the time her bare feet had landed on the floor this morning, dropped the hose and crossed her arms over her chest. "I could have known about him, told the other kids about him, not been called those creepy names, if you'd just told me."

"I said I was sorry."

Caitlyn lifted her chin challengingly. "Will I go spend weekends with him like Nora Petrelli does with her dad?"

"No! Oh, I honestly don't know how this is going to play out." Sam stretched the hose taut. "We'll just have to see."

"I'm gonna call Tommy and Sarah and—"

"Not yet, honey, okay? Not until we tell the family. You and I'll go talk to Grandma today, and we'll let Kyle tell his brothers and sisters." She couldn't begin to imagine what the rest of the Fortune clan would think.

"Do I have cousins?" Caitlyn picked up her hose again and sprayed water on some withering tomato plants.

"Probably a thousand of them."

"Oh, wow!" A smile split Caitlyn's face as she realized that there was a much wider family she was a part of. "When can I meet them?"

"As soon as Kyle tells everyone." The knell of doom

struck deep in Sam's heart as she realized that from this day forward she'd never again be able to make a decision concerning her daughter's future without Kyle's input.

The sun slid beneath the western horizon as Kyle wiped the grease from his hands. After setting fence posts in the morning, he'd spent the afternoon doing his own kind of inventory—looking over machinery and buildings, figuring out what needed to be sold and what could be repaired, assessing how much money he'd have to sink into this place in order to keep it running for six months before he could sell it for top dollar.

As if someone was going to buy it in the dead of winter. Kate might have made the stipulation that he live six months on the ranch before selling it, but realistically, he was probably stuck here for nearly a year, so he'd better make a go of it.

In the past week, he'd met three hired hands who lived nearby and had been on the ranch payroll for several years. Randy Herdstrom, a big, strapping man with two kids and a small place of his own, looked more than capable of handling the cattle, running the equipment and dealing with prospective livestock buyers. The other two guys, Carson and Russ, were young and green, rough around the edges, the kind of muscular guys who could work all day cutting, wrestling, castrating and branding and then, come quitting time, spend all their hard-earned wages on beer, gambling and the women that hung out at the Lone Elder Tavern on the outskirts of town. Not that what they did on their time off was any of Kyle's business. He only cared about how they performed on the job.

Still working the grease from his fingers, he leaned against a fence post and looked at part of his herd, short-legged, thick-bodied cattle in a mixture of colors. Most of the animals had the markings of Herefords, their faces white or mottled. But black- or dun-colored coats were interspersed with the red hides of the stock and hinted at different bulls the ranch had used over the years. Lumbering across the fields in the twilight, lowing every once in a while, the cattle seemed content, an emotion that had escaped Kyle for as long as he could remember.

He'd always been so damned restless, but if the truth were known, his most peaceful days had been those summers on these vast, savage acres, riding, roping, raising Cain or making love to Sam. Always Sam. The mother of his daughter.

Why hadn't she shown up today? He'd expected her to stop by and work with Joker. He'd listened for her truck, kept an eye out for both Sam and Caitlyn and, just before sunset, talked himself out of driving over to her place. Now that he knew Caitlyn was his kid, he could barely keep away. It was bad enough, this obsession he had with Sam, but now his kid was involved.

He'd forced himself to stay away from Sam's house because he figured mother and daughter needed time and space to sort things out.

And yet he hadn't been able to forget his daughter's simple question: *can't you get married?* Both he and Sam had sidestepped that one, but there was a part of him—probably the guilt-riddled part—that considered Caitlyn's suggestion with more than a little interest. So he and Sam weren't in love. So what? People got married for lots of reasons, some of which were a darned sight worse than for the benefit of a child. They wouldn't even have to live together. He could provide financial support, live with them when he was in Wyoming.... Nah, that wouldn't work. He'd want to be close to his daughter all the time, and he couldn't imagine Sam moving to Minneapolis.

He took in the night-darkened panorama, the shadows of mountains rising high above dry fields. Could he live here—day in, day out? With Sam? A smile touched the corners of his mouth as he imagined sleeping in her bed, making hot, hard love to her well into the late hours of the night and waking up with her snuggled in his arms. He imagined her scent lingering with him throughout the day, her laughter touching the deepest part of him, her sexy little smile teasing him, until each night he undressed her slowly. The moonlight would stream through the windows as each piece of her clothing pooled on the floor, as he explored and loved every inch of her body. He would touch her in the most intimate of places, feel her heat, taste her moisture, and when she was ready, thrust into her with all the primitive passion of a randy stallion claiming a wild mare as his own.

"Boy, you've got it bad, Fortune," he chided. He was already starting to get hard just at the mental image of her warm skin pressed to his. Sweat collected on his upper lip and between his shoulder blades. His mouth was so dry he couldn't work up any spit. The idea of spending the rest of his nights with Sam nestled in his arms was sweet, sweet torture.

But could he do it? Walk down the aisle again? Swear his faithfulness for the rest of his days in front of God and family? He'd failed before, but he'd failed because of Sam. Now he'd be with her. Forever.

As quickly as the idiotic thought struck, it disappeared. Sam deserved better than a marriage of convenience. She wanted and needed true love, and Kyle knew that he was incapable of love, the kind a woman read about in fairy tales.

He frowned into the night. The idea of marrying Sam to give Caitlyn his name chased through his head. If the marriage thing was going to work, he'd have to give up other women, which wasn't a problem. He'd have to forget life in the fast lane in Minneapolis, which he'd outgrown anyway, and he'd have to quit being quite so selfish. That part might prove harder than he imagined, at least if you believed what his sisters had to say about him.

Above all else, he would somehow have to convince mule-headed Samantha that it would be best for the three of them to be a family. He doubted if she'd accept any kind of marriage proposal anyway, and he wasn't certain marriage was what he wanted. He remembered all too well how strangled he'd felt in his few months of being a husband to Donna. But with Sam... God, he'd cut off his right leg to spend time in her bed and wake up to see the morning sunlight set her hair on fire.

"Oh, hell," he growled, kicking at a fence post in frustration. It would never work. Any chance he'd had with her he'd blown ten years ago. She'd made that crystal clear. Even if they did share a child.

At the thought of Caitlyn, he grinned. Full of the devil, that imp of a girl had boundless energy, an infectious grin and the earmarks of becoming prettier than any woman had the right to be. Sam had done a great job with her, but now it was definitely time for him to step in.

Marriage was out of the question. He knew it, Sam knew it and eventually Caitlyn would understand.

His stomach growled and he remembered that he hadn't eaten anything since breakfast, which had consisted of a couple of slices of toast and two cups of coffee. Maybe he should call Sam and offer to buy her and

Caitlyn dinner. He turned toward the house, ready to pick up the phone, then spied Grant's truck roaring down the lane. With a spray of gravel and screech of tires, his stepbrother parked near his own truck.

Grant, grimy from head to foot, shot out of his pickup. "I tried to call, but you didn't answer."

"Been outside. What happened to you?"

"A long story involving my idiot neighbor's runaway bull, my fence and my truck," Grant said, his jaw hard as granite, his eyes angry slits. "It's not been a good day."

Kyle laughed. "Come on, let me buy you a drink. Nothing fancy, just some of Ben's old stuff."

"Sounds good."

Kyle clapped his stepbrother on the back as they headed into the house. "Now tell me about the guys who work here."

They walked onto the back porch. "Randy's smart, a hard worker who understands the business. Russ and Carson—they're young, got their minds on women all the time. You remember how it was."

Was and is, Kyle thought. Ever since seeing Sam again, he couldn't push her out of his mind. During the day he was tempted to chase her down, and at night he ached, his body hot and anxious for her. Now that they had the link of a daughter, his thoughts strayed to her constantly. And Caitlyn...it was all he could do not to race over there and demand partial custody.

"The hands around here are honest and that's more than you can say for some of the guys working these parts." Hanging his hat on a peg near the back door, Grant added, "They'll do their best, work hard until quittin' time, then watch out."

He settled into a kitchen chair while Kyle fished

around for a bottle. He poured them each a stiff shot and handed one glass to Grant.

"Here's to ranchin', the best and worst job on this planet." Grant clinked the rim of his glass to Kyle's, took a long swallow and leaned his head back.

Kyle kicked out a chair. "I don't know about the best, but I'll vouch for the worst." He tossed back his drink. The liquor splashed against the back of his throat, then, like a bolt of lightning, scorched a hot trail to his stomach. Considering his lack of food, this was probably not a good idea.

"You don't get it, do you?"

"Get what?"

"That Kate left you this place with that stipulation so you'd finally find out what's important in life and put down some permanent roots."

Oh, he got it all right. Not so much because of Kate or the ranch, but because of Sam. Time to change the subject. "How about dinner?"

"You got a cook stashed away here someplace?" Grant grinned.

"Nah. I thought we'd go into town, find a place that serves two-inch steaks."

"You buyin'?"

"Oh, sure, I'm rich now that I'm a rancher."

They finished their drinks, washed some of the grime from their skin, and Kyle drove into town. On the way, he decided to unburden himself, and while his stepbrother listened in silence, he explained about his relationship with Sam and Caitlyn.

"I'll be damned," Grant said under his breath. Rubbing the stubble on his jaw, he added, "I never would have guessed. Everyone in town assumed the kid was Tadd Richter's and that Caitlyn takes after her ma, but now that you mention it...hell's bells, who would've thought?''

They pulled into a parking lot near a low-slung restaurant on the main drag, and Kyle cut the engine. A huge set of antlers was displayed over the door, and a dog, a cross between a Lab and a German shepherd, lay on the sidewalk near the entrance.

''So what're you gonna do now?''

''I don't know.'' Kyle pocketed his keys. ''I'm afraid whatever I decide will go against Samantha's grain.''

Grant's strong fingers curled over Kyle's forearm as he reached for the door. ''No matter what you want, Kyle, you've got to think of Sam and her daughter first. They've done fine without you for nine or ten years now, so you can't just bulldoze into their lives like a runaway truck.''

''She's my daughter, Grant. I have a right to claim her.''

''Yeah, as long as you don't hurt her in the process.'' He let go of Kyle's arm. ''Just use your head for once, and keep this to yourself, at least until Sam and Caitlyn get used to the idea of having you around.''

''So now you're *Dear Abby?*''

''Nah—just someone who cares.''

''Well, that is the question, isn't it?'' Kyle asked as he stepped out of the pickup and into the warm summer evening. Cars and trucks rumbled through the middle of town and streetlights were bright enough to block out the stars. Country music and cigarette smoke filtered through the doors of the restaurant. ''Just who is it you care so much about? Me or Sam?''

''Neither of you. You're adults. It's Caitlyn who concerns me. It wouldn't take much to break her little heart.''

''I wouldn't do that. As a matter of fact, I want to ask

you if she can ride Joker. She's been on me about it since the first day I saw her.''

"Long as it's okay with her ma and she's supervised. That stallion's got a wild streak.''

"I'll be there.''

"Okay, so remember to tread lightly around the kid. If you plan to be a father she can count on, fine. But if you're thinkin' about being a part-time daddy, I'd say you're no damned good.''

"Thanks for the vote of confidence.'' Kyle slammed the truck's door. The old dog flicked his ears, but didn't move. Kyle had to step around the animal to shoulder open the door of the restaurant.

Grant was only a stride behind him. "Face it, Kyle,'' he said from somewhere near his left shoulder, "your track record with women and commitment isn't great.''

Eight

"Do you still love him?"

Caitlyn's question echoed through the bathroom as Samantha combed the tangles from her daughter's hair. Caitlyn was old enough to shower and towel off by herself, but she still had trouble combing out her hair, and as she had tonight, usually left a trail of water from the tub to the sink, where she sat on the counter.

"Do I love him?" Sam dragged the comb through her daughter's hair again. "That's not an easy question."

"Ouch! What's not easy about it?"

"Love is complicated. A lot of emotions involved," she explained, thankful that her daughter's mood had improved.

"You love me."

"Of course."

"And you always have."

"I know, but—"

"Then why not Mr.—Kyle... What should I call him?"

"Oh, Lord, Caitlyn, I don't know," Sam admitted. She finished with the comb and stared into the foggy mirror, as if in her steamy reflection she could find answers to her daughter's probing questions.

"*Daddy* sounds weird."

"Amen. Why don't you let him decide, and then, if you're not comfortable with whatever he comes up with,

suggest something else? He's a pretty reasonable guy—
well, most of the time.'' That was a little bit of a lie.
Kyle Fortune was about as reasonable as a cornered cou-
gar at times. Sam suspected this issue—dealing with his
daughter—would be a situation that would make him
downright irritable.

"Would you marry him if he asked you?"

"What?" Sam swallowed hard.

"I said would you—"

"I know, I heard you the first time. I just couldn't
believe you were asking that. Come on, let me help you
down."

"But *would* you?" Caitlyn insisted.

Gently, Sam held her daughter's shoulders. "I don't
think so, honey. What we had, your dad and I…it was a
long time ago and things change." Noticing the defeat
rising in her daughter's eyes, Sam silently swore at herself. But she couldn't lie.

"That doesn't mean things can't change back again."
Caitlyn was nothing if not resilient. She hopped to the
floor, and Sam didn't have the heart to tell her that it
would be a cold day in Hades before Kyle Fortune ever
proposed, and an even icier night before she'd say yes.

Together Sam and Caitlyn swabbed up her trail of water with two of the towels the girl had used to dry herself.
The third was wrapped around her body, and she held it
in place as she sprinted up the stairs to her room. Samantha hung a damp towel over the bar on the back of
the door and carried the sopping ones to the laundry room
off the back porch, where she tossed them into a plastic
basket. She glanced toward the Fortune Ranch and
sighed. Kyle hadn't been over all day, and deliberately,
she hadn't dropped by.

They both needed time to adjust to the thought of being parents, perhaps sharing custody, working through Caitlyn's dawning adolescence together. A peculiar pain knifed through Sam, and though she knew that it was only right to allow Kyle to be a part of his daughter's life, a part of her resented the intrusion. Where had he been during the long months of her pregnancy, when curious as well as condemning stares had been cast in her direction? Where had he been during the twenty hours of labor, when the doctors were trying to decide if she needed a cesarean section, and she was certain she was dying? Had he ever comforted her? Held her as she, frightened of the responsibility of caring for a baby alone, had cried into her pillow at night?

No. He'd been marrying someone else—someone who was his social equal, someone who wasn't pregnant and needy and desperate. And later, when the insults had been hurled at Caitlyn, the raised eyebrows, the snickers and knowing glances sent her way, Kyle Fortune hadn't had to explain to his daughter why she was different from all of her friends.

"Oh, God, Rawlings, now you're sounding pathetic and self-pitying, the kind of woman you hate," she told herself as she climbed the stairs. As terrified of the future as she'd been, Sam had been around to see Caitlyn's first smile, her first tooth, her first tentative steps. It had been she who had kissed her daughter's bruises and scrapes, she who had watched Caitlyn struggle to ride a bike, she who had sat proudly in the gymnasium when her daughter had scored the first basket on her basketball team this past year. Yes, Sam had suffered the heartaches alone, but she'd never had to share the limelight when Caitlyn had proved herself so special.

She tucked Caitlyn into bed, left the hall light burning and made her way downstairs.

Kyle was waiting for her.

Slouched on a chair at her kitchen table, one booted foot propped on the seat of another, he studied her with unreadable eyes.

Her heart nearly stopped, and it was all she could do to keep her steps from faltering at the sight of him, sitting there as if he belonged, as if he truly was part of their little family. "You scared me," she said, trying to recover. "How'd you—"

"Back door wasn't locked."

"I never lock it until I go to bed. But I should have heard your truck...." She glanced to the window, where the blue light of a security lamp cast eerie shadows over the yard.

"I walked. Needed time to clear my head."

"And Fang didn't bark?" She eyed the dog, and Fang, lying near the back door, had the good sense to look sheepish. "What kind of watchdog are you?" she demanded.

Head resting between his paws, Fang thumped his tail on the worn linoleum.

"I'm surprised you didn't come up and watch me tuck Caitlyn in."

Kyle's jaw worked, as if he was grappling with emotions that were foreign to him. "I wanted to. Thought it would be best to talk to you alone."

A pang of despair slid through her heart. "Why?"

"We've got a lot to discuss."

"Now?"

"Yep."

Intending to argue with him, she opened her mouth, then snapped it shut and held her tongue. She couldn't disagree. Their lives had changed; now they had to do something about the future, and yet she felt trapped and scared. Her well-planned life, though not ideal by some-one else's standards, suited her. Still, she needed a little time to pull herself together. "All right, but pour yourself a cup of coffee while I finish the chores. I'll be back in fifteen minutes."

"I'll come with you."

Again she started to object, only to stop herself before she said something she'd regret, something that would bring back all the pain, all the lies. With Kyle, she had to tread softly. "Suit yourself."

Under a star-studded sky, they walked silently across the gravel driveway, neither saying a word as their boots crunched on the crushed rock and a chorus of crickets was interrupted by the anxious bawling of a half-grown calf penned in the barn.

"You'll be okay," Sam said, as she clicked on the lights. The calf bellowed again, and Sam clucked her tongue. Somehow, probably by trying to join the Fortune herd, this particular animal had gotten himself tangled in a barbed-wire fence. One of his front legs was cut badly enough that Sam had decided to keep him inside until the wounds healed a bit. Now he was bawling, making enough of a ruckus to wake the dead in the next county.

"He's not happy here." Kyle leaned a shoulder against one of the posts supporting the hayloft as he eyed the calf's rough hide, stained in places by yellow disinfectant.

"Doesn't like to be penned up," she agreed, reaching into her pocket for a jackknife. Opening the blade, she bent over a bale of hay and sliced through the twine.

"Don't blame him."

Snapping her knife closed, she pocketed it again and reached for a pitchfork hung on the wall. Kyle grabbed it first and tossed a forkful of loose hay into the calf's manger. The hungry animal thrust his nose into the sweet-smelling hay, his complaints quieted for the moment.

"Are you talking about yourself now?" Sam asked, trying to sound indifferent, while her stupid pulse jumped. What did she care if he liked being penned up or not? She already knew the answer to that one, didn't she? *Commitment* wasn't a word in Kyle Fortune's vocabulary. She shot a glance in his direction and caught him staring at her so intently her breath stilled for an instant. With suddenly sweating hands, she reached for a bucket and walked to the tap mounted just inside the door.

"You didn't come to work with Joker today." Kyle's words chased through her mind.

She'd known he would notice her absence, expected him to bring it up, but she didn't like explaining herself. She twisted on the faucet and icy water splashed into the bottom of the galvanized pail. "I needed time to think."

"I figured."

When the bucket was full, she turned off the water and walked back to the stall. Kyle was leaning on the handle of the pitchfork, the angles of his face set and hard. "What did you decide?"

"About Caitlyn?" She partially filled a small trough with the water from her bucket.

"What else?"

"No decisions. I really don't know what to do." She cleared her throat. If only he would quit staring at her with his mesmerizing eyes. Slipping out of the stall, she locked the gate behind her. She was hanging the bucket on a peg near the window when Kyle's fingers covered hers, wrapping around her smaller fist as she hung on to the handle.

With his other hand he jabbed the pitchfork into a bale of straw. "Okay, I gave you your chance. Now it's my turn." His breath was hot against her nape. Turning, she came face-to-face with him, so close she noticed the first signs of stubble on his chin, saw the ghost of desire pass through his eyes. His fingers tightened.

Her heart pounded, and involuntarily, her gaze slid to his lips—blade thin and sensual. Determined.

"I've given it a lot of thought and decided that fate's handed me a gift. I cursed my grandmother for making me live on the ranch for six months as part of my inheritance, but now I think it could be a blessing. I have time to get to know my daughter and—" his mouth tightened at the corners "—and I get to know you again."

Old scars opened as easily as if he'd peeled away the scabs.

"You already knew me, Kyle, and you didn't want me then." She couldn't help the bite in her words, the lingering traces of pain. She tried to draw her hand away, but his grip tightened. The bucket swung between them.

"You know, I might have been young and foolish." He shifted even closer to her, and her heart gave a kick. He was too near, too damned sexy. His body, long and lean, was too male, and she was way too susceptible to him.

"And stupid?" she said, her silly pulse quickening.

"Maybe."

"No maybes about it," she said, hating the breathless quality in her voice. "We made a lot of mistakes—it's just what happens."

"But you don't regret what happened between us?" His gaze lingered on hers.

"No." Her heart was hammering now, her blood racing. The air in the barn seemed suddenly hot and close, making breathing impossible under the unforgiving glare of the dangling bulbs. "I have Caitlyn. I'll never regret having…been with you." She swallowed. "Because of her."

"Is that the only reason?" With one large hand, he touched her shoulder, and she started, nearly jumping out of her skin.

"Yes." She had to be firm and protect her heart, which bruised so easily around him. "If you expect me to say that I'm glad we had an affair, that suffering through the pain of your leaving and marrying someone else was one of my most beautiful memories, then you're wrong. I can't say that I'm not happy I got to know you, to have had sex with you, but only because of Caitlyn. Without you, I wouldn't have had her. Other than that, I think our relationship was a big mistake. Big."

"It wasn't all that bad." His hand was hot, scorching her flesh where his fingertips pressed into her skin. "Was it?"

"It was hell."

He seemed to wince, and she flung his arm aside. The bucket clattered to the floor and rolled. From outside, Fang let out a startled bark.

"Leave me alone, Kyle. Just because you found out that you fathered a kid doesn't mean anything's changed between us. I told you—"

"I know what you said, and as I told you before, you're a lousy liar, Samantha." He leaned forward, his gaze locking with hers, his arms wrapping around her despite her resistance. She tried to step away, but her rump and shoulders met the rough boards of the barn wall. What was he doing? Why was he toying with her?

"Kyle, don't. If you have a single shred of decency in your body—"

"I don't. We both know it." His lips claimed hers then, hard, impatient and demanding. His arms tightened around her and somehow caused the floor to buckle, because her legs were suddenly weak, her skin on fire. All her protests died before she could utter a word.

Kyle, don't do this to me, not when I've tried for ten years to forget you!

But the words were unformed and forgotten as her lips parted slightly.

She'd never experienced anything like this reaction— the hot wanting, the tingling of her flesh, the images of lying beneath him and watching the tensing of his muscles as he'd made love to her, the corded strength of his arms, the flat washboard of his abdomen, his firm, supple hips and buttocks. He'd whispered words of love then, kissing her, touching her, loving her as he'd broken through the barrier of her virginity and thrust deep into the hot, welcoming warmth that even now was beginning to heat deep inside her.

With a soft moan, she gave in to the kiss, opening her mouth as his tongue slid past her teeth, explored deeper, touching its counterpart, flicking and stroking, touching and mating until the world seemed to swim and her insides trembled for more...so much more.

But she couldn't. This was dangerous fire that was licking through her blood.

Lifting his head, he placed both hands on her cheeks. Passion turned his eyes the color of midnight. "Sam, Sam, Sam," he groaned. "Why do you do this to me?"

"Me? Do this to you? Oh, Kyle..." She caught her breath for a second and tried to clear her head. Being alone with him, touching him, kissing him was wrong. Wrong, wrong, wrong! She couldn't become involved with him ever again. Just because he was Caitlyn's father was no reason to…

But he kissed her again, and all her protests scattered on the hot Wyoming wind. As naturally as if they'd been lovers for all these past ten years, she wound her arms around his neck, ignoring the warnings that rang dully in her mind, listening not to her head but to her body and the long-dormant fires that he so easily stoked. After one kiss she ached for more of his touch. His lips were hard and insistent, his fingers strong, his smell all male and musk, a bittersweet memory.

"Kyle…" Her protest sounded like a plea.

Lifting her from her feet, he carried her outside, where the air was clear and a breeze stirred the branches of the apple tree near the back door. A half-moon was riding high in the sky, where thousands of stars had already been sprayed, but Sam hardly noticed as Kyle kissed her and carried her to a shadowy spot on the far side of the house, where the grass was dry, the air scented with faded roses and columbine.

A primitive noise escaped his throat as they tumbled to the ground. Her own cry was an echo of his, just as primal and needy. With fevered lips he brushed anxious kisses over her skin, skimming her eyelids, her cheeks and her throat.

"Do you remember?" he asked, his breath hot against her ear.

"Yes. Oh, yes." She was trembling as he held her.

He traced the shell of her ear with his tongue, and her back bowed like a supple stalk of wheat in the wind. "Sweet Samantha. My girl."

All the old lies raced through her mind. *Stop, Sam! Use your head! Being with Kyle Fortune is dangerous. Stop him now before it's too late!* But she couldn't. The tingle of her skin as his lips and tongue slid down her neck was too delicious to ignore. He parted the neckline of her blouse and placed a hot, wet kiss on her breast-bone. Desire sped through her blood and she moaned in anticipation as he slid each button from her blouse, allowing the fabric to part slowly, exposing the pale skin above the line of her bra.

His tongue slid along the lacy scrap of fabric, and her nipples tightened, pressing against the soft cotton until his mouth found one and kissed it through the lacy cup.

She arched and he held her closer still, kissing her as he lowered the strap of her bra, letting her breast spill over the cup and his breath tickle her skin as he stared at the dark peak beckoning him.

Heat pulsed through Samantha. Desire sailed through her blood to throb in the deepest part of her.

"You're more beautiful than I remembered," he said, his voice low and throaty as he leaned forward and placed a chaste kiss on the tip of her anxious nipple.

She waited, expecting more, her body aching for his touch and tongue, but he just stared at her moon-washed flesh, as if fascinated.

"Kyle..."

He kissed her nipple again, and heat swirled deep within her. The pressure of his mouth was harder this time, wet, hot, anxious, but again he teased her by lifting his head.

"Please..." *Oh, no, she wasn't begging him, was she?* But passion thundered through her body, causing her to quiver as he settled beside her and, holding her close, brought her body to his lips. She cradled his head instinctively and he suckled, drinking as if he could draw sweet milk from her breast, his hands splayed over the small of her back and holding her so close to him that through her jeans and his she could feel his erection pressing into her thighs.

This was crazy. Dangerous. Explosive. But she couldn't stop. She'd never let another man touch her, not since Kyle, and after ten years of denial, she couldn't hold back the tide of desire that flooded her, crashing like a powerful waterfall through every cell of her being.

She touched him, opening his shirt, letting her fingers tangle in the thick curls of his chest hair, brushing his nipples, feeling his abdomen ripple in response. He sucked in his breath as she pulled his shirt from his waistband. "Sam, Sam, Sam...do you know what you do to me?"

She swallowed hard. "I don't think I want to know."

"Don't you?" One eyebrow rose wickedly, and then he kissed her so hard she couldn't breathe.

Yanking her blouse from her pants, he discarded the unwanted garment and unfastened her bra deftly. It fluttered away as he tossed it aside. Instinctively she tried to cover up, but he held her hands down and gazed at her naked torso, her flesh white in the moon glow, her nipples puckering beneath his gaze. "It's indecent how gorgeous you are," he said, and she blushed. Still holding down her hands, he bent over and kissed each ripe button.

Closing her eyes, she quivered beneath him, her back again bowing instinctively.

"That's it," he whispered. "That's it."

Oh, God, she couldn't think, could barely breathe as his hands and mouth played with her, tormented her, pleased her. She writhed, and he chuckled low in his throat. "Slow down," he whispered in her ear. "We've got all night." He rubbed his jeans-clad leg against hers, and she felt how much he wanted her. Though his hands held her like manacles, they trembled, and when he pressed his face into her abdomen she cried out.

"Kyle," she whispered in a voice unlike her own.

Releasing one of her hands, he reached for the button at the waistband of her jeans. The zipper slid down with a soft hiss. Cool air touched her skin above the elastic of her panties, and then he kissed her, his mouth and tongue touching that scrap of fabric, hot breath seeping through the cotton. She let out a soft moan.

He kissed her again, but just then the phone rang, shrill, loud and insistent through the open window.

"Leave it," he growled.

"No, I can't." Maternal instincts cut through desire. "Don't you have a machine?"

"Caitlyn will wake up...." Sam was rolling away from him, zipping up her pants in one quick motion.

"Samantha—"

The phone rang again and she grabbed her blouse, forcing her hands into the sleeves and buttoning as she ran into the house.

"For the love of Mike, Sam—"

The third ring was short, and by the time Sam clambered up the back steps and flew into the kitchen, she knew Caitlyn had answered it. "Hello?" she said, snagging the receiver.

"...Tommy Wilkins thinks you're a slut—"

"Who is this?" Sam demanded of the whiny voice.

Silence.

"Are you still there? Do you hear me? You quit calling and harassing us or I'll phone the police and your mother because, believe me, I'll find out who you are." She heard footsteps on the porch and knew that Kyle could hear her end of the conversation from the porch. The screen door creaked as he entered.

''Mom...'' Caitlyn's voice, shaking, came through the receiver.

''Hang up the extension, honey,'' Sam said, gnashing her teeth and silently swearing at the little brat on the other end of the line. ''I have a few more things I'd like to say—''

''No, Mom—''

Click.

''Are you still there?'' Sam demanded, pounding a fist against the wall in frustration. ''Do you hear me, you little—''

''They hung up,'' Caitlyn said.

''Good. They'd better stay hung up. I'll be up in a second.''

Slamming down the receiver, she headed for the stairs. Her emotions, already running high from her lovemaking with Kyle, were now on overload.

''Trouble?'' he asked, following her as she ran up the stairs.

''Yeah. Some little creep thinks it's cool to harass our daughter.''

''What do you mean?''

''Calling at all hours. Insulting Caitlyn or not responding at all when we answer,'' she said over her shoulder.

''They have caller ID, you know—a box that tells you who called, and there's a service where you can dial a certain number and it will reconnect you with the number that last called you.''

''Not here, they don't.'' She strode into her bedroom, where her daughter, the receiver still clutched in her fingers, was sitting on the edge of the bed. The covers were pulled to her chin and tears tracked from her eyes. ''Oh, honey...'' Sam, her own heart breaking, took the receiver from Caitlyn's fingers, hung up the phone and hugged her daughter fiercely. Pain and anger surged through her. "It's all right," she said.

"They called me that name again."

"Don't listen to them."

"What name?" Kyle stood in the doorway, the hall light burning behind him, throwing his silhouette into stark relief. Sam couldn't see his expression, but his voice was low and deadly.

She shook her head. "It doesn't matter."

"What name?" he demanded.

"Stay out of it, Kyle."

"I think I've stayed out of it too long already. What did the person on the phone say to you, Caitlyn?"

A broken sob escaped from her throat. Hot tears splashed against the front of Sam's blouse. "They said it again," she said in a choked voice. "They called me a bastard."

"Who?" Kyle demanded. "Who called?"

"We don't know. I thought I already explained all that," Sam said, still holding her daughter and rocking her as Caitlyn's sobs disintegrated into hiccups.

"I think it's Jenny." Caitlyn sniffed, but managed to blot her eyes dry.

"Who's Jenny?" Kyle demanded, intent on strangling the wretch. For the first time in his life he felt impotent and vulnerable. His child was hurting, and there wasn't much he could do to help her.

"Jenny Peterkin," Sam said, "a classmate of Caitlyn's."

"Why would she call?"

"You know how kids are."

"'Cause she's mean," Caitlyn said, then added, "And Mrs. Johnson picked me to go on a special science trip to Portland, and I beat Jenny at basketball and in the Junior Olympics.''

In spite of his anger, Kyle felt a smidgen of pride. This little imp had grit. A girl who'd rather catch tadpoles than play with Barbie dolls, Caitlyn Rawlings—oh, hell, that would have to be changed to Caitlyn Fortune—was a firecracker. A girl who would've made her great-grandmother proud.

"Jenny doesn't like to lose," Sam said. "She's a spoiled rich kid who's used to getting her way. But remember, we can't prove who called. You're all right, aren't you?" she asked her daughter, and Caitlyn gave a little nod.

"Don't let anyone get the better of you." Kyle took one of her small hands in his. "All your life you'll come across people who would like nothing better than to show you up. Some of 'em will be downright nasty, others will smile in your face while they're knifing you in your back and sometimes even your best friend, or someone you trust, might turn on you, be it intentional or not." He stared at Sam for a heart-stopping second before turning back to his daughter. "But you've got to hold your head high, keep right on going and believe in yourself. Most people aren't mean, at least not all the time, but there are a few out there that can cause you to lose faith. Never do, Caitlyn."

She smiled through her tears. "I hate Jenny Peterkin."

"Oh, honey, no," Sam said, but Kyle bent on one knee and looked his daughter squarely in the eye.

"Go ahead and hate her. At least for now."

"I want to call her up and tell her she's a stuck-up snot who doesn't have the brains of a flea!"

Kyle laughed. "I'm sure you do, but you shouldn't. Not yet. It'll only make things worse. The more of a reaction this kid gets from you, the more she'll keep egging you on, and you'll end up looking like a fool. So just ignore her. Believe me, the Jenny Peterkinses of the world hate nothing more than for someone to act as if they don't exist.'' Slowly he released Caitlyn's hand.

Samantha sighed. ''Okay. Crisis over. Why don't you go back to bed?''

''But it's still early!''

''You were half-asleep when the phone rang.'' With a little cajoling, and Kyle's promise to see her the next day, Caitlyn curled up in her bed and was asleep within seconds. With Kyle watching from the hallway, Sam turned off the light.

''Does this happen often?'' he asked once they were downstairs.

''More than it should.'' She stood at the sink, staring out the kitchen window, her fingers gripping the lip of the counter. ''Sometimes they call and don't say anything—just hang up the phone quickly. Little creeps.''

A tiny worry wormed into Kyle's heart. ''The same person calls?''

She lifted a shoulder. ''I think so.''

''But you're not sure?''

''No, why?''

As she turned, he saw the concern etched in her features, the furrows between her arched eyebrows, the pinched corner of her lips, and he silently cursed whoever it was who could cause her such distress. *Like you did? No one hurt her with quite the same amount of pain as you did, Fortune.* ''It doesn't sound like a ten-year-old to call and say nothing. More likely to insult than hang up. But maybe it's just a couple of different kids.''

Kyle glanced around the cozy room. ''Until we figure it out, I think I'd better stick around.''

"Why?"

"In case you need me."

She laughed nervously. "We've done fine by ourselves for over nine years, Kyle. I think we can handle things."

"But I didn't know I had a daughter before. Now I do, and I'll be damned if I'm going to leave her—or you, for that matter—alone."

"Your concern is a little late, don't you think?"

"Better late than never," he muttered, eyeing the windows and doors and latching them all as he walked through the rooms on the first floor.

"You're paranoid," she complained, following him.

"Family trait. It comes with the territory."

"Meaning?"

"That when your family has a lot of money and some fame or notoriety, or whatever you want to call it, there's always a chance for some nut to think he can make some pocket change. Kidnapping and blackmail are prime sources."

"This is sick...."

He strode into the bathroom and slammed the window shut. Flipping the latch, he turned and nearly ran into her. "Get used to it."

"Why?"

"Because Caitlyn's a Fortune."

"No one knows that."

"Yet." He flashed her a ghost of a smile. "Only a matter of time."

"And then what, Kyle? Do you think suddenly she'll be a target? Is that what you're saying?" Dear God, this was unreal. She and Caitlyn had lived such a carefree and idyllic existence for the most part. Sure, there were taunts and insults, but the two of them had always been safe out here in what Sam thought of as God's country.

The fears she'd had for her child included the usual concerns about accidents or problems at school, or the cruelty of other children, but Kyle's concerns were much more complex and chilling.

"I think you're jumping at shadows. Just because we got a couple of prank calls doesn't mean anyone's going to hurt Caitlyn."

"I hope you're right," he said, "but just in case you're not, I'll be here."

"Dear Lord, Kyle, don't you think this is a little over the top? Melodramatic?"

He turned then and backed her up against the wall. "Are you willing to gamble our daughter's future on it, Sam?" he asked, his eyes narrowing for a second.

"Of course not."

"Then you'll let me sleep here."

"I—I don't think that would be such a good idea."

His lips stretched into a smile that was nearly sinful. "How're you going to stop me? Throw me out bodily? Pull your dad's shotgun on me? Call the police?"

"Actually, I thought I'd seduce you," she said evenly, her gaze never flinching. "Invite you into my bed, make love to you so long that you're panting for air and crying for mercy, then when you're so weak you can barely move, call the paramedics to drag you away in an ambulance."

He laughed and touched the side of her face with one long finger. "Funny," he said, his eyes a dark, erotic shade of blue, "that's exactly the torture I planned to put you through, but if you think you're woman enough to do everything you promised, then so be it. I'm at your mercy."

"Just the way it should be," she said, suppressing a giggle as she reached behind her and opened the door to a hall closet. As he leaned forward to kiss her, she withdrew an old army blanket and a pillow that smelled of mothballs. "Here you go, cowboy," she teased, shoving the bundle into his abdomen. "If you want to stay here, fine, but you've got the couch."

"So what was all the talk about wild, passionate lovemaking?"

"A lie," she said, and when he leaned forward again to kiss her, she placed her hands on his shoulders and shook her head. "This is too soon, Kyle. All kidding aside, I don't think I'm ready to get tangled up with you."

"How do you know?"

Her smile turned cold. "You know what they say—once burned, twice shy. I think I've been burned enough to last me a lifetime."

He stepped aside and let her pass. "I don't think so, Sam, and deep down, if you think about it long and hard, you don't, either."

"Turn out the lights, would you?"

"Sam—"

"Good night, Kyle."

"What time's breakfast?"

"Whenever you make it. I like scrambled eggs. Caitlyn's partial to pancakes, but whatever you fix will do just fine."

He heard a door slam at the top of the stairs, and he told himself that if he were half a man he would climb up there, strip off his clothes and share her bed. He'd felt her respond tonight. She'd shuddered beneath his touch, quivered with want, been as hot with desire as he was. It wouldn't take much to convince her to let him sleep with her, kiss her, make love to her all night long. He could imagine the way her legs would feel wrapped around his ribs as he plunged into the sweet, hot moistness of her. He'd lift her hips and she'd moan his name and…oh, hell, he was getting aroused.

Muttering a string of curses under his breath, he made his way to the couch, threw down the blanket and flopped on the worn cushions. The old camelback was lumpy, but discomfort wouldn't keep him awake. The knowledge that Sam was only a few feet away would.

Nine

She woke up to the smell of coffee wafting up the stairs. "Wha—?" Pushing her hair out of her eyes and yawning, Sam remembered that Kyle was in the house. He'd spent the night. Why that knowledge was comforting was beyond her. She didn't need Kyle Fortune. She didn't want Kyle Fortune. The less she had to do with him the better.

Her room was still dark, the light of dawn just beginning to creep through the open window. Snagging her robe from the hook on the closet door, she dashed barefoot down the stairs and found Kyle, a shadow of a beard darkening his jaw, his hair rumpled from sleep, his eyes as clear and blue as the sky on a new Wyoming day.

"Mornin'," he drawled, leaning back in one of her chairs. Fang was curled at his feet, and the coffeemaker was done dripping.

"Good morning." Arching an eyebrow, she walked to the pot, poured herself a cup and sat in a chair opposite him. "I never thought I'd see the day," she said, cradling her mug. "Kyle Fortune—the picture of domesticity."

"There's a lot you don't know about me, Sam." He eyed her over the rim of his own cup.

"Oh? Tell me."

"Okay." He leaned back in the chair, rocking it on two legs. "I think a basic thing you should understand is that spending the night in the same house with you and not marching up the stairs and breaking down the door took a hell of a lot of willpower. I spent half the night arguing with myself. In the end, nobility won out over basic sexual urges, but I can't promise it'll always end up that way. In fact, I'll guarantee you it won't.''

Her throat suddenly dry as a dust storm, she took a swallow of the hot brew and silently prayed for strength. Nothing, not even waking up in the morning, was ever easy with this man. ''What makes you think there'll be a next time?''

''What makes you think there won't?''

''We can't live like this, running from shadows, having you camp out here to protect us. Caitlyn and I...we're fine.''

Maddeningly, he took another long swallow of coffee and didn't respond, just stared at her with determination etching his jaw.

''We've made it this far alone.''

''Because I didn't know I had a daughter.'' Setting his cup on the table, he folded his arms over his chest and tipped the chair back even farther. ''Now I do, and there's no way—not legally or physically—that you can keep me out of her life.''

''I didn't say that's what I wanted.''

''Good point, Samantha. Let's hear it. What is it you want?'' The chair clattered forward. Fang scooted out of the way. Suddenly Kyle was halfway across the table, nose to nose with her, animosity seething from him.

''That's an easy one, Kyle.'' She didn't hesitate, nor did she blink as she set her half-drunk cup of coffee on the table. Splaying her hands on the nicked Formica, she declared, ''I want my daughter to be happy.''

''Without a father?''

''No, I think that would be foolish. I never really

wanted you out of her life, but the circumstances, such as they were, made it seem like that was inevitable. Now it's not." Finally, twisting her fingers, she looked away and sighed. "What a mess."

"It doesn't have to be. Come on." Circling her wrist with his strong fingers, he pulled her out of the chair and through the door to the porch. Dew still clung to the grass and turned a spiderweb to a shimmering crystal net that bridged a small gap between the eave and downspout. Leaning his hips against the rail, he drew her into the circle of his arms and held her close enough that she could smell the maleness of him, feel his warmth through her thin robe, hear the steady drum of his heart. Somewhere in the distance a late-rising rooster crowed. "We don't always have to fight."

She rested her head against his shoulder. His lips brushed her temple and she shivered a bit.

"I only want the same things you do for Caitlyn." His breath was as warm as a summer wind.

"Do you?"

"Her happiness comes first."

"Really?" She wanted desperately to believe him, but thinking clearly while being this close to him was difficult, nearly impossible.

"Trust me, Sam. This time things will be better."

"*This* time?" she repeated, realizing that he was talking about their relationship. Oh, it was all so complicated and tangled, both in the past and the present. Could there be enough happiness today to wash away the pain of yesterday?

Footsteps clattered down the stairs, and Sam bolted away from Kyle before Caitlyn could catch them embracing and leap to the wrong conclusion about her mother and father.

"Mom?" she called. "Mom..."

"Out here, honey."

Still in pajamas, Caitlyn dashed across the kitchen and shot through the door, only to slide to a stop when she encountered Kyle.

"You're *still* here?" Was there a little bit of hope in her voice?

"Yep. Your ma can't seem to get rid of me."

"He spent the night on the couch." Samantha wanted her daughter to understand that there was nothing romantic in their relationship. Any dreams she'd had of romance he'd dashed long before.

"Why didn't you go home?" Caitlyn eyed each of her parents with a skeptical gaze.

"I was worried about you."

"About me?"

"Because of the phone call," Sam explained.

Caitlyn made a disgusted noise in the back of her throat. She was definitely braver in the light of a new day. "Jenny Peterkin is a dweeb. She can go suck pond scum!"

"Uh, maybe it would be better to say she can go jump in a lake," Sam suggested.

"Okay, she can go jump in a lake *and* suck pond scum."

Kyle, damn him, laughed. "That's the spirit. Don't let any little snot get the better of you."

"We don't say 'snot' or 'suck' or—"

"It's all right," Kyle interjected, smiling down on his daughter. "You should hear the things I say when I'm mad."

"What?" Caitlyn, eyes bright, was intrigued.

"Another time." Sam shot Kyle a warning look.

"Let's just hope we never make him mad so we hear it the hard way."

"Jenny's stupid," Caitlyn decided, hoisting herself up on the rail and swinging her bare feet. "She can say whatever she wants about me, because it's not true anymore, right?"

"Right," Kyle agreed.

"It never was true," Sam said hurriedly, afraid of the direction of the conversation. Already Caitlyn was seeing herself as part of a normal, two-parent family, when nothing had changed. For all Sam knew, Kyle was still the same irresponsible, spoiled playboy he'd been years ago. And just as she was attracted to him then, she found him impossible to resist now, even though he still wasn't husband or father material.

Startling herself with the turn of her thoughts, she rubbed her palms on the front of her robe and realized what she must look like. Her hair was disheveled from sleep, her nightgown peeked from the lapels of her housecoat and her legs were bare.

This was crazy. He had no business sleeping here in her house, nearly making love to her, brewing coffee in the morning, almost as if they were lovers....

She glanced into his hooded blue eyes and caught him staring at her with such undisguised lust she could barely think straight. She licked her lips and realized from the spark in his eyes that the action was provocative. Steadfastly she looked away. This was wrong. All wrong. What kind of mixed messages were they sending to their daughter? To each other? There was nothing between them, *nothing*. Everything they'd once shared was gone, carelessly tossed away years before.

Clearing her throat, Sam reached for the door handle. She had to break this spell he seemed to cast whenever they were together. No matter how much effort it took, she had to grab hold of her composure when she was with him. "Caitlyn," she said, her voice more breathless than normal, "hurry and get dressed and I'll fix you both some breakfast."

"But—"

"Now."

"Don't argue with your mother," Kyle interjected. "Besides, we've got a lot to do today, the three of us."

"We do?" Sam was instantly suspicious.

"Yeah, but later." He tousled Caitlyn's hair. "First I've got some business to attend to."

Kyle pressed on the doorbell and waited on the wide porch where hanging boxes of petunias, fuchsias and geraniums were suspended. Roses lined the drive, and the lawn, lush and green, contrasted starkly with the surrounding fields. The house was white clapboard with brick trim, three stories tall and as out of place in this part of Wyoming as a diamond tiara worn by a steer-wrestling cowboy.

He heard footsteps, saw a worried, pretty face pressed to the etched-glass window next to the door, then waited as locks clicked open.

"Kyle Fortune!" Shawna Davies Peterkin stood in the doorway, neat and trim, not a hair out of place, a smile tugging at the corners of her glossy pink lips. "I heard you were back in Clear Springs, but I didn't expect... Oh, come in, come in. I've got tea or coffee or something stronger." She actually blushed like a schoolgirl.

She'd always been a phony. Even ten years before, when she'd done everything but strip down to her birthday suit to gain his attention. Right now she was fairly oozing charm, as if he were the most interesting person to have ever set foot on her doorstep.

"Thanks, but I don't have a lot of time," he said, refusing to give an inch.

"Oh, sure you do." Her fingers, manicured neatly and decorated with several rings, fluttered at her throat a trifle nervously.

"This really isn't a social call."

"What?" A shadow of doubt crept into her honey-colored eyes and some of the warmth left her smile. "Is something wrong?"

Behind her mother, lurking on the stairs, was a girl about Caitlyn's age, all big eyes and dark hair, with a figure just starting to show. "Someone's been making crank calls to Caitlyn Rawlings, and I'm not sure who the culprit is, but Jenny's name was mentioned as a possibility."

The girl visibly blanched.

"My Jenny?" Shawna shook her head and not a hair stirred. "I'm sure you're mistaken." Her smile disappeared completely. "Jenny's a good girl, Kyle, and I don't know what kind of lies you've heard from Samantha Rawlings and her wild kid, but I can assure you that Jenny's never made any of those calls."

"You're positive?" Kyle's gaze flicked to the girl on the stairs.

"Absolutely!" Shawna's chin elevated a fraction, but her gaze slid away from his. "Jenny's too busy for such nonsense, what with her piano and swimming. She's kind to everyone, even the Rawlings girl."

"Even her?" Kyle's temper sparked.

"Yes. That kid's out of control, I'll tell you. Comes from being allowed to run wild like a..." Her voice faded and she wrapped her arms around her waist. One finely arched eyebrow lifted a fraction and her mouth pulled into a puckered pout as surely as if someone had tugged on invisible strings. "Don't tell me. Samantha sent you over here to do her dirty work."

Kyle shook his head, his eyes narrowing a fraction, enough to make Shawna pause. "Nope. Took it as my own personal mission."

"Why?"

Kyle stared at her so hard she blushed again. "Because I like that kid of hers and I wouldn't want Caitlyn to get hurt or run into any trouble. You might mention this to Jenny and her friends, let them know that when I find out who's been calling, I'll make sure it doesn't happen again." The girl, biting her lower lip, slunk up the stairs noiselessly, probably to come up with a likely lie when her mother gave her the third degree.

"Let me get this straight, Kyle, so I can tell my husband when he gets home. You're threatening my daughter?"

"Wouldn't dream of it, Shawna," he drawled, watching her prickle a little more. Oh, she knew what kind of a kid she had, all right; he read it in the worry reflected in her eyes. "I just thought you and she—well, yeah, maybe your husband, too, come to think of it—would want to know. Maybe Jenny has got an idea who's been getting a petty little thrill by making the calls."

"No way. The crowd she hangs around with are good kids, from good families. You're barking up the wrong tree."

"If you say so." Kyle left her standing at the door, clutching her throat, trying to convince herself that her precious little girl wouldn't do anything so nasty.

After seeing the kid, Kyle would bet ten to one that Jenny Peterkin's index finger was cramped from dialing the phone and playing cruel practical jokes. He'd also wager that they were about to stop.

"This is how it's done," Kyle instructed, wrapping his fingers around the thick rope that he'd tied to an over-hanging branch of a lone oak tree. "You take a long run and swing out. Right over the swimming hole, you let go."

"I don't know about this," Sam said, eyeing the dangling hemp with a wary eye.

Ignoring her, Kyle, wearing only jeans, let out a whoop, ran barefoot across the dry grass and, holding on to the new rope, swung out over the river. Just as the rope tightened, he let go and dropped feetfirst into the slow-moving current. Water splashed high beneath the leafy branches.

Caitlyn giggled as Kyle surfaced, tossed water from his hair and swam easily to the bank. "Your turn," he said to Samantha as he climbed up the shore. Drops of water, sparkling in the afternoon sun, clung to his hair and rolled lazily down his face, neck and torso. Sam tried not to stare at the corded muscles of his chest and shoulders or the way his jeans, already low-slung, nearly slid over his buttocks with the weight of the river water. His tan line was visible and below that...

With a start, she glanced upward to eyes as blue as a mountain lake. His grin was positively wicked, as if he could read her every thought. "Come on, Sam, give it a try."

"No way."

"Spoilsport." His eyes glinted and she half expected him to physically drag her into the water.

"Come on, Mommy!" Caitlyn's eyes were bright on this, their first family get-together. Again, it would be false advertising if Caitlyn got the impression they were truly a family unit. Sam had packed a picnic lunch, Kyle had donated the horses and they'd ridden along the ridge, then deep into the valley to a swimming hole Kyle remembered from his youth. But they were still little more than strangers trying to fit themselves into an awkward situation cast upon them by fate.

"Mommy, please..." Caitlyn wheedled.

"Okay, okay." Feeling trapped, but seeing no way out, Sam decided not to be a cold blanket on the fun. She grabbed hold of the rope Kyle held out to her, walked backward, and with a rush of adrenaline, took a run, swung out over the river and dropped as the rope arced. Ice-cold water rushed up at her as she fell rapidly, submerging completely. Her skin tingled. Air bubbles rose to the surface. Holding her breath, she shot upward toward the shimmering sunlight and shadowy branches of the trees overhead. As she found air again, she tossed her hair from her eyes and let out her breath.

"You did it, Mommy!" Caitlyn yelled in delight. She and Kyle already had hold of the rope again. "You did it."

"How is it?" Kyle asked, his rumpled jeans still dripping.

"Cold!"

"Sissy," he teased. "Come on, Caitlyn. Let's show your mom how it's done." He wrapped one steely arm around his daughter and captured the rope in his free hand. With his wild whoop and a squeal of pure joy from Caitlyn, they sailed over the water, pausing for a fraction of a second, then dropped with a splash into the pool.

Watching them together, hearing their laughter, seeing her daughter finally find the father she'd asked about, Sam felt her heart give a tug. But what about the future?

If Caitlyn became close to Kyle over the next six months, if she grew to love him, how would she feel come winter, when he planned to sell his ranch and leave? Would she want to go with him? Would Kyle want an exuberant nine-year-old chasing after him? What about school? Oh, Lord, what a mess! Dripping wet, Sam crawled up to the blanket and let the late-afternoon sun dry her skin. She watched father and daughter splashing and laughing in the sun-dappled water and wondered how her life would have been different had she and Kyle stayed together.

But that was impossible, she reminded herself. He had married another woman just months after making wonderful, passionate love to her. He'd betrayed her. Treated her as if what they'd shared had been unimportant.

Sighing, she scratched in the dust with her bare toe and wondered if she would ever be able to put that painful truth to rest. She picked a dandelion gone to seed and blew its fluff into the wind. Her heart ached with the fear that history was repeating itself. Try as she might to prevent it, the inevitable truth was that she was still attracted to Kyle Fortune—as attracted as she'd ever been. This time there was no chance that the emotions he inspired were something as simple or as fleeting as a schoolgirl crush. No, she was beginning to view him as a man, not a boy, and that man did things to her mind that were downright dangerous. Like it or not, she was falling for Kyle Fortune again, and there didn't seem to be much she could do about it.

Sam frowned when she realized she couldn't control her stubborn heart. Like a freight train racing toward a sheer cliff with no bridge, she was headed for certain disaster. She couldn't trust him, couldn't love him, had to remind herself that his interest in her these days was only because of Caitlyn. Sooner or later they'd have to come to a decision about their child's future.

And he's going to leave. Remember that he's only biding his time until he can sell this place. And what then? What would he want to do about Caitlyn?

That troubling thought gnawed at her for the rest of what was supposed to be a carefree afternoon.

Dusk had painted the sky a deep purple hue by the time Kyle parked his pickup near the back porch of Sam's house. Caitlyn, exhausted from a day of swimming and horseback riding, had fallen asleep in the truck during the short ride from the Fortune Ranch. Rather than rouse her, Kyle carried his daughter into the house, where he tucked her into her bed for the first time in his life.

Observing father and daughter from the doorway, Sam felt a painful lump form in her throat. She watched as his big, tanned hands tenderly pulled the covers to Caitlyn's chin. The girl's eyes fluttered open a second and she sighed. "Thanks, Daddy. I love you," she said, then fell back into a dreamless sleep.

Sam's heart turned over. Kyle was going to hurt his daughter. Intentionally or not, no matter what he did, he would disappoint and wound her.

Kyle, towering over Caitlyn's bed, stood motionless for a minute, as if he couldn't believe what he'd just heard. Clearing his throat, he turned, his expression grim, his jaw set in stone. "We'd better talk," he said as he switched off the light and started down the stairs. Sam was right behind him, noticing the tension in his neck and shoulders, his determined tread. Dreading the conversation, she started forming her excuses, because she knew, deep in the darkest part of her heart, that Kyle was going to assert his paternal rights and take Caitlyn away.

Obviously he was captivated by his daughter and wouldn't rest until he had full or partial custody.

Throat dry, mind numb, dread pounding in her heart, Sam followed him downstairs and outside, where the air had cooled and millions of stars spangled the night sky. Somewhere far away an owl hooted softly.

"I know what you're going to say." She caught up with him at the last remaining buck-and-rail fence on the place. The rails, from old lodgepole pines, had silvered with the passing years but had stood the test of time.

"Do you?" Turning, he stared at her with a gaze so intense that for a second she forgot what she was going to say. Her eyes traveled to the powerful width of his shoulders as he crossed his arms over his chest. "What?"

"That—that you want Caitlyn with you, that you're going to sue me for custody, that...oh, God, Kyle, don't. Just don't!"

"You think I would try and steal her away from you?" He snorted in disgust, and in the shadowy light his face seemed more rugged and craggy, his lips pressed into a thin, angry line, his eyes slits.

"You wouldn't think of it as stealing."

His jaw worked and he rammed stiff fingers through his hair. "I'm not that much of a bastard."

"I didn't say—"

"So what do you think we should do?" The question seemed to shiver in the wind.

"Oh, God, Kyle, I wish I knew," she said honestly, her throat raw, her insides disintegrating at the thought of losing Caitlyn.

"So do I."

She bit her lip for fear she might break down and watched as his gaze moved to the hollow of her throat. With one callused finger, he traced the circle of bones surrounding her wildly erratic pulse. "What is it with us?" he asked as she felt her blood begin to heat.

"I don't know."

She should step away, put some distance between her body and his, keep a clear head. But as he lowered his face to hers, she tilted her chin upward, eager and expectant. "This is either a blessing or a curse, but I don't know which." His lips brushed over hers and hesitated.

"A curse," she whispered.

With a groan, he kissed her, his lips claiming hers in a caress that was as desperate as it was passionate. His arms surrounded her, holding her close, hands splayed over her back. She didn't try to pull away, didn't argue with the yearning in her soul. The years reeled backward in a blur and she was young again, eager and hopeful, with the boy she loved.

"Samantha! Oh, God," he whispered, as she linked her arms around his neck and he slid a hand to her ribs, feeling the weight of her breast between the span of his index finger and thumb. "This is crazy."

"Idiotic," she agreed, her mind swimming, her doubts already fleeing into the night. His face was washed in the silver light of the moon and he smelled of musk and soap and all things male. Memories of a heavenly summer in his arms dashed through her mind in vivid, scattered images of love gained and lost. "I don't want—"

"Me, neither."

"Kyle!"

"Oh, Sam, what am I gonna do with you?" His mouth swooped down on hers again, and she was ready. Her lips parted easily to the gentle pressure of his tongue. Nothing that felt this right could be wrong. He was her lover, the father of her daughter, the only man who had ever touched her.

Closing her eyes, she felt his fingers caress her, hot skin scorching her flesh through her shirt and bra. Rough thumbs teased her nipples, and heat that started low in her abdomen slowly spiraled upward, tingling her skin, causing a need—wanton and wild—to throb between her legs.

"My Samantha," he said into the shell of her ear. "It's been so long...."

Her knees gave way just as he pulled her to the ground. Dry grass brushed against her temple as he slid open the buttons of her blouse. His hands trembled, her heart beat wildly as he pushed her unwanted garments aside. His mouth was warm, his tongue provocative as he kissed her skin, tenderly at first and then more fiercely as his restraint eroded.

She stripped him of his clothes as well, feeling the hard, strident muscles of his arms and chest, kissing him as feverishly as he kissed her, touching and rediscovering this man who had stolen her heart, her youth and her virginity, all of which she would gladly part with again.

He rolled so that she was on top of him and her breasts, silvered by the light of the moon, hung before him. He kissed each one with agonizing tenderness before he finally latched on and buried his face in the warmth of her flesh, tongue, lips and teeth toying with her nipples.

Ripples of desire sped through her blood. Hot shivers of need caused her head to spin, her breathing to accelerate, her hands to explore the furry mat covering his chest, the flat buds buried therein, the line of hair that disappeared beneath his jeans....

"Sweet, sweet Samantha," he said, drawing her closer and kissing the valley between her breasts. She moaned low in her throat, wanting more as his hands lowered to smooth the denim fabric over her rump, fingers skimming the inside of her legs.

"This—this…is dangerous."

"I know."

"And—and…"

"Shh."

His finger dipped below the waistband of her jeans, skimming her bare buttocks as he helped her wiggle out of the denim. Cool air caressed her skin and still he kissed and toyed with her breasts, sending chills down her spine, creating a swirling pool of heat rising deep within her.

Naked, lying atop him, she writhed as he touched her, perspiration dampening her skin, air caught in her lungs. With gentle fingers, he stroked her, finding the most intimate places only he had dared explore before.

Sam moaned and gave herself up to the pure, vital pleasure that he offered. This was what she wanted—to be loved by him, to feel her breasts in his mouth as he readied her with his hands.

"Samantha," he breathed across her wet skin. "Let me, please…"

She needed no more encouragement. His fly opened with a series of soft pops as the buttons gave way and his erection, hidden only by boxer shorts, rubbed against her. She touched him as intimately as he did her, stroking him until he cried out. "Sam, I—ooh, wait, darlin', please, not yet!"

Breathing hard, a throbbing vein evidence of his faltering self-control, he took care of protecting her then rolled her onto her back and parted her legs with his body, kissing her cheeks, her throat, her abdomen and the inside of her thighs as his fingers skimmed her calves and feet.

She cried out when his breath fanned the sensitive folds of her body and his lips kissed her in the most private of spots. "Please," she whispered, her skin on fire, her insides pulsing with desire as his mouth worked a magic she hadn't remembered existed. She lost control, writhing and gasping, biting her lip as the stars in the heavens swirled behind her eyes. Just when she was certain she would climax, he stopped, leaving her aching for a second before he shifted onto his arms and drove deep into her warmth.

She gasped as he moved, then caught his rhythm and held on tight as the world spun into a new, starry orbit and the earth collided in a series of spasms that shook her entire body. "Kyle," she cried, but her voice was lost in his own primitive, hoarse cry, which reverberated through her heart. "Sam. Oh, I've missed you. Sam. Sam." With a mighty groan he fell against her, breathing hard, his sweat mingling with hers.

Tears rained from her eyes and she struggled to hold back her sobs. Tenderly he folded her in his arms, holding her close, cradling her body with his own. "Shh, sweetheart. It's going to be all right," he promised, kissing her temple. "Everything's going to be all right."

"Will it?"

"We can make it right."

He rolled to his side and drew her against him, spoonlike. "Remember when you told me you knew what I was going to say?" he asked, his breath fanning her cheek.

Here it comes, she thought, bracing herself.

"Well, you were wrong. What I was going to do was ask you to marry me."

"What?" Her heart stopped for an instant.

"You heard me, Sam. This time I think we should do it right. I want you to be my wife."

"You—you can't be serious," she said, but her mind was already spinning ahead with images of them together, the three of them. Kyle, Samantha and Caitlyn, a family at last—a dream that could never come true.

"Believe me, Sam, I'm more serious than I've ever been in my life."

"But where would we live? You're planning to sell the ranch, right? So are you going to live here with me? Or do you think that Caitlyn and I will move to wherever it is you live?"

"I've got a penthouse in Minneapolis."

"Oh, and we'd fit right in."

"I wouldn't expect you to move."

"Good, because I wouldn't. I couldn't. It wouldn't be fair to Caitlyn." This was all happening too quickly, and yet it was also past due—ten years past due. Sam tried to wiggle out of his arms, but his hands held her tight. "So would this be one of those long-distance marriages, where you drop by when you're out here in Wyoming?"

He lifted a shoulder. "It would be what it would have to be. Nothing more, nothing less."

"A marriage in name only," she said, a deadweight settling in her heart.

"Caitlyn would have a name—a father."

"But just a part-time dad. Kind of like a father of convenience."

"You don't have to look at it that way."

It was the only way she could. He'd made no mention of love. Hadn't spoken one word of commitment. Just revealed a latent sense of duty. A little bit of hope withered deep in her soul. "Caitlyn and I belong here."

His mouth turned down at the corners. "She needs a father."

"Oh, I see—we should go wherever you want to, be available when you need *us* rather than the other way around."

"I didn't say that."

"You said enough, Kyle, and if you didn't understand it before, get this—I'm not the kind of woman to come running at your beck and call, nor is Caitlyn. If you think—"

"I think we should be together. For Caitlyn's sake."

She let out a long, angry breath and wrenched herself free. With one hand she scooped up her clothes. "I've got news for you. Caitlyn and I were doing just fine before you showed up and we'll get along when you leave. You don't have to come up with some overdue marriage proposal to help fix things." She yanked on her jeans and thrust her arms through the sleeves of her blouse. "I don't want her raised by some part-time daddy whose only reason to be married to her mommy is to salve his guilty conscience. So if that's what you've got in mind, O great lord and master, you can just forget it!"

"Caitlyn needs a father."

"Does she? Would it really be so good to tack on Fortune to her name so that people could see what a low-life, miserable, self-involved jerk her father really is?"

"You're getting this all wrong," he said, as he stuffed one long leg into his own pair of Levi's. "I'm older and wiser now."

"That's the trouble, isn't it? So am I! I won't be burned twice, at least not by the same man. And believe me, I'll never, *never* let you do anything to hurt our child."

"I wouldn't—"

"Wouldn't you? You can't just turn on the charm here and make her adore you, only to go running away again!"

He glowered at her as he zipped his fly. "I really did a number on you, didn't I?"

"Yeah, you did. But I'm a grown woman and I can handle it." That was more than a little bit of a lie, but she wasn't averse to stretching the truth to protect her heart. Tucking her boots under her arm, she headed for the front porch and added, "Caitlyn can't. Good night, Kyle."

She let the door bang shut behind her and fought the urge to cry. He'd offered to marry her—*marry* her, for crying out loud—but it wasn't good enough. A marriage of convenience was like a glass ring, a fake diamond sure to crack at the first sign of trouble. Nope, she'd be damned before she accepted Kyle's offer. She didn't need him. Neither did Caitlyn.

Through the window she watched the twin taillights of his truck disappear down the lane and wondered if he was out of her life forever. No one turned down a Fortune.

As she turned off the lights, she caught a glimpse of her own reflection in the window—tousled hair, swollen lips, nipples visible beneath her shirt—and was reminded of their recent lovemaking.

What kind of an idiot was she? A woman who spurned marriage from a millionaire, but couldn't resist making love to him. A mother whose daughter needed to know her father. Suddenly weary, she sighed. "You're a fool, Sam," she chided herself as she bent over and scratched Fang behind his ears. "Nothing more than a damned, prideful fool."

The worst of it was, she didn't know what she wanted.

Ten

Kyle gave a final tug on the wrench and hoped that the nut and old washer would finally hold against a leak that had, from the looks of rust stains running along the pipe, been in existence for several seasons. With a silent prayer, he turned on the tap, and water sprayed into the trough, filling the concrete tub without dripping down the pipe. "Hallelujah and amen!"

The horses—mares with the foals, mostly—watched him with only mild interest. They'd become accustomed to him as he fixed up the ranch, painting sun-blistered boards, replacing shingles on the barn roof, shoring up sagging porches and stretching miles of barbed wire along fence lines. The animals barely flicked their ears or lifted their noses from the stubble on which they grazed as he went about his business.

Today he was hell-bent on fixing all the pipes that leaked. Tomorrow he'd work on the baler, which seemed to break down each haying season, according to Randy, and finally he'd start recaulking and painting around the house. The maintenance on the place was endless, but surprisingly, he didn't mind. In fact, now that his muscles had quit protesting and aching from the hours of hard labor, he was beginning to enjoy life here in the wilds of Wyoming.

And all the hard work kept him busy, used up his energy, helped him hold on to his temper.

Three nights before, he'd asked Sam to marry him, and since then he hadn't seen much of her. She'd come over, worked with the damned horse, managed to be polite, or at the very least civil, but hadn't bothered to smile. Caitlyn had come along. She was still as interested in him as ever, and the fact that her parents' conversation was charged, that the very air between them seemed electrified with unspoken accusations, couldn't have been lost on her. But so far she hadn't brought up the fact that her parents were behaving like teenagers.

Since that night, Kyle had not so much as kissed Sam, prickly as she was. She was careful not to allow any time when they were alone together, nor did she touch him lightly on the sleeve or even offer him much of a greeting. Hell, she seemed to be punishing him for proposing to her. True, there hadn't been a lot of romance in his suggestion, but she didn't really expect *that,* did she? Who could fathom that woman?

When the trough was full, he turned off the faucets, noting with pride that they hadn't leaked a single drop. Most tasks around here were simple, but created a sense of accomplishment he'd never felt while working for the family company in Minneapolis.

A curious buckskin colt scampered close to him and tested the water with his muzzle, only to race away, black legs flying, dun coat gleaming in the afternoon sun. High overhead a hawk circled in a cloudless sky. The Tetons, still sprinkled with snow, knifed upward with a stark power he'd never noticed before. Yep, this savage land with its raw beauty was getting to him. Because of the kid. Because of Sam. But he didn't belong here. Never had. Never would.

Grabbing the shirt he'd hung over a fence post, he slapped his wrench into the tool belt slung over his hips and headed for the house. He'd accomplished a lot in the past week. Randy Herdstrom had agreed to keep overseeing the ranch, while Carson and Russ would still be part of the crew. Joker was calming down a bit as Sam worked with the headstrong beast, and Caitlyn trusted Kyle implicitly.

Sam didn't. That much was obvious.

He slapped a fence post in frustration. Locking the gate behind him, he thought about his grandmother. "Maybe you were right," he muttered under his breath, as if Kate could hear him. "Maybe I do belong here." But as he uttered the words, he knew they were wrong. The problem was he never believed he belonged anywhere. Not here in the wilds of Wyoming or in the high rises of Minneapolis. The only time he felt as if he was at home was when Sam was cradled in his arms and— "Stop it!" he growled, angry with the turn of his thoughts.

But what about Caitlyn? That kid was really something. She tagged after him each day, chattering on and on, asking a stream of questions and begging to ride the damned horse. Saw had allowed their daughter to sit on Joker's back just the other day, but that hadn't been good enough. No, sir. Caitlyn had been disappointed when her mother wouldn't let the Appaloosa off his lead rope. The tyke had put up a fuss, claiming she was old enough to handle any horse, but Sam hadn't budged.

He heard her truck before he saw it, and he couldn't help the skip of his heartbeat. Hell, he was a fool where she was concerned. Shading his eyes with one hand, he spied the old pickup speeding along the drive, leaving a plume of dust behind until Sam stood on the brakes and squealed to a shuddering stop. Kyle felt a grin tug at the corners of his mouth. She was driving like the proverbial maniac.

He walked to the parking lot as she flew out of the truck and cast a quick look around. Her furious gaze landed full force on him. Her strides were long and rapid, her hair billowing behind her, her small jaw set in concrete. "There you are!"

"Been here all afternoon."

Pointing a damning finger at his bare chest, she fairly quivered with rage. "You had no right," she said, green eyes snapping fire, "*no right* to make accusations against Jennifer Peterkin!"

"Hey—"

"Don't bother denying it, either, because I just ran into Shawna in the store, and she couldn't wait to tell me all about it and warn me that if you or I stepped foot on her property again she'd sue us for slander, criminal trespass, harassment and about fifty other charges!"

"I'd like to see her try," he drawled, and watched as her gaze slid down his naked torso for a second before returning to his eyes. There was a moment's pause, a hesitation that he read as a positive sign. Damn, but she was beautiful when she was mad.

"That's not the point, Kyle. You went over there behind my back and you didn't even tell me about it."

"I figured you might get mad or try to stop me."

"Bingo! I am mad. In fact, way past mad. I'm angry, irritated and disgusted all the way to furious!"

"Caitlyn's my kid, too."

"That doesn't give you the right to accuse—"

"Sure it does." Kyle grabbed the hand poking at his bare chest. Strong fingers tightened over hers. "No one's gonna bother Caitlyn anymore. I saw Jenny lurking on the stairs behind her mother's back when I was over there. That little kid's guilty as sin."

"Probably. But you have no proof."

"Have you had any more crank calls?" he demanded, his own volatile temper sparking.

"What?"

"In the past few days. Has anyone called and given Caitlyn a hard time, or just hung on the phone, breathing heavily?"

"No, but—"

He felt a glimmer of satisfaction. "You might say thanks instead of coming over here and reading me the riot act."

"Wait a minute."

"No, you wait a minute!" His own temper went up in flames. "As long as I'm around no one's going to hurt my kid. No one!"

"And how long will that be, hmm?" she asked, trying not to notice the beads of sweat rolling down his sun-bronzed torso, the play of light on his shoulders or the way his tool belt hung low on his hips.

"That's up to you, Sam. I'll be around as long as you let me."

"Even though the clock's ticking and you're planning to sell the ranch in what—a little over five months?" Her eyes narrowed as she glared up at him. "Don't worry about anyone else hurting Caitlyn, okay? Because you're the one who's going to break her heart when you leave."

"I offered to marry you." His breath, hot and angry, fanned her face, and a vein in his neck stood out. He stared at her so hard she wanted to step away. "The offer still stands, Sam."

If only the answer were so simple. If only the pain and scars of the past didn't cut so deep. At times she felt like she was seventeen again—young, naive, hopelessly in love, the world at her feet because Kyle was back. But those illusions easily shattered when she took a hard look around and reminded herself of the grim facts of life. She was a single mother. The father of her daughter was a rich playboy who had left her years before to marry another woman. Though she was falling in love with him all over again, she was certain he would leave—not just her this time, but his daughter as well.

But he wants to marry you, Sam. How many times does he have to ask? How many times will he? What are you waiting for? This is it, the brass ring, the key to your happiness! Grab it before it's too late.

"Come into the house, I'll buy you a drink." He glanced at the truck. "Where's Caitlyn?"

"Over at Sarah's for the afternoon."

"Then we have time alone." His blue eyes glinted mischievously and she knew she was in trouble. Corded muscles gleamed provocatively, disreputable jeans framed an abdomen that was flat and hard and lean. She couldn't resist him, never had been able to. Loving Kyle Fortune was her own private curse.

Seeing her hesitation, he draped an arm over her shoulder and touched his forehead to hers. "I don't bite."

"I do."

"I noticed."

"And you're not afraid?"

"Shakin' in my damned boots."

She couldn't help but laugh. So angry she wanted to strangle him minutes before, now she wanted to relax, laugh with him, enjoy a few minutes....

"You know, Fortune, if you're not the biting kind, then I'm definitely not interested."

"Wicked woman." With a groan, he pulled her into the circle of his strong arms and gathered her close, pressing his warm, sinewy flesh to the cotton of her T-shirt, his lips claiming hers in a possessive kiss that stole her breath.

"Kyle, please..."

"Whatever you want."

"I wish I knew what that was," she admitted.

"Come to bed with me, Samantha." His voice was low and husky, inviting.

"Not a good idea."

"A great idea."

"It's the middle of the afternoon," she protested. Becoming intimate with him would only make her weaker at a time when she needed to be strong.

"I know." He didn't wait for her to object any further. "Best time." Sweeping her off her feet with those steely arms, he carried her into the ranch house.

"This is a mistake."

"Just one more."

He smelled of sweat and soap, leather and that particular male scent that was undeniably his. His arms were strong; his breath, skimming the top of her head, was warm. Up the stairs and through double doors he carried her, to a room where a king-size bed dominated one pine-paneled wall. Indian prints and a hand-pieced quilt were hung on the walls, and a braided rug added warmth to the scuffed oak floor.

With a contented sigh, Sam gave herself up to him, kicking off her boots and clothes as he placed her on a sheepskin coverlet that had been folded atop the bed.

His tool belt dropped with a clunk.

His hands and lips were magic, touching her where her clothes had once been, skimming her body with a new familiarity that created a swirling heat deep inside her. She moved against him, feeling corded muscles rub her softer flesh. A newfound ache spread through her as he discarded his jeans. She was anxious, throbbing, and he was only too willing to fill her, delve deeply into her, drive away the demon lust with his skilled ministrations. Vaguely she wondered if she was a slave to his mastery, but knew that he, too, lost control, that she often had the upper hand. When she touched him with her fingers, slid her tongue along the washboard of his abdomen or tickled him with her hair, he was her willing servant. Tit for tat, and oh, it felt so good.

"Oh, darlin'," he cried, thrusting into her and driving all thought from her mind. She was his and nothing else mattered for the moment. As sunlight streamed through the dormers and the old gauze curtains fluttered in the soft summer breeze, she loved him with wild abandon and refused to think of the future, of losing him come December, of knowing that his natural restlessness would force him back to Minnesota. Instead she gave herself to him, body and soul.

Kyle heard the ringing, distant at first, then more insistent as he opened a bleary eye and realized that he'd dozed off. Samantha, still naked, was snuggled against him, and the phone, damn it, was downstairs. He hadn't yet had the place rewired for new jacks, and the answering machine he'd told himself to buy hadn't yet been purchased.

Sam's eyes flew open. "The phone," she murmured against him as she stretched with feline grace.

"Let it ring." He kissed her again, but she pushed him away.

"It could be Caitlyn." She was already out of the bed and scooping up her clothes. "Welcome to parenthood."

Grumbling under his breath, Kyle slid into his jeans and dashed out of the room. Whoever was on the other end was being persistent, for he snatched up the receiver on the sixth ring. "Hello?"

"Where in God's name have you been?" a smooth female voice intoned. "I've been calling you for days."

"Caroline?"

"You remembered," his cousin said with a laugh. "Ever since you flew to Wyoming, no one here at the company has heard a peep from you."

"Hard work and clean livin'," he drawled, winking at Sam as she, disheveled from their loving, entered the room. She was still buttoning her shirt and he scowled, anxious for another look at her glorious breasts.

"Yeah, right. You live about as clean as Satan himself."

"Caitlyn?" Sam mouthed, lines of worry etching between her eyebrows. He shook his head and grabbed hold of her wrists, pulling her close and smelling the perfume of her hair. He kissed her crown and felt her sag against him.

"Don't give me any story about hard work, Kyle. I know you. If you've been busy, it's probably because of some woman."

"Watch out, Caro, your claws are showing." He imagined his cousin, recently married to a Fortune Cosmetics chemist, stretching the phone cord in her private office at the headquarters of the company. Cool, controlled Caroline had relaxed a lot since she'd wed Nick Valkov.

Sam wiggled out of his arms and picked up the morning's pot of coffee. As Kyle talked, she scrounged in the cupboards, found a couple of cups and filled them with the remainder of the brew.

"The reason I called was to remind you of the board meeting on Friday," Caro said.

Kyle, distracted by watching Sam's jeans-clad rump as

she set coffee mugs in the microwave, found it difficult to concentrate on the family business, a topic that had, ever since he'd been a kid, bored him senseless. "This Friday?"

"Um-hmm. Just because I fired you as my assistant doesn't mean you're not part of the business. Everyone in the family who owns shares—and we all do—has to attend."

"Why?"

"Because we need to discuss a lot of issues. The new ad campaign, the value of the stock since the company reorganization—and there's the youth formula to discuss. Everything's been on hold since Kate died.... Oh, damn, I still can't say that without cringing inside."

"Amen."

Caroline cleared her throat. "There's more. Nick can't get any farther with his formula for the youth cream without the key ingredient—"

"I know, I know," Kyle interrupted, a headache forming behind his eyes. It was the same headache that pounded at his temples whenever any of the family company's problems were called to his attention. Whereas Caroline had always been fascinated with the corporation and had groomed herself to run it one day, only to fall in love with and marry Nicolai Valkov, Kyle hadn't cared a lick about business, profit-and-loss statements, beauty creams or marketing. He'd tried for a while, but just didn't have the same interest. Maybe his grandmother had been right in leaving him this ranch, far from the rest of the family and company headquarters. He still didn't want to think about the supposed youth formula, the key ingredient of which was growing somewhere deep in the Amazon rain forest and had been the reason Kate Fortune had flown to Brazil and ultimately died.

The microwave buzzer sounded and Sam reached inside. The scent of coffee teased Kyle's nostrils. Sam handed Kyle one cup and blew across the other.

"There's another reason I want you to come home, Kyle," Caroline said, her voice more serious. "It's Rebecca."

"Don't tell me. She thinks there might have been foul play and that Kate was possibly murdered." Kyle took a sip of the warm brew and winked at Sam. "Rebecca already called me."

"Did she tell you that she's hired a private investigator, a man by the name of Gabriel Devereax, to help her look into it?"

"She said she was moving on it."

"Well, I'm not against hiring the guy, I guess. I suppose if there was anything suspicious about the plane crash, we should know about it. But I don't think it would be wise for the press to get wind of it. Rebecca's theory, loose as it is, smacks of company espionage and the kind of publicity Fortune Cosmetics doesn't need or want. That fire in the lab a few months ago already got the attention of the press and made some of the stockholders nervous." Caroline's voice had an edge to it. "Maybe I'm overreacting because of Rebecca's insistence that Grandma was killed on purpose."

"Hey, Caro, slow down. Rebecca's still only got a theory, and a thin one at that."

"But the press—"

"Is the least of our worries." He set his cup on the counter, wishing she hadn't called. Why did the family feel compelled to drag him back into the corporate fold? Hell, what could he do?

"You see why you need to come home."

"Yeah, you've made your point." Shifting from one

foot to the other, he considered returning to Minnesota. The thought settled like lead in his stomach. Life back in the city was far removed from his new existence here in the shadow of the Tetons. ''What time's the meeting?'' he asked.

''Nine sharp.''

''I'll be there,'' he said, meeting Sam's eyes and seeing the corners of her mouth turn down as she absently swirled cream into her cup. ''Besides, I have some news of my own.''

Sam's head shot up.

''Good or bad?'' Caroline asked.

''Definitely good.''

''No!'' Sam was shaking her head, her coffee forgotten, the spoon clattering onto the table. ''Kyle, no—''

''Well, what is it?''

Sam was on her feet, her skin white as birch bark. ''Kyle, don't, not now. This isn't the time—''

''I was going to phone Dad and break the news to him first, but since you called, you may as well know that I've got a family.''

''What?'' Caroline demanded.

Sam gasped and looked as if the world had suddenly collapsed.

Kyle barged on. ''A daughter. Nine years old.''

There was dead silence on the phone line, and Sam reached for the receiver, determined to hang it up.

''Excuse me, Kyle,'' Caroline said. ''You've got a...?''

''A girl. Her name's Caitlyn,'' he said, turning so that Sam couldn't reach the phone.

''Oh, Kyle, no! Stop this!'' Sam was frantic, staring at the telephone as if it were the embodiment of evil.

''You remember Samantha Rawlings?''

"Yes..."

"She and I were involved a long time ago.... Oh, hell, it's complicated. But I'm bringing them both back to Minneapolis and we'll straighten everything out then."

"Good Lord." Caroline's voice was barely a whisper.

"See you Friday."

He hung up, and Sam, her pale face suddenly surging scarlet with rage, stood trembling before him. Her fists were clenched in frustration, her eyes wide and snapping green fire. "How dare you?"

"They have to know."

"But not like that."

"Then how?" He stood, jeans zipped but not buttoned, thumbs hooked in the empty belt loops.

"I don't know, but there has to be a better way."

"Name it."

"Oh, God, Kyle. You can't just spring this on people—"

"We'll tell them together."

The thought of his family—his rich family—staring at her turned her blood to ice. She would never put Caitlyn through such an ordeal and couldn't imagine suffering through it by herself.

"I asked you to marry me," he reminded her.

"To make things proper?" she said, disgusted.

"To make things easier."

"Sometimes easier isn't better."

He reached for her but she backed away, too angry to let him touch her. "We can get married and you can come back to meet the family," he suggested.

"I have a ranch to run."

"We'll get someone to oversee it for a few days."

"I'm not ready, Kyle."

"You've had ten years."

"But this—this is all too fast." Shaking her head, she held up a hand as if to cut off any further protests forming on his tongue. "I don't want you to marry me just because we have a child, to give Caitlyn a name, to do something noble to ease your guilt, okay? I'm old enough to stand on my own and I don't need any halfhearted proposal to make me feel good about myself."

"What's that supposed to mean?"

"That you can't use me to get to my—er, our daughter. I won't have you toying with my emotions or hers. I already told you I'm not interested in some piece of paper claiming that we're husband and wife. A marriage is more than a scrap of paper signed by a justice of the peace." She held out her hands and shook her head. "All this talk is crazy. Besides, married or not, I can't just up and leave."

"The family will be expecting you."

"The family can damned well hang for all I care. I've got Caitlyn to consider and I'm not taking her to a strange place filled with gawking relatives, anxious reporters and questions she can't begin to answer. I won't let her be part of some sideshow for curiosity seekers in the Midwest." All of her decade-old worries swam frantically to the surface and she rubbed her arms, feeling a sudden, doom-filled chill. "How were you planning to introduce her?"

"As my daughter."

"Your illegitimate daughter who was conceived right before you married someone other than her mother?"

"So we're back to that."

"Afraid so."

His jaw turned to steel. "Sooner or later I've got to tell my family that—"

"Later, okay?" she retorted. Her composure was long

gone, impossible to snatch back, and yet the smell of him still lingered on her skin. Only a few minutes before they had been lying together naked, limbs tangled, as if they were already wed, as if there were some kind of commitment between them, as if they loved each other.

"When?"

"I don't know!"

His chest muscles twitched and he thrust his jaw forward at an uncompromising, don't-tread-on-me angle. "Just what is it you want from me, Sam?"

"Time and space to think things through."

"Ten years in the middle of one of the most unpopulated areas of the country isn't enough?"

"Don't joke with me."

"It wasn't a joke."

Eyes thinned suspiciously, he rubbed the stubble on his jaw, the same bristles that had brushed her soft skin so recently. "You once accused me of being a coward, Sam, but I think you're the one who's afraid. What is it about me that scares you so much?"

That you don't love me; that you could hurt me again; that, damn it, you could hurt your daughter, who's starting to adore you.

"I—I just don't want to make a mistake."

"You know, Sam," he said, hoisting himself up on the counter and staring down at her with damning eyes that had always seen deep into her soul. "I told you once you were a lousy liar, and that hasn't changed. You're avoiding the truth. You've never been the kind of person to back away from a challenge, to duck a dare, to worry about stepping into a river that was too deep or swift."

Her smile was like ice. "You're confusing me with someone you used to know. A girl who trusted, a girl who didn't have a child dependent upon her, a girl who was carefree and—''

''No way! I'm talking about a girl who took the fall over and over for her dad, a drunk. A girl who could handle just about anything life dished out to her. A girl who trusted and loved. I'm talking about you, Sam, and don't lie to me and say that you've changed all that much, that I hurt you and scarred you and you can't find that girl buried deep inside you, because that's a pile of pseudopsychological crap and we both know it. Come on, Samantha. Admit it. You don't want to marry me because you think that by walking down the aisle with me you'll have given up, fallen in with the enemy, abandoned your personal quest to raise your daughter by yourself. Your pride's so big you're tripping over it.''

''And your ego makes you blind!''

He hopped down from the counter, but she was already halfway to the door, intent on spending several hours with Joker and then leaving Kyle and his incredibly inflated ego behind. Before she said something she'd regret, she strode onto the porch. Late-afternoon heat hit her like a furnace blast.

The screen door slapped closed, but Kyle's voice followed after her. ''If you think you can win this battle, Sam, you're wrong.'' She spun around and found him on the other side of the mesh, his body rigid and imposing, all hard, determined muscle and raw, unbridled energy. His eyes were dark and furious, his lips blade thin. ''I don't know what kind of game you're playing, but you'd better face the fact that I'm in Caitlyn's life and that's the way it's gonna stay.''

''Are you?''

''Absolutely.''

"Tell me, Kyle, do you work hard at being a bastard or does it come natural to you?"

"Natural, Sam," he said as she marched away from the house, his words thundering after her. "It's natural and you know it!"

"We've got a problem. Kyle is returning to Minneapolis for a company meeting." The stranger leaned heavily against the dusty glass of the phone booth, where four-letter words had been written with a smudged finger. Ignoring the filth, he mopped his brow. He was tired of this cloak-and-dagger business. He wasn't a young man any longer, and the trips between Minneapolis and Clear Springs were becoming more difficult.

His partner sighed audibly. "He'll go back to the ranch."

"You're certain of it?"

"Absolutely. He knows he's a father now, doesn't he?"

"I think so. He sure spends a lot of time with Samantha Rawlings and the girl."

"Perfect. I knew it would work."

"You hope. As I said, he's returning to Minneapolis. Who knows if he'll come back here?"

"He will. He's made of stronger stuff than anyone knows and he's never felt comfortable in Minnesota. Never."

"Humph." He wasn't convinced, but wouldn't argue. "Well, that's not the worst of it anyway. Our biggest concern at the moment is that Rebecca is suspicious. She thinks something's up. She's hired a private detective to start poking around, looking into the accident, searching for clues. She's convinced there's some kind of cover-up in her grandmother's death."

"Interesting."

"Is that all you can say? This isn't an idle curiosity, you know. If Rebecca starts digging up information she shouldn't, things could get out of hand. There could be more trouble and our plan could be exposed. What then?"

"Things will get dangerous."

"My point exactly."

"For everyone." There was a long pause as his partner considered all sides of the issue. "Well, no one's proved anything yet. As far as everyone knows, Kate Fortune had a bad accident. Her luck ran out."

"Until Rebecca and that private investigator she hired find out the truth."

"You worry too much."

"You pay me to worry," he retorted as he stared through the smudged glass. Traffic chugged by at the slow, rural pace that made him edgy. He missed the city—the noise, the crowds, the excitement that was Minneapolis.

"Let's not borrow trouble."

"We don't have to borrow it. Lately it seems to find us."

"Rebecca won't discover anything. At least not for a while. As for Kyle, don't worry about him. He'll be back in Wyoming before you can blink, and then the first phase of our plan will be in place."

"I'll cross my fingers."

"Ever the skeptic. Just stay the course. You know, that's been my motto."

"I know." *And look where it's gotten you,* he added silently before hanging up and tugging at his collar. Sweat dripped down his spine. The temperature had to be near ninety and he was sweltering in his crisp jeans and plaid shirt. Catching his reflection in the glass of his rented Ford Explorer, he scowled. The sooner this was over, the better.

"You're leaving?" Caitlyn watched as Kyle tossed his overnight bag into the back of Sam's pickup.

"Just for a little while." Kyle helped her into the passenger side of the truck, then slid onto the bench seat. "I'll be back Monday night or Tuesday morning."

Sam, sitting behind the steering wheel, forced a smile she didn't feel as she twisted on the ignition and the truck's engine ground, then roared to life. Against her better judgment, but attempting to appear as if she wasn't holding a grudge, she had agreed to drive Kyle to the airport in Jackson. Though she and Kyle had said barely ten words since their argument the other day, she was determined that Caitlyn be fooled into believing that everything was fine—well, as fine as it could be, considering the circumstances—between her parents. What good would it do for her daughter to know that Sam wanted to throttle Kyle? Never mind that she was in love with him.

Kyle slammed the door shut and squirmed under his daughter's worried gaze. Good. Let him feel what all sides of being a parent were about.

"Why do you have to go?" Caitlyn demanded as Sam rammed the truck into gear.

"It's business."

"I thought you owned the ranch." Thunderclouds rolled in Caitlyn's blue eyes. "Isn't that your business?"

"Yeah, but it's more complicated than that. I own shares in a company—" He broke off and ruffled Caitlyn's hair as the truck bumped down the lane. "Look, honey, don't worry about it. I'll be back in a few days."

He shot a glance at Sam, which, she decided, was supposed to make her feel bad for not joining him. She didn't.

"But what if your plane crashes?" Caitlyn was known to belabor a point.

"It won't."

"Mrs. Kate was a pilot and her airplane crashed and she died." Caitlyn's lower lip trembled.

Sam's heart ripped a bit as Kyle draped an arm over his daughter's shoulders and hugged her close. They were on the highway now, tires singing north to Jackson. "Nothing's gonna happen to me, I promise. I'll be back to bug your ma before you can say Minneapolis, Minnesota."

"I can say it pretty fast," Caitlyn said, sniffing away her tears.

"See, it only goes to show you that you won't even miss me." He slid Sam a glance. "Now, on the other hand, your mom, she's gonna miss me a lot."

Caitlyn's head swiveled as she looked from one parent to the other. "How can you tell?"

Sam's smile was so tight and phony it hurt.

"Oh, I can tell," Kyle drawled, his lips stretched into a wide grin that taunted her, as if he had the upper hand.

Sam stepped on the brakes and shifted down as they entered the city limits of Jackson. Kyle's eyes, staring intently at her, nearly burned her skin, daring her to respond.

Good. She was always glad to give him a piece of her mind. "Your dad thinks he knows all about me, but he still has a lot to learn."

"Do I? Well, I think I'll enjoy doing just that." He leaned against the passenger door.

"But you will come back?" Caitlyn demanded, biting her lower lip.

"Count on it!" He winked at his daughter before his eyes centered on Sam again. "You know, darlin', you couldn't get rid of me if you tried."

Eleven

As she hummed along to an old Bruce Springsteen ballad playing on the radio, Sam twisted off the faucets, then wrung the water from her hair. She stepped out of the shower and cracked the window open to let some of the steam escape from the bathroom as the mirror over the sink cleared of condensation.

Her tired muscles felt better from the hot water, and the grime that had covered her face and body after hours in the saddle was washed away. She'd spent the better part of the day checking on the cattle and making sure that the once-injured calf had reestablished himself in the herd, then she'd tackled the barn, cleaning out manure, old straw and dirt. Every muscle in her body had protested at the hard work, but she needed to keep busy, to throw herself into each and every task so that she wouldn't think about Kyle and the fact that he was so far away.

What did it matter? If he never came back, she would have lost nothing and Caitlyn would adjust. Kids were resilient, weren't they? Sam and her daughter would drift back into their normal life, the one without Kyle, and though Caitlyn would miss her dad, at least she knew who he was.

And what about you? What will you do to chase away the memories of laughing with him, touching him, making love to him?

"Stop it," she grumbled, tired of the little voice in her mind that even dared suggest she might still love a millionaire playboy who had left her once before.

"Caitlyn," she called through the closed doors. While Sam had shoveled out the barn, Caitlyn had been playing in the hayloft, and when Sam had finished, she'd left her daughter playing in the shade of the apple tree. Fang had been at the girl's side. "What do you say we go out for dinner tonight?" she asked as she buffed her skin with a towel and combed the tangles from her hair. She didn't want to heat up the stove as well as the kitchen, where she would subconsciously wait for Kyle to call. He'd been gone less than twenty-four hours and damn it, she missed him already. What was she going to do when he left for good? When he demanded partial custody of Caitlyn?

"Cross that rickety bridge when you come to it," she admonished, snapping her hair into a rubber band. *Or you could marry him.* Her eyes found her reflection behind drops of condensation. *It would never work. Or would it?* Lord, how had life become so complicated? Could she accept a marriage without love, a long-distance union that was only for show? Maybe she was just romantic and naive to think that people still married for love, for the joy of sharing the rest of their lives. "Hey," she called again. "How about pizza?"

No answer. Caitlyn was probably still outside. She threw on clean jeans and a T-shirt, then slid into a pair of sandals. "Caitlyn?" she called as she walked through the hallway toward the kitchen.

The house was quiet, aside from the ever-present hum of the refrigerator and the steady ticking of the clock in the living room. Fang was snoozing on the back porch, but Caitlyn, who had been swinging not fifteen minutes before, was nowhere in sight.

"Caitlyn?" Sam called through the open kitchen window. No answer except for a startled jackrabbit that disappeared among the cornstalks in the garden. "Let's go into town, meet Grandma and grab a pizza or something...."

No answering whoop and running footsteps. "Honey?" Sam glanced around the yard but saw no sign of her daughter. "Caitlyn?" Had she come into the house and sneaked up the stairs—maybe fallen asleep while reading or looking through magazines? Sam checked the living room and Caitlyn's bedroom, but the house was still quiet. Too quiet. *Don't panic,* she warned herself. Caitlyn was somewhere nearby, but Sam's heart began to pound and a sprinkling of sweat collected at the base of her neck. Caitlyn wasn't the kind of kid who was content playing cards or watching TV. She was always into something and was probably outside, or in one of the outbuildings out of earshot.

So why did Sam feel a rising sense of anxiety as she hurried through the house and onto the back porch, where Fang, lifting his head, gave a couple of obligatory thumps with his tail. "Yeah, a lot of help you are," she chided. "Where's Caitlyn?" The old dog yawned and rolled onto his back as if expecting a belly rub. "Later."

Stay calm. She's nearby. She has to be.

Shading her eyes against the setting sun, Sam stared at the outbuildings and fields. Sometimes Caitlyn wandered off, chasing butterflies or grasshoppers. Desperation slid a cold finger down her soul. What about all those phone calls where the caller had hung up? What about Caitlyn's worries that she was being watched?

Sam's mouth turned to sand as she ran from one of

Caitlyn's favorite haunts to another. But her daughter wasn't casting stones into the creek or building a fort in the hayloft or hiding under the old chicken coop. Fear striking a new and chilling chord in her heart, Sam searched the garden, where Caitlyn sometimes sought refuge in the tall stalks of corn or the shady alcove created by the pole beans. "Caitlyn?" she repeated, then, under her breath, "Where the devil are you?" Despair soured her stomach, but she told herself to remain calm, that she'd seen the girl less than half an hour earlier. Nothing could happen.

"Caitlyn!" she called again, an edge to her voice. *Don't lose it—she's around here. She has to be!* But Sam's walk became a half trot and she licked her lips nervously. Once again she checked the house, the barn, the toolshed, the fence line, the outbuildings.

Sweat broke out on her forehead and between her shoulder blades and the mind-numbing fear that she'd angrily pushed aside scaled her ribs to burrow into her heart. *Where are you, Caitlyn? Where?* Inside the house again, she reached for the phone. Kyle. She had to call Kyle. She'd started dialing when she realized he was out of town, as was Grant, the other man she could rely upon—far away in Minneapolis. "Damn." She slammed the receiver back into its cradle. Her fingers tapped nervously on the counter. There was no reason to call her mother. If Caitlyn had ridden her bike into town, she would have called the minute she landed on Bess Rawlings's doorstep. Caitlyn's grandmother would have insisted that she check in.

Biting her lip and forcing back the fear that was gnawing at her stomach, Sam studied the horizon as she chewed on the tip of one of her fingernails. Her gaze landed on the Fortune Ranch, spreading out as if the vast acres stretched to forever. More often than not, lately, Caitlyn had climbed the fence and walked to Kyle's house, either to visit her newfound father or to try to con someone into letting her ride Joker, her obsession.... Oh, God.

Sam's stomach hit floor.

Heart in her throat, she snagged her keys from the counter and flew out of the kitchen to her pickup.

"Please let me find her," she prayed as she leapt into the rig, jabbed her key into the ignition and stomped on the throttle. In a spray of gravel, she took off, images of Caitlyn and Joker flashing through her mind.

At the turn to the county road, she barely slowed, swinging wide. Foot to the floor, she drove like a crazy woman to the Fortunes' long drive. Trees and fence posts sped by until she slowed at the yard. She didn't bother turning off the ignition but jumped out of the truck when she spied her daughter astride the damned stallion. Joker was snorting, racing from one end of the enclosure to the other, and Caitlyn was clinging to him like a burr.

"Hold on," Sam whispered, remaining outwardly calm, determined to swallow back her rising sense of panic as she half ran to the corral. *Don't let the horse feel your worry.*

But her heart was in her throat, her gaze steady on her daughter, as Caitlyn, red-blond hair flying, face pale as chalk, saw her. "Mommy!"

"Hang on."

Joker, sweat glistening on his dark hide, reared just then, and Caitlyn screamed.

"No!"

When his front hooves hit the ground again, the stallion took off like a proverbial shot, racing to the far end of the enclosure.

"Mommy...!" Caitlyn clung to his mane.

"Oh, God. Oh, God. Oh, God." *Calm down, Sam. Don't fall apart now. Take control, damn it!*

"Whoa, boy," she said, her throat clutching as she opened the gate and slipped into the paddock. The stallion was out of control, his eyes white rimmed, his nostrils and muscles quivering. "It's all right. Gonna be all right," she said in the same smooth voice, and she didn't know if she was talking to herself, the stallion or her daughter.

Joker let out a sharp whistle and pawed the ground.

"Caitlyn, if you could just slide off..."

With a snort, the stallion reared again. Sam stopped dead in her tracks.

"Mommy—"

The horse took off again, racing past Sam like a bullet, dust stirring beneath his frantic hooves, his tail streaming out like a silky black banner.

"Caitlyn!" Sam cried. "Hang on. I'll get you."

"No!"

Joker, with a high, piercing whistle, reared again. Caitlyn squealed.

"Hang on, honey!" Sam called, hurrying forward, trying to calm the horse, while inside she was scared to death. Joker rolled white-rimmed eyes in her direction. "Slow down, boy," she said, reaching forward, hoping to grab hold of his halter.

With a snort, Joker twisted into the air and bolted, only to stop short and buck. Caitlyn's hands flew upward. Her body jerked, fingers losing their grip. She pitched forward over the stallion's lowered head.

"No!" Sam ran, boots slipping.

Caitlyn landed with a hard, sickening thud, her head striking the dry earth. Dust flew. Joker tried to jump over her, but one hoof struck her shoulder. With a cry, Caitlyn crumpled even more. "Oh, God. Caitlyn..." Sam reached her daughter and fell to her knees, praying that Caitlyn wasn't injured. From the corner of her eye Sam saw Joker gallop through the gate that hadn't latched behind her, but she didn't care. All that mattered was Caitlyn. Nothing else.

"Caitlyn, honey, oh, God..." Sam cradled her daughter's head, dusty blond hair falling over her arms. "Sweetheart," she whispered, tears standing in her eyes. "Caitlyn, oh, baby, can you hear me?"

Caitlyn moaned, but didn't open her eyes. "You'll be okay," Sam whispered, tears of fear rolling down her cheeks as she gathered her daughter close and prayed. "You hang in there," she said, her throat choked with emotion.

She heard the tractor before she saw it come chugging around the barn. Randy Herdstrom glanced her direction, mouthed a stream of invectives and jumped from the old John Deere. His boots pounded across the dry ground. "God Almighty, what happened?"

"Call an ambulance!" Caitlyn ordered.

The foreman took off like a shot and was back within seconds. "What happened?" he asked again, running experienced fingers around Caitlyn's shoulder, ribs and arm.

Riddled with guilt for letting her daughter out of her sight, Sam explained how Caitlyn had wandered over here and tried to ride the half-wild stallion. "...I ran to her and Joker galloped out of the corral and—and you showed up, thank God."

An ambulance siren wailed far in the distance.

Randy placed a huge, dirty hand on her shoulder. "Sounds like the cavalry is on its way." Sam thought she might break down completely, but he said reassuringly, "She's a tough cookie, just like her ma. She'll be all right."

Sam crossed her fingers and said a prayer, hoping beyond hope that Randy had some kind of window into the future.

His mood as black as midnight, Kyle suffered through the business meeting.

The boardroom, even with its bank of windows and panoramic view of the city, seemed tight and claustrophobic. Kyle tugged at his collar, loosened his tie, unbuttoned the top button of his shirt. How had he ever stood living here? He'd never felt quite so tied down, so suffocated. It was true he'd always been restless, never settled-in or happy, but now he was going mad. Already he'd cast several votes, offered his opinion a couple of times and was more weary than if he'd been setting posts for days in the rocky, unforgiving acres near Clear Springs.

While his father, uncle, aunts, brothers, sisters and cousins sat with him around the table, discussing everything from the company logo to the profit margin on a tube of mascara, Kyle drummed his fingers, tried to pay attention and felt as if he might crawl out of his skin. They discussed, pondered, argued and even laughed on rare occasion, but for the most part were so damned serious about every little detail that Kyle thought he might go stark, raving mad. As far as he was concerned the company could fold tomorrow and it wouldn't affect him. Even if it meant that all the assets including his ranch had to be sold, he could deal with it. If he'd learned anything in the past month it was that his life couldn't be measured by assets and net worth or even the valuable acres in Clear Springs. No, his very existence had changed, and at the center of it all were Sam and Caitlyn. That Sam wouldn't marry him burned like acid in his gut. She cared for him, maybe even loved him. He sensed it and yet she wouldn't accept what he so willingly offered.

Because, you stupid bastard, you acted as if you were doing her a favor instead of the other way around.

He twisted the ring on his right hand and sneaked a peek at his watch.

As the discussion turned to the damned youth formula—the cornerstone for Fortune Cosmetics's new line—a pall settled over the table. No one had forgotten that Kate had lost her life in her search for the secret ingredient. If Kyle were calling the shots, he'd scrap the whole project, but the general consensus was that the new formula would not only make big profits but benefit consumers as well. With company stock prices falling, the success of the damned youth formula was essential.

The good news was that so far there hadn't been time to discuss personal lives. Kyle had walked into the boardroom two minutes before the meeting started and found a chair around the gleaming, cherry-wood table. Grant sat to his left, his cousin Rocky to his right. The Westerners, rebels who didn't fit into the Fortune family niche here in the Midwest, were all crowded together. Across from him, Caroline, forever devoted to the company and vice president of marketing, was flanked by her new husband, Nicolai Valkov, and Allie the Beautiful. Though a twin to Rocky, Allie made the most of her God-given beauty, while Rocky tended to downplay her classic cheekbones, long neck and thick, wine red hair. Allie was a model and Rocky a pilot.

At the head of the table, with his children, siblings and

nieces and nephews scattered around him, Jake, Kyle's uncle, was explaining about last quarter's profits and losses and how the downward trend could be stopped by—you guessed it—the new youth formula.

Kyle couldn't give two cents, and he figured his body language—slouching in his chair, his arms folded over his chest—conveyed his disinterest. He noticed Rocky doodling on her notepad, and Grant, clearly having trouble sitting still, glanced at his watch every two or three minutes. "I thought you were going to bring Sam," he whispered.

"So did I."

Grant managed a knowing grin. "Stubborn thing, isn't she?"

Kyle slid him a look. "Should fit right into the family."

"Into the family?" Grant's thick brows slammed together. "You two gettin' hitched?"

Kyle scowled as he turned the question over in his mind. Deep in his heart he doubted that Sam would ever marry him. He'd blown it years before and even though she cared for him—he knew she did, damn it—her pride wouldn't let her stoop to the marriage of convenience he'd suggested.

For the first time in his life, he realized, something he wanted desperately was beyond his reach. And, oh, how he wanted Sam and Caitlyn, to claim them as his own. *Like searing brands on cattle,* he could almost hear Sam taunt.

His thoughts darker still, he ignored Grant's question and tried to rustle up some enthusiasm for Jake's lecture and the flowchart propped on the end of the table. Projected Earnings was the title, and it seemed that with the sales of the youth formula, profits were predicted to rise like a rocket to the stratosphere.

Of course, everything depended upon procuring and cultivating a rare plant found only in the Amazon rain forest. Jake paused, and once again Kate's demise, so recent and brutally unnecessary, loomed like a specter over the whole family.

"It's a bitch," Grant said softly. Kate had always treated him as if he were her own flesh and blood, no different from her other grandchildren.

Kyle didn't disagree and glanced across the table, where Caroline met his gaze. Her demeanor had changed slightly. Usually all-business, she seemed to have mellowed since her marriage to Nick. At one time Kyle would have called Caroline bossy, and he never would have expected that her marriage, arranged for the express purpose of keeping the Russian chemist in the country, would have blossomed into love. But judging from the way her husband held her hand and the slight smile that played upon Caroline's lips, things had changed. She'd even forgone her usual upswept and severe hairstyle, allowing her thick, sable brown waves to brush her shoulders.

Nick touched her elbow and her face lightened. Who would have thought tough-as-nails Caroline would fall so hard and fast?

After several breaks and a catered lunch, Jake gave up the floor to Sterling Foster, who had been Kate's lawyer and confidant. Now Sterling worked closely with Nathaniel, Kyle's father and the official company attor-ney. Sterling spoke about a few problems with lawsuits slapped on the company, dismissed most of them as bothersome but nothing to worry about and flashed his confident smile. He seemed less grief stricken than the last time Kyle had seen him, at the reading of the will, but there was something odd about the man. For all his oratory skills, never once during the entire time he stood and talked about company politics and litigation did he ever so much as glance at Kyle. Not so with the rest of his siblings and cousins, but for a reason Kyle couldn't begin to fathom, Sterling avoided eye contact with him.

Why?

Kyle leaned forward, interested for the first time since stepping foot into the room. What was it about Foster? The elder lawyer seemed different than the last time they'd met—in his office, with the whole family drained and reeling with grief. Sterling, like the rest of them, had been clearly devastated. But in the past month he appeared to have picked up the pieces of his life and moved forward.

"I know this is a difficult time for all of you, trying to run the company, keep your busy lives on schedule and deal with your grief." Sterling's gaze moved slowly around the table, and when he reached Kyle, he seemed to pause for a second before hurrying along. "Kate would have wanted you to put that grief behind you and get on with the business of living, of raising your own children, of keeping Fortune Cosmetics on track.

"Now there's been some discussion as to the circumstances of Kate's death. I know this is difficult, but we have to face the fact that she's gone—prematurely, yes, but gone. The accident was disturbing and unsettling, I know, but there was no foul play involved. I've seen the police reports from Brazil and, if you would like, you may each have a copy." He cleared his throat at the morbid topic. "In my opinion, it wouldn't be wise to spend time, energy or funds on searching for some kind of vague conspiracy in this tragic incident. Kate wouldn't have wanted—''

''Wait a minute!'' Rebecca shot to her feet, as if listening to one more word was too much for her. ''I just want answers, Nate. You're a lawyer, for crying out loud. Surely you can understand. There's a lot left unexplained.''

''What?''

''Maybe she was murdered.''

Nate dropped his pen. ''Murdered? Oh, for the love of God, don't tell me you're beginning to believe those mysteries you write.''

''This has nothing to do with my work—''

''Let's not get into a fight here,'' Jake interrupted.

''She's playing Nancy Drew again,'' Nate grumbled.

Kyle leaned back in his chair, interested for the first time in the family theatrics. ''What does it hurt if she hires an investigator?''

Sterling tried to take charge. ''Is this what Kate would have wanted—all this bickering?''

''Yep,'' Kyle said before anyone else could answer. ''She liked a good, heated discussion—the hotter the better. She never ducked an argument and wouldn't want her murderer to go free.''

''*If* there was a murderer,'' Jake reminded everyone. ''Listen to you—''

Kyle leaned forward and pinned his uncle with a relentless glare. ''Kate would certainly want Rebecca to do what she thought was best.''

''That's right,'' Jane agreed heartily. Tossing her ginger-colored hair off her face, she showed some of the same spirit associated with Kate Fortune. ''If Grandma taught us anything, it was to follow our hearts.''

''Are we talking about the same woman?'' Michael

demanded, casting a look that could melt steel toward his dreamy sister. "Grandma was reasonable and pragmatic. She wasn't known to go off chasing rainbows or—" he turned his glare onto Rebecca "—ghosts. Come on, let's be realistic for a minute—"

"I'm with Kyle." Kristina finally joined the conversation, surprising both her brothers. Usually self-absorbed, Kris didn't get into many of the family squabbles. "What does it hurt? Grandma would have wanted us to look into all the possibilities. *That's* the way *she* would have handled the situation. She wouldn't have been afraid—"

"Amen," Kyle offered.

"—or worried about what other people thought. So let Rebecca hire an investigator. It's the least we can do for Kate."

Kyle grinned at his blond sister. He'd never have thought she could feel anything so passionately.

There was some more grumbling and arguing, especially from Sterling, but in the end, as expected, a truce was reached and Rebecca kept Gabriel Devereax on the payroll. Devereax's job was to determine if Kate had died in an accident or by more nefarious means. He was to look into any and all questions surrounding her death, as well as anything vaguely hinting at company espionage. No one asked what would happen if the investigator did turn up the grisly fact that Kate had been killed. That someone wanted Fortune Cosmetics to fail and was willing to commit murder to that end.

Kyle left the board meeting feeling dead inside. All the talk about profit and loss and secret formulas and Kate's death depressed him. He wanted Sam. Now. Only she could take the ache out of his heart. Only she could lift his spirits. Only she could offer him the companionship and solace he so sorely needed.

He closed his eyes for a second and imagined her face, fresh, scrubbed and smiling; her green eyes bright with the reflection of the summer sun; her lips curved into a grin that was both provocative and warm.

God, how he loved her.

The thought hit him squarely in the gut. He stopped dead in his tracks.

He loved her.

How had he not recognized that single earth-shattering emotion until this very moment?

His heart pounded and sweat broke out over his upper lip with the startling realization that he'd loved her for a long, long time. He'd just been too arrogantly stupid to face the truth.

"Oh, God," he whispered. Why had he been such a blind, unbending fool?

Running a hand over a day's worth of beard stubble, he rimmed dry lips with his tongue as he walked to the bank of elevators. The offices were empty, most of his family having rushed home after the long meeting. Their lives were here in Minneapolis, but he didn't belong. Not here. No, he finally understood that he was destined to live at the base of the Tetons on a windswept ranch with a freckle-faced cowgirl and his—their—daughter.

He slapped the elevator call button and was suddenly anxious to drive to his apartment—the one he'd left when he'd moved temporarily to Wyoming—and call Sam and beg her to marry him. He wouldn't propose out of a sense of duty, but because he loved her.

But would she believe him? Or hang up on him? No, it would be best to see her face-to-face, look into her eyes, hold her as he told her he couldn't live another second without her.

And if she said no?

He could strongarm her, threaten to take Caitlyn from her to make her capitulate. The thought brought the taste of bile to his throat, and he leaned on the call button again, filled with disgust. He'd never take Caitlyn away from her mother, but Sam didn't know that. She still thought he was an egomaniac with no concern for anyone else's feelings. Not that he blamed her. Then again, he couldn't start a marriage on the wrong foot; no, he'd just have to convince her that he loved her, she loved him, they both loved their daughter and Caitlyn needed—they all needed—to be part of a family.

A soft bell sounded and the doors whisked open.

"Hold the elevator!" Rocky yelled, racing to catch up with him.

Her voice surprised him. "I thought you took off," he said as she dashed into the car and pressed the button for the lobby.

"I did. Forgot my umbrella." She held it up for him to see. "I hate these things. Usually I just depend on a hooded parka, but when in Rome…"

"Yeah, yeah, I know."

"Let's have a drink," she offered as the elevator sped to the first floor.

He leaned a shoulder against the polished brass walls. "Do I look like I could use one?"

"A double," she teased as the doors opened into the lobby.

"You buying?"

"Me? No way. You're the rich cowboy with the ranch. You're picking up the tab." She was one of his favorite cousins, and her smile was infectious.

"I'm not good company tonight." He was anxious to call Sam and make arrangements to return to Wyoming.

"When are you ever?" she countered as they walked through the lobby of the building their grandparents had purchased years before. A security guard stationed behind a rounded desk nodded as they passed. Glass doors opened to the street, still bustling with activity. Cars, taxis, trucks and pedestrians scurried past. The temperature was still high, the air heavy with humidity. A few fat raindrops began to fall, and following Rocky's lead, Kyle hurried two blocks to a high rise with a staircase leading to a lower floor. Rocky swept down the flight of brick steps ahead of him and through an oak-and-glass door to a cozy English pub. A cloud of cigarette smoke and the buzz of conversation muffled music from a single piano player.

Rocky found a corner booth near a couple of older men who were playing darts as if their fortunes depended upon the outcome. A waitress dressed in gray slacks and white blouse with a red tie took their orders without cracking a smile, left a couple of paper coasters on the oak table and disappeared. All the while glasses clinked, billiard balls clicked on a nearby table and the bartender poured pints of ale and glasses of dark whiskey.

"So I hear you've got a daughter." Rocky settled deeper into the tufted cushions of the booth.

Kyle lifted an eyebrow. "News travels fast."

"In this family."

"And you never were one to mince words."

She grabbed a handful of peanuts. "A waste of time." As she plopped a salty nut into her mouth, she leaned forward, her eyes wide. "Come on, Kyle, tell me about her."

"Looks like I don't have much of a choice."

"None." She plopped another peanut into her mouth.

"Okay. Well, she's nine."

"And I suppose she's got a name?"

"Caitlyn." He couldn't help but smile. "Caitlyn Rawlings, until I change it legally."

"Sam will go for that?" Rocky asked dubiously. She'd known Samantha years before and apparently, from her reaction, already knew most of the information she was asking about. No doubt Grant had filled her in.

"I'm working on it."

"Good luck."

"Have you met my daughter?" he asked, suddenly realizing that Rachel could have bumped into Sam and Caitlyn.

She shook her head, her wine red hair shimmering under the soft lights. "Don't think so. Even though I'm in Clear Springs on occasion, I don't see much of Samantha. But from what I remember about her from when we were kids and would visit the ranch, I doubt that she's a woman who would embrace being told what to do. She spent a lot of years working hard and trying to keep her father sober."

"You knew about that?" Kyle asked.

"Yeah. I think Kate did, too. Probably Ben, as well, but the guy was such a hard worker and he had a wife and kid to support...." She lifted a shoulder. "I never said a word to anyone. I figured it wasn't any of my business. Anyway, I suspect that Sam, who had to grow up faster than the rest of us, is a woman with a mind of her own. I doubt that she's a woman who would embrace being told what to do."

"She's not." He shifted uncomfortably, as if he wanted to squirm away from Rocky's prying eyes. "I'd show you a picture of Caitlyn, but, of course, I don't have one on me. Truth is, I don't have any.''

''So tell me about her,'' Rachel suggested as the waitress deposited sweating glass mugs of ale on the table, then turned her attention to some demanding customers near the bar.

''I don't know what to say. She's a tomboy, gorgeous like her mother, just as stubborn and...'' He studied his glass and frowned. ''Oh, hell, the truth of the matter is I want to marry Sam, claim Caitlyn and start from the beginning.''

''Is that possible?''

''Not yet.'' He took a swallow and scowled at his glass, as if the liquor were the source of all his troubles. ''I've already lost nine years—ten if you count Sam's pregnancy. But she wants to take it slow. Not make any mistakes.''

''Sounds like a smart woman.''

''Or a mule-headed one.''

Rocky had the nerve to laugh. ''What's it they say? Something like it takes one to know one?''

''Yeah, yeah, well, I feel like time is running out. Besides they're living alone out there in the middle of nowhere....''

''Oh, and you want to be their knight in shining armor and save them from...what? A crazed coyote? Or maybe a cattle stampede from the domestic stock? Maybe an out-of-control tumbleweed!'' Her laughter caused several heads to swivel in their direction.

''Wyoming isn't the end of the world. There are creeps there, too. Caitlyn's having trouble with a girl in her class who's using her for a mental punching bag and she also told me that she feels like someone's following her...

well, more like watching her. I don't know what, but it makes me nervous.''

Rachel, who hadn't even tasted her ale, leaned forward. ''You think she's being stalked? In Clear Springs?''

''I don't know what to think, but it worries me.'' He took a long swallow of ale. ''It worries me a lot.''

''Boy, have you got it bad.''

''What?''

She smiled. ''Don't try to fool me, Kyle. I never would have believed it if I hadn't seen it with my own eyes and heard it with my own ears, but you're in love with Samantha, aren't you? This isn't just about your kid. You want to marry her because you love her.''

His jaw tightened.

''It's not a crime, you know.'' She scooped up another handful of peanuts. ''Have you told Sam how you feel about her?''

Hesitating, he turned the glass around, watching the ring it made on the dark planks of the table.

''Oh, God, Kyle, you haven't told her you love her?''

''She knows it.''

''Does she? Or does she think you're just doing all this for your daughter? You left her once before, you know.''

''Yeah, I know,'' he admitted, more anxious than ever to talk to Sam. ''I've tried to explain everything to her.'' Kyle felt that particular jab of guilt he always did when reminded of his past and the mistakes he'd made.

''I'll bet. Kyle Fortune, the great communicator!'' Rocky took a sip from her glass. ''Don't you think she might suspect your ten-years-late proposal is kind of an act of duty?''

He didn't respond.

"I assume she knows about Donna?"

"Yep."

"So Sam feels that you abandoned her, left her pregnant and married another woman."

"I didn't know she was pregnant."

"Doesn't matter. You were involved with her and then turned around and married someone else. I wouldn't be surprised if she never forgives you."

Kyle winced. "That's what I like about you, Rocky, you really know how to lift a guy's spirits."

"You did this to yourself."

"But I can't change the past."

"Just the future."

"Believe me, I'm trying."

Rachel took another swallow from her mug. "Okay, not to belabor a point, but have you told her that you love her, that the sun rises and sets on her, that—"

"I'm not good with those kinds of words." He knew his cousin was right, though, and as soon as he could he planned to used all of his powers of persuasion to make Sam see how much he loved her.

"I know, but I think it's time you practiced. Right now Samantha's holding all the cards. Years ago, you had the upper hand, but the tables have turned, and my guess is that Sam's not risking her heart, or her kid's, on a man with a track record of loving and leaving."

"I didn't realize it was your personal mission to browbeat me into a pulp," he grumbled.

"Always has been. Why should I change now?" She touched the rim of her glass to his. "Cheers, cousin."

The streets were damp, headlights gleaming on the road and buildings as Kyle drove to his apartment. The city, his Porsche, the condo were all familiar, but seemed empty and without life, no longer a part of him.

Inside the suite of rooms he'd called home for several years, he felt no sense of relief, no feeling of homecoming. He poured a drink from his mirrored bar and caught his reflection in the beveled glass—a tall, lean husk of a man with no purpose in this town. A stranger in his own home. Because he no longer belonged. Maybe he never had. His suit, tailored by a European designer, felt stiff and uncomfortable. His leather furniture seemed cold and the view from his penthouse window inspired no awe in him. Rain drizzled down the glass and lightning flashed in the distance.

He noticed the red light flashing on his answering machine, and without much interest, rewound the tape.

Why was it that everything he'd had here—the series of jobs, the few relationships with women so unlike Sam they seemed mannequins now, the places he'd lived— were so easily forgotten? Had the past ten years been such a waste?

The recorder beeped as a month's worth of messages bombarded him.

"Kyle, it's Frank. How about a game of squash next week?"

"Hi, Kyle, it's Cindy. Call me."

Grinding his teeth together, he only half listened to call after call—short messages from people he didn't really care about.

He took a long swallow of the Scotch he'd poured, jiggling ice cubes as the recorder bleeped again and Sam's voice filled the room. "Kyle, are you there? If you are, pick up. Please." He straightened as he heard the desperation, the pure, dark fear in her voice. "It—it's Caitlyn. There's been an accident. She was thrown from

Joker—'' his heart stopped ''—and it looks like she's going to need surgery. On her left arm and shoulder, maybe more, depending on—on if there's any internal damage or bleeding.''

He could almost see her sag with the effort of leaving this message, and his throat closed as he reached for the jacket he'd tossed over the back of his couch. His keys were still in his pocket.

''They—they think she needs a specialist...for her spine, if it's damaged, but they're not sure yet. Oh, God, they're talking about flying her to Salt Lake City to see a doctor there, but that's only if her spine's involved, and I don't know. I just don't know. I'll know more soon, I hope. I—I'll try to call again....''

Click.

The recorder stopped and the apartment was silent as death.

Twelve

Watching the clock and flipping through old magazines, Samantha sat in the waiting room of the hospital in Jackson. A cup of tepid coffee rested on the table next to the old vinyl couch that she'd claimed for the past few hours, but she hadn't touched a sip of the brew.

She couldn't eat, couldn't drink, couldn't think of anything save the fact that Caitlyn was down the hall and through double doors in surgery. A doctor she'd never met before, supposedly the best in Jackson, was overseeing the procedure, but at least it seemed as if Caitlyn wouldn't be sent to Salt Lake City or Boise or a bigger hospital. Dr. Renfro felt confident that her spine hadn't been affected by the accident, though her back was bruised, a muscle possibly torn. For that Samantha was grateful. All Caitlyn's other injuries would eventually heal once the surgery was over and successful.

So why was she so upset, so worried that the doctor was wrong, that his hands weren't as skilled as they should be, that her daughter wouldn't survive? It was silly, and yet the fear, dark and numbing, couldn't be driven away by common sense or faith.

Rubbing a chill from her arms, Sam climbed out of her seat and paced absently, her thoughts with Caitlyn, her prayers unending, her worries eating at the edge of her consciousness. "Please, God, be with her," she whispered, the same prayer springing to her lips over and over again.

"Sam?"

Kyle's voice reached her above the sounds of rattling medication carts, pagers and the gentle hum of conversation. Turning, she saw him striding toward her, his jaw dark with shadow, his suit wrinkled, the jacket thrown over one arm, his tie askew and shirtsleeves shoved up to his elbows. Worry was etched in the lines of his face, his shaded eyes anxious.

She was on her feet in an instant. "Oh, God, Kyle." She flung herself at him.

He caught her in an embrace and she wilted against him, the tears she'd held at bay suddenly burning her eyes and flowing down her cheeks. Relief flooded over her, and she didn't protest as he wrapped his arms around her, fingers curling in her hair as he buried his head in the crook of her neck. "Is she all right?"

"I don't know," she squeaked, clinging to him as if she could draw on his strength. "But thank God you're here."

"Where is she?"

"In surgery."

"Son of a bitch." He closed his eyes for a second, as if to find an inner source of strength. "What kind of surgery? Who's the doctor? Is he the damned specialist you told me about?"

"He's a good man—Dr. Renfro, the best they've got in all of Jackson."

"Why didn't they take her to a specialist in Salt Lake?"

"It—it wasn't necessary."

"I can afford the best damned doctor in the country, in the world—"

"It wasn't a matter of money, Kyle!" she snapped, angry that he, as always, thought the almighty dollar could fix anything.

"Okay, okay," he said, backing off of the fight and holding her close again. "Just tell me what happened."

They stood by the window overlooking the parking lot. Eerie blue illumination from the security lamps shimmered like water on the cars and trucks below as Samantha slowly, trying not to break down, told him about the accident, the horrifying ride in the ambulance, the decision to keep Caitlyn here with Dr. Ned Renfro. But she didn't tell him how she'd nearly fainted, had been more frightened than she'd ever been in her life, had felt unable to cope with the fear for her child. "...They have to put a pin, maybe two, in her arm and set her shoulder and collarbone. She'll have at least one temporary cast and a brace and, once the swelling goes down, probably another cast. But they think, at least they told me, that she'll be all right—that...that her spinal cord wasn't injured."

"Thank God," he whispered. He blinked rapidly, almost paralyzed with fear, sick with worry.

"Oh, God, I hope they weren't lying, that they don't find anything else...." He felt hot tears stain the front of his shirt and knew that Sam hadn't broken down until she'd seen him. Only then had she allowed herself to collapse.

"Have faith," he chided, though his own was shaken. He kissed her temple and held her fast. "We'll get through this. The three of us."

Sam felt like she was falling apart. She clung to Kyle and tried not to voice her fears, her despair. She was still worried that the surgery would expose some kind of internal injury the doctors hadn't foreseen. What if they were wrong? What if Caitlyn's spinal cord was bruised or worse? Even the best doctors made mistakes. Was it possible that the impish tomboy might never skip stones across the creek, catch crawdads, ride a horse or walk again?

If only Sam hadn't been so careless. If only she'd seen Caitlyn leave. If only she hadn't had the radio playing loudly. If only she'd figured out that her daughter had taken off through the fields as she had a hundred times before. But Sam had been slow to react, and by the time she'd spied Caitlyn astride Joker, it had been too late. *She'll be fine, she has to be,* Sam told herself, but couldn't shake her jittery worries. "I just wish I'd found her before she climbed on the horse—"

"Don't beat yourself up over this," Kyle whispered against her ear. "You're not guilty of anything."

"But—"

"But nothing," he said, his voice husky, his face lined with his own concern. "You're the best mother a kid could ask for. Come on." His arm was clamped firmly over her shoulder. "You'd better sit down."

As they sat together on the tired vinyl couch, ancient magazines and cold cups of coffee ignored, she looked at him and understood that if nothing else, he was devoted to their child.

The seconds ticked slowly by, and Sam thought she would go out of her mind. Without Kyle's presence and strength she would have lost her sanity, but he kept her from crawling out of her skin. "Don't worry," he said over and over again, when the shadows in his own eyes reflected the fear in hers.

"You know I lost Joker."

"Randy'll find him."

Her throat closed in on itself, feeling raw. "I saw

Caitlyn riding him and I ran through the gate. I guess it didn't latch behind me, but I always check. I—I don't know what I was thinking.''

''You were thinking about our daughter. Hell, the horse didn't matter. Still doesn't.''

''But he's valuable. He belongs to Grant and—''

''And I'd like to shoot the miserable son of a bitch. Joker's been a pain in my ass from day one.'' Kyle's fists clenched in frustration.

''You can't pull a Rhett Butler and blame the horse for Caitlyn's accident.'' Sam shoved a handful of hair out of her eyes.

''Why not?''

''Because it was my fault,'' she said firmly, determined to shoulder the blame. ''I should have been more careful.''

''You were in the shower.''

''Yes, and I didn't hear her yell through the door that she was going over to your place. I wouldn't have let her, not alone, but with the door locked, the radio playing and the water running, I didn't even realize that she was trying to tell me something. I only found out on the ride to the hospital, when she her eyes opened for a few seconds and told me. Oh, God, if I'd only…'' Her voice cracked and tears collected in the corners of her eyes.

''Shh. Quit beating yourself up over it.'' He threaded tense fingers through hers. ''I should have been around. If I hadn't gone to the damned board meeting in Minneapolis—''

''But you did, and Caitlyn knew better than to go over to the ranch when you weren't home.''

''It won't happen again,'' Kyle vowed, staring at her with worried blue eyes.

"Sure." She shook her head, knowing full well how stubborn her daughter was. "How can you stop it?"

"I won't let her out of my sight."

"Oh, right..."

"I mean it, Sam. I did a lot of thinking when I was in Minneapolis, and then after you called, on the plane back here. I've gone over our situation every way possible and the only answer is that we get married. The right way. No damned marriage of convenience."

"What?" Her head snapped up and she stared straight into his rugged, determined face.

"You heard me. I love you, Sam. I want you to marry me."

Love? He *loved* her? Swallowing hard, she was certain she hadn't heard correctly, but her heart nearly burst at the honesty and hope in his eyes. But could she trust him? Believe in him? She'd already lost her heart to him, but to take a chance on marriage?

"Kyle..."

Standing, he pulled her to her feet. "Did you hear me?"

"Yes, but..."

Disappointment darkened his gaze. "I love you, damn it, and I want to marry you!"

"Oh, God, I love you, too," she admitted, happiness swelling deep in her heart as his arms surrounded her and he kissed her until she was breathless, until the promise of the future chased away any of the doubts hidden deep in the corners of her mind.

"Listen, Sam," he said, lifting his head. "There's more."

"More?"

"I want to claim Caitlyn as my daughter, do whatever

I have to do legally to change her name to Fortune. I want to marry you and have you both move in with me.''

"With you?" Her heart dropped. The thought of moving to the city stopped her cold, but if it meant marrying Kyle, then she'd do it. He was right. Being part of a normal, two-parent family would be best for Caitlyn. And Sam knew she didn't want to live the rest of her life without him. "I don't know how Caitlyn will like Minneapolis.''

"Oh, I'm sure she'd hate it." His fingers tightened over hers. "Not Minnesota. I'm talking about you two moving to the ranch.''

She couldn't believe her ears. "Here? In Wyoming?"

He grinned. "Is that so hard to understand?"

"But you're going to sell the place and move back to—''

"Never!" he interrupted swiftly, his face harsh with renewed determination. "I finally figured out that this is home, with you and my daughter, on our ranch. I'll never sell the place.''

"You'll change your mind," she said. "Winters here are severe. The temperature drops, the wind howls, the snow—''

"So I'll take up skiing or…what's it they do now? Snowboarding? Sounds like something I can do with Caitlyn." He glanced down the hallway, worried again. "That is, if she's healed by then.''

"She will be." Sam was suddenly certain.

"So?" he asked, his arms tightening around her. "What's it gonna be, Sam? Will you marry me?"

"In a Wyoming minute," she said, and flung her arms around his neck. Kyle laughed and spun her around, causing a scene as Dr. Renfro, chart in hand, approached. Sweat stained his scrubs, but his face was set in an easy smile.

"Ms. Rawlings?"

"How is she?" Sam asked, her heart in her throat.

Kyle's arms tightened around her.

"She'll be fine eventually."

"Eventually?" Sam's knees threatened to buckle again.

"Your daughter came through everything. We set her shoulder, arm and ribs. The arm was the most difficult, requiring pins in both the radius and the ulna as the fracture was compound, the bones splintered."

"What about her spine?"

His smile was patient. "I told you there was nothing serious. She'll be fine, though she will be in quite a bit of pain for a while. I've written a prescription for something to take the edge off it for the next few days, but then she'll be anxious to be up and around. Your biggest problem will be keeping her off her feet."

They listened to his instructions, and Sam, relief sweeping through her, broke down again. Always strong and in control, she suddenly was limp with joy. Tears streamed from her eyes, and if it hadn't been for Kyle's strong arms supporting her, she would have slid to the floor.

"Just remember," Renfro continued, "this will take time. She's pretty shaken up." He explained everything in great detail, answering Kyle's questions as well as her own. But throughout the conversation, Sam wanted only to be with her child. The doctor agreed. "As soon as she's out of recovery, you can see her. She'll be in room 301."

* * *

"You're here." Caitlyn's eyes fluttered open and she stared up at Kyle. His heart ripped a little at the surprise in her gaze. "I—I thought you left."

"Just for a few days."

"Because of me," she said, still groggy. She ran a thick tongue around her teeth and yawned.

"You?"

"You didn't want me. That's what Jenny Peterkin said—that my daddy didn't want me."

"What? Oh, honey, no—"

"You left Mommy before. Because of me." Her eyelids seemed heavy again.

A great darkness stole through his heart. "I made a mistake when I left. But I didn't know about you, honey. I only found out about you a few weeks ago...."

But she'd drifted off again, thick blond curls framing her face, her tanned skin sallow, the freckles sprinkled across the bridge of her nose more visible. "What's this all about?" he asked Sam.

"I don't know. She never said a word to me."

"We've got to fix things and fast. Caitlyn?"

"Hmm?"

"Your mother and I are getting married."

Again her eyelids fluttered open. "Wha—?"

"That's right, honey," Sam said, reaching over the metal rail of Caitlyn's hospital bed to touch her uninjured hand. "Kyle and I are going to ask Reverend Pease to marry us as soon as you get out of here. Kyle's going to be your daddy."

Blue eyes sought out Kyle's. "You're not just saying this 'cause I'm in here?"

"I've been trying to talk your mother into it for a while now," Kyle asserted.

"You didn't want to be married?" Caitlyn, still struggling against the cobwebs clouding her mind, blinked at her mother.

"I just wanted to be sure."

"No one asked *me!*"

Kyle held his breath.

"Well, would you like us to be a family?" Sam asked.

"A real family?"

Kyle's throat was hot and dry. "Yep, kiddo. If you want."

She rolled her eyes. "Can I have a horse of my own?"

"Anything you want."

Sam shot him a look. "Within reason."

"Will my name be Caitlyn Fortune?"

"Caitlyn Rawlings Fortune," Sam said, blinking against the tears starring her lashes.

Kyle touched his daughter gently on the head. "So you just get yourself well, okay?"

"Okay," she said, drifting off, a small smile toying at her lips. "Okay, Daddy."

"...I'd like to present to you Mr. and Mrs. Kyle Fortune," the preacher said, as Kyle and Samantha turned to face the congregation. Sam was radiant in her raw-silk-and-pearl gown, and Kyle had never felt happier in his life. Caitlyn, positively beaming, was standing near her grandmother in the first row of pews. The church was packed with family and friends, and Kyle grinned as he saw the smiling faces of his own father and stepmother, as well as the tear-streaked cheeks of his sisters and some of his cousins.

He knew most of the guests, but as his gaze met that of a slight, elderly man in the back pew, he felt a moment's recognition, then realized he didn't know the mustached stranger in the linen suit, black tie and dark glasses.

The pianist broke into the recessional, and Kyle and Sam, together as husband and wife, walked through the church and out into the warm Wyoming sunshine. With the Tetons in the distance, they stood in the shade of a solitary cottonwood tree by the front doors of the church and greeted each guest filing out of the church.

Kyle's family wasn't shy. Each member was ready to pump his hand and tell him how lucky he was to have a bride as beautiful as Sam. His sisters were thrilled, glad that one of their headstrong brothers was finally "off their hands." Jane, an antique brooch at her throat, winked at Sam. "Welcome to the family," she said with a grin. "And don't let Kyle boss you around."

"Wouldn't dream of it," she answered.

"Good," Kristina exclaimed, brushing a kiss across her brother's cheek, her blond hair shining in the sunlight, "because he can be a stubborn son of a gun when he wants to be."

"Can he?" Sam teased, smiling widely. "I would never have guessed."

"Give me a break," Kyle muttered.

Mike couldn't help but say, "So you finally got smart."

"Finally," Kyle admitted.

"Isn't it a tradition to kiss the bride?" Grant didn't wait for an answer, but nearly bent Sam over backward as he pressed his lips to hers.

Samantha giggled, but Kyle's blood boiled, and Grant, squaring his Stetson on his head, grinned widely at his stepsister-in-law and offered her a lazy wink. "You could have had me," he teased, and Sam laughed gaily, slipping her arm through that of her husband. "You just made a bad choice. If this guy—'' he hooked a thumb at Kyle ''—ever gives you any trouble, you can always call me.''

''Don't hold your breath,'' Kyle warned with a hard grin.

Grant, spying Caitlyn, picked her up. ''Still wearing this damned contraption?'' He tapped on the brace hidden beneath her new rose-colored dress.

''Yeah.'' Caitlyn's crown of rosebuds tumbled to the ground as she nodded her head. In one swift motion, Kyle scooped the fragrant halo from the grass and placed it around his daughter's curls.

''Here, let me help.'' Sam adjusted the ring of flowers. ''There you go. Caitlyn only has to wear the brace a few more weeks.''

''Sounds like forever,'' Caitlyn grumbled.

''Oh, it'll go fast.'' Grant set her onto the ground. ''Besides, I've got a surprise for you. Well, it's really a surprise for you and your mommy.''

''What?'' Caitlyn clasped her hands together in pure delight.

''I can't wait,'' Samantha said, eyeing her husband. ''I take it you're in on this, too.''

Kyle gave her an exaggerated wink. ''My idea.''

''Uh-oh.''

''Remember when Joker got free, the day of your accident?'' Kyle asked.

Caitlyn nodded soberly and looked at the ground.

Kyle bent a knee so that he could look his daughter squarely in the eyes. ''You know that Joker's okay. Grant found him a couple of days later with those wild mares— the ones he rounded up and bought from the government?''

"Yeah?" Caitlyn said, lifting her face, her eyes suddenly shining.

Grant clapped his stepbrother on the back. "There's a good chance some of those mares are going to have old Joker's foals come next spring, and your daddy and I, we thought you might want one."

"Could I?" Caitlyn said, gasping in delight, her crown of rosebuds falling off again as she jumped up and down.

Kyle hugged his daughter. "You bet."

"Mommy?"

Sam sighed. "I don't think I can talk either you or your father out of this one."

Caitlyn let out a whoop of sheer joy and Sam clucked her tongue at her new husband. "Between you and Uncle Grant, you're going to spoil her rotten."

"Exactly my plan," Kyle said, picking up Caitlyn and kissing her on the cheek until she squealed.

"So, it looks like we've lost you." Allie, dressed in shimmering black silk, eyed her cousin. Arching a perfect eyebrow, she sighed as Kyle set his daughter on the ground and watched her run toward a group of friends.

"Who would have thought?" Allie brushed his cheek with her lips. A broad-brimmed hat shaded her face as she smiled at Sam. "I know I'm supposed to say something like I haven't lost a cousin, I've gained a friend, but I have this feeling that Kyle's not going to come back to Minneapolis often. I think we really have lost him."

"Oh, don't be silly. Kyle'll be back. He has to," Barbara, his stepmother, insisted as she moved forward in the reception line. Always down-to-earth, she'd accepted Nathaniel's children from his first wife as her own, and she'd loved Kyle more than his own mother had.

Sheila, Nathaniel's first wife, had declined her son's invitation to the wedding. Though over twenty years had passed, she was still bitter over the divorce and what she saw as her loss of social stature and wealth. She'd told Kyle in stiff tones over the phone that she wished him the best, but couldn't possibly interrupt a tour of Europe for his wedding. He'd accepted her dismissal. Some things never changed.

"We'll expect you. At least for the holidays," Barbara insisted. "I'm a country girl at heart, but Christmas in the city is special."

"I thought the whole clan would come out here for the holidays," Kyle argued. "We'll have snow and pine trees and—"

"Temperatures in the subzeros." Allie, mock shivering, laughed. "Thanks but no thanks. I can just see us braving the elements to go out and feed the stock. Sorry, Kyle."

Spying the mischief in Allie's eyes, Sam swallowed a smile. It would be good to have this large, extended family in their lives. She'd been an only child, and Caitlyn...well, so far she didn't have any siblings, so she welcomed all of Kyle's family with open arms, including regal Allie, who often seemed aloof and disinterested.

Sam suspected that under her breathtakingly beautiful surface, Kyle's cousin had a deeper core, something vital lurking beneath the supermodel-slim body and head-turning face. Strong-willed like her grandmother Kate, Allie Fortune, whether she knew it or not, was just waiting for the right man to cross her path.

Sam shook multitudinous hands, accepted many warm wishes, murmured words of gratitude and realized as they drove back to the ranch and the reception that everyone seemed willing, even eager, to accept her as part of the Fortune clan.

"We're really not so bad," Rebecca told her later, after the family had assembled for pictures and the cake had been cut. Champagne flowed from a silver fountain positioned near the stairs, and notes from a piano on the back porch reached their ears.

Lovingly, Rebecca ran a hand along one of the windowsills. "You know, my mother loved this place. It was her sanctuary. I'm glad she gave it to Kyle, but I'm sorry she wasn't here, wasn't a part of the ceremony."

"Me, too," Sam said, sipping from a fluted glass. Glowing candles were reflected in the windows and outside as the moon rose high in the vast Wyoming sky.

Sighing, Rebecca glanced through the windowpane and lifted her own glass. "To Kate," she said.

Sam clinked the rim of her glass to Rebecca's just as Kyle joined them. "You know," he admitted, looking sheepish, "I realize this sounds like I've completely lost it, but today, at the church, I felt as if she was there. As we came down the steps I could have sworn that she was in the crowd." An embarrassed flush swept up the back of his neck. "Listen to me. I'm starting to sound like you, Rebecca."

"I guess we can think that she was there in spirit."

"I felt it, too," Sam admitted.

Rebecca rolled her eyes. "Oh, wow, and *I'm* the one that everyone in the family thinks is a kook."

"Not a kook, just an eccentric. Every family needs one," Caroline said with a laugh as she joined them. With a knowing grin, she eyed Kyle. "I think everyone's expecting you to lead your bride in the traditional wedding dance."

"Does the band know 'Turkey in the Straw'?" Michael asked, urging the newlyweds outside to the dance floor that had been assembled near the rose garden. The pianist gave up his position to a band that was tuning up.

Guests gathered around the dance floor clapped as Kyle pulled not only Sam, but Caitlyn as well, onto the smooth surface. The band played "The Anniversary Waltz," and with the two women he loved in his arms, Kyle moved around the makeshift floor. The scents of sagebrush and pine mingled with Sam's perfume, and the wind whistled softly off the mountains, causing the colored lanterns strung along the eaves of the back porch to sway. Kyle held tightly to his family and realized that he'd finally come home. The path had been long, with painful turns and blind alleys, but now he was where he belonged.

Thanks, Kate, he thought, for his grandmother, in her death, had given him what he needed in life: a family of his own and a ranch in the wilds of Wyoming. Other couples joined them, and Grant pried Caitlyn from Kyle's arms.

"Just one dance with the little lady," his stepbrother said, whisking her away.

Sam laughed, and the sound echoed through Kyle's heart. Holding his new bride tightly, he kissed her cheek. "I'm afraid you've done it now, Sam," he admonished, touching the gold band on her ring finger. "After today, you'll never get rid of me."

"Uh-oh. You mean this was forever? Oh, darn."

He squeezed her, and her laughter rippled above the music. "You're playing with fire, woman."

"Am I?"

"You could get burned." His warning was a breathy tease.

"Oh, I plan on it," she said silkily, "and I intend to do some burning myself." She kissed his neck, leaving a wet impression. "It'll be so hot, husband, you'll have trouble putting out that fire."

He groaned low in his throat. "If you don't stop this,

I'll carry you upstairs right now in front of my family, your mother, our daughter, God and everybody!''

"Promises, promises," she said blithely, and in one swift motion, he lifted her from her feet, slipped an arm under her knees and started for the stairs. Samantha laughed deep in her throat, but struggled to get free. "First things first, cowboy," she said, and when he set her on her feet, she grabbed her bridal bouquet from a table and raced to the landing. With a flip of her wrist, she tossed the nosegay over her shoulder. The flowers arced high into the air, nearly hitting the rafters of the foyer before landing squarely in Allie's open hands.

"What in the world?" Allie, stunned, stared at the beribboned roses and carnations caught in her fingers.

Kyle laughed. "Fitting," he said, amused at the surprise on his cousin's pretty face. Then, unable to wait a second longer, he chased his fleeing bride up the remainder of the stairs to their bedroom. Once inside, he slammed the door behind him and twisted the lock. Loosening his tie as he advanced slowly upon her, he asked, "What should we do now?"

Her green eyes twinkled with devilment. "Use your imagination," she suggested, just as a little fist pounded upon the door.

"Mommy? Daddy? Are you in there?"

Sam laughed. "Yeah, honey, just a minute." With a lift of one eyebrow, she eyed her husband, crossed the room and unlocked the door. "Welcome to parenthood, Kyle Fortune. I think your daughter needs you."

Epilogue

"Haven't you learned your lesson? Isn't one near-death accident enough to convince you to be careful?" Sterling was obviously agitated. His lips were a grim, distrustful line and he rubbed a hand around the back of his neck, pulling at his shirt collar.

She chided herself for making him spend so many hours in Wyoming checking up on Kyle, Samantha and Caitlyn, but it had been necessary.

Seated at his massive desk, the panorama that was Minneapolis visible through the windows of his corner office, he glared at her as if she were a disobedient child—or more precisely, a partner who couldn't be trusted. "Everyone in your family thinks you're dead, Kate," he reminded her. "Sad as it may be to keep up this hoax, it's the only way to insure your safety."

"So you say."

"You agreed, remember? This was your idea, I believe." Taking off his reading glasses, he rubbed the bridge of his nose. He was tired. The past few months had taken their toll on him.

"No one knows any differently. Unfortunately, everyone who ever cared about me, aside from you, thinks I've passed through the pearly gates."

He wasn't deterred. "Going to the wedding in Wyoming was foolhardy. Too risky. What were you thinking?"

"I slipped into a back pew dressed as a man. No one recognized me."

"You'll be the death of me yet, Kate," he muttered, and she chuckled at the irony. "I spent the past six weeks flying to and from Clear Springs, reporting to you, so that no one would suspect you were alive, and then you just up and go out there yourself, when everyone in your family's present. Hell's bells, Kate, I'm starting to wonder if the plane crash affected your brain." Concern edged the corners of his mouth.

"Don't worry so much, Sterling. Everything's fine. You know as well as I do that there was no way on earth I was going to miss my grandson's wedding."

"But—"

"Didn't I tell you that leaving Kyle the ranch as his inheritance would fix things up between Samantha and him?" She tapped her fingers on the cane she'd used since the accident—the fiery plane crash that was supposed to have taken her life. Luckily, the hijacker who had hidden in the plane, then, at about the time she was preparing to land, had emerged from his hiding spot and pointed a gun to her head, had lost control of the situation. They'd struggled, and during their fight, with no one manning the controls, the plane had lost altitude. At the first jolt of the fuselage striking the rain-forest canopy, Kate had been thrown free of the wreckage, and her attacker had been burned beyond recognition in the fireball that had exploded when the plane slammed into the earth.

Kate had been unconscious when local natives found her. They had taken her to their village, where they had nursed her back to health. In the ensuing months everyone, including Sterling, had presumed the body burned in the wreckage had been hers. She'd nearly sent him to his own grave when she'd turned up very much alive, with the idea of remaining "dead" so that whoever had paid an assassin to kill her would reveal himself.

The worst part was that she was going out of her mind with worry for her family. Staying away from her children and grandchildren was proving to be harder than she'd anticipated, and there was no way this side of hell she would have missed Kyle's wedding. The same was true for the rest of her brood. She would just have to find a way to attend weddings, christenings and, God forbid, funerals.

Sterling rotated his head, relieving a kink in his neck. "How did you know Caitlyn was Kyle's child?"

"That was easy." Kate sighed. "That baby had Fortune stamped all over her from the moment she was born. I knew it the first time I saw her, and the timing was perfect—the birth being nine months after Kyle visited the ranch. While he was in Clear Springs that summer he was completely smitten with Samantha and she with him." Kate toyed distractedly with the single strand of pearls at her throat. "Kyle just couldn't face that a woman was controlling his emotions rather than the other way around. He returned to Minneapolis and married someone he thought would make him happy, the right kind of girl from the right social circles. They were miserable together, you know.

"I didn't dare let on that I thought Sam's baby was his. Even after the annulment of his marriage to Donna, he refused to return to Wyoming."

"Until you forced him back there by leaving him the ranch with the condition that he had to live there for six months." Sterling shook his head, as if amazed that she could be so manipulative.

"It worked, didn't it?"

"Like a charm. He's back there for good. Rumor is

that he's vowed he's never going to sell the place. That he plans on raising as many kids as Sam will have there.''

Kate chuckled, pleased with herself. ''Good. So everything isn't so gloomy, now, is it?''

Sterling wasn't convinced. ''What about Rebecca and that private investigator she's hired?''

''They're not my first concern,'' Kate admitted thoughtfully.

''No?'' Sterling's eyes thinned. ''I don't suppose I want to know what is.''

Standing with the help of her cane, she felt a twinge of pain from the accident, but ignored it. Bothersome, that's all it was. She had more important matters to discuss. ''It's Allison,'' she admitted.

''Allie?''

''Hmm. I saw her at the wedding. She didn't look happy.'' Kate remembered the sadness that seemed to play at her corners of Allison's full lips, the distracted expression on her face when she thought no one was paying any attention to her.

''Don't start borrowing trouble. Allie's perfectly happy, and why wouldn't she be? She's beautiful, bright—the spokesperson and chief model for Fortune Cosmetics, for God's sake. Believe me, Allie Fortune is the envy of every woman in America. She's got it made.''

''I wonder.'' Kate frowned. ''There was something in her eyes.... You know, I think she never really got over her broken engagement with—''

''Don't even say it—you've meddled enough. Allie's a big girl. She can take care of herself.''

''The way Kyle did?''

Sterling walked around the desk and stopped just short of her. Towering over his petite partner, he wagged a finger in front of her nose. "I don't like that gleam in your eye, Kate. Remember, you're supposed to be dead, and the reason for that is because someone tried to kill you. We don't know if or when whoever wanted you dead might strike again if you should suddenly appear and announce that there was a terrible mistake in Brazil and someone else's body is buried in the family plot. The assassin in the plane was probably just a hired gun, and until we find out who was paying him, you're in danger."

"Unless I'm dead." The thought was so depressing.

"It's the only way we'll find out who's behind the hijacking. So don't fret about Allison."

Kate drummed her fingers on the curved handle of her cane and clucked her tongue. She felt her backbone stiffen as it always did whenever she was challenged. "Now, Sterling, you know very well that when it comes to my family, I'll do whatever it takes to keep them all happy."

"Don't even suggest it," he warned.

"Oh, I won't do anything for now. I'll just keep my eye on—well, your eye on—Allison. That's all."

"Maybe I should get that in writing," Sterling said as he rested a hip against his desk and folded his hands over his knee.

"Don't be silly," she retorted with a laugh. "What good would a dead lady's signature do?"

"Kate…"

"Just keep me informed about Allison, Sterling," Kate insisted. "As for whoever tried to do me in, well, they just didn't realize who they were up against, did they?" She picked up her purse and tucked it under her arm. "We'll just have to beat them at their own game."

"Is that all?" he mocked.

She couldn't help the smile that curved her lips as her

thoughts turned back to Kyle, Samantha and Caitlyn. "Just remember what I keep telling you. Nothing in life is impossible."

"You're amazing." He chuckled and slid her arm through his. "Even for a dead woman."

"As long as you don't forget it, Sterling," she said, her eyes sparkling, "you and I will continue to get along just fine."

*   *   *   *   *

The next book in the exciting new
Fortune's Children series is

BEAUTY AND THE BODYGUARD

by **Merline Lovelace**
Available this month

Here's an exciting sneak preview....

Beauty and the Bodyguard

She noticed his tie first.

Having spent ten of her twenty-five years as a model, Allie Fortune had seen every extreme of fashion. During her career, she'd glided down runways wearing items from collections the most generous critic could only describe as eclectic.

This particular piece of neckwear went well beyond eclectic, however, and got lost somewhere on the other side of atrocious.

Wondering what kind of man would combine such an outrageous tie with conservative black slacks, a pale blue cotton shirt and a cream-colored linen sport coat that stretched at the seams of his impressive shoulders, Allie raised her eyes to his face.

She'd never met him before. She would have remembered him if she had. He stood out, even among the diverse crowd of advertising executives, art directors, photographers, chemists and production engineers gathered at the party her older sister had thrown for the people involved in launching Fortune Cosmetics's new line. Under his neatly trimmed midnight hair, his face was lean and tanned and striking, despite the scars on his chin and neck...or perhaps because of them. Certainly she would have remembered his eyes. Silvery blue and framed by black lashes a good number of her friends would have committed serious mayhem for, they riveted hers across the crowded room.

For several long seconds, those cool blue eyes held her pinned. To Allie's considerable surprise, his scrutiny sent a spine-tingling tension arcing through her. The tiny hairs at her nape lifted, as though stirred by an unseen breeze. A sort of prickly awareness drifted across her shoulders and down her back, left bare by the plunge of her dress. For a moment, the excited buzz of conversation about Fortune Cosmetics's new product line seemed to lose its sharp-edged focus.

Being watched wasn't a particularly unique experience for a woman who'd spent most of her adult life under the harsh, unforgiving eyes of makeup artists and stylists and photographers. Yet an inexplicable little shiver shimmied along Allie's nerves as the awareness intensified. With the ease of long practice, she maintained an unruffled poise as she returned his stare, then walked out onto the terrace.

She turned and saw him still watching, then he began to move toward her. Slowly, deliberately, as he came closer his gaze traveled from the top of her upswept hair, down the soft lines of her lemon-colored chiffon tank dress, to the tips of her open-toed sandals.

When his gaze finally made it back to her face, his eyes held a predatory male gleam that Allie recognized instantly. A slow, liquid disappointment spilled through her.

This man's cool detachment had intrigued her almost as much as his tie. For a few moments, she'd imagined he was different. That he didn't care about appearances. She'd actually let herself believe he was trying to see past the image she projected to the person within when he pinned her with that look.

She extended her free hand. "I'm—"

"I know who you are, Miss Fortune."

Her hand dropped slowly. The fact that this stranger knew her name didn't particularly surprise her. The explosion of media interest in the lives of top models had made them into the superstars of the nineties. As a result, Allie's face usually garnered instant recognition whenever she walked into a room.

Lately, it had garnered something else, as well. Something dark and frightening.

An echo of the call that had dragged Allie from sleep only last night whispered through her mind. She bit her lip as her inexplicable preoccupation with the man standing before her slipped, like a car skidding on a patch of ice, then skidded into unease.

Etched by moonlight, his face showed no softness, only sharp, uncompromising angles. A square chin, darkened by late-night shadow. A nose that had collided with some solid object once or twice in its past. Lean cheeks. And those scars on the left side of his chin and neck...

Swallowing to clear a suddenly dry throat, Allie broke the silence. "Well, you may know me, but I don't know you. Who *are* you, and what are you doing here?"

"My name's Rafe Stone. And I'm your bodyguard."

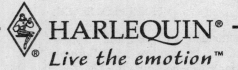

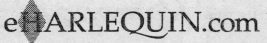

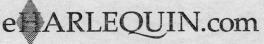

Harlequin Historicals®
Historical Romantic Adventure!

From rugged lawmen and valiant knights to defiant heiresses and spirited frontierswomen, Harlequin Historicals will capture your imagination with their dramatic scope, passion and adventure.

Harlequin Historicals... they're too good to miss!

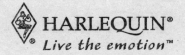